GIRL IN THE REFLECTION

MONICA ARYA

To my beautiful children, Mila and Ari. Thank you for letting me have the front seat in your own stories. I cannot wait to watch them continue to unfold and be as amazing as you both are. My moon and stars, I love you eternally.

To those who look at their reflection and don't recognize the person they once were. May you find the strength and courage to find the missing piece of your own puzzle and be proud of the one staring back at you. This is our now.

Milari Publishing

CHAPTER ONE

"*S*erena?" I heard the soft whisper fall against my ear. Turning away, I pulled the warm blanket over my face. The sunlight trickled in through our sheer curtains. I felt that I had only just went to bed. Groaning dramatically, I bundled myself tightly. Why did I stay up past midnight watching those crime documentaries? It was a vicious cycle. I'd swear to myself day after day that I'd go to bed by ten, but once the house had no movement, and the light was replaced by the dark night sky, all I wanted to do was relish in it.

I craved silence and time alone after a day full of noise and commotion. The stillness around me when everyone was deep asleep allowed me to think clearly, without my racing thoughts being blurred with everyone else around me. Some days I felt extremely agitated, like I could never have a moment to just… *think.* Someone always needed me or something from me.

"Serena?" Eric whispered again, his lips grazing my neck. The morning scruff on his jawline pricked at my delicate skin. He began tickling my exposed abdomen, and I couldn't help but burst into laughter, quickly suppressing it into my pillow. I lifted my phone and saw six a.m. displayed brightly. *She will be up any time now.* I rolled over to Eric and saw his eager green eyes. Reaching up, I brushed my hand through his hair and pulled him closer. We kissed hurriedly, peeling our pajamas off. I let my fingers trail against his cheek, tilting my face upward for our lips to intertwine.

"Mommy!" Our door abruptly opened, followed by a flop onto our covered legs. Eric quickly rolled off me, discreetly sliding his pants back on. I scrunched my nose at him, shaking my head with a light laugh. *Marriage after children.*

"Hi, my little love!" My hand met the bouncy, golden blonde curls of our three-year-old daughter, Lola. She climbed closer to us, squeezing in between her father and I.

Eric kissed the top of her head. "There's my beautiful girl."

"I hungry." She grabbed her stomach, sticking her tongue out.

"We can definitely fix that. How about some pancakes with chocolate chips for our best girl?" Eric tried to reach for her in an embrace, but Lola excitedly jumped up and down on our fluffy white comforter.

I smiled and leaned back, allowing my head to meet the oversized pillow. It took us years of trying, praying, and finally, intense fertility treatments to have Lola. She was our miracle baby. *Unexplained infertility.* The same label I had spewed out countless times to distraught patients, had become my own reality. It just hurt more when you were on the receiving end of the obsolete diagnosis.

Looking at my husband and daughter, I suddenly felt revived without my morning cup of coffee. Everything I could have ever wanted was right here... right here in front of me. Gratitude covered me in warmth and a burst of energy. Taking a deep breath in, another day had begun... another sprint. They say life is a marathon, not a sprint. *Bullshit.* It's how many roles you can cram into a day. Balancing a demanding career, while still making it home in time to magically be the perfect mom, wife, and human being. Okay, so maybe I needed to be more glass-half full this early in the morning, but it was the truth. My feet hit the cold floor as I tapped around until I could find my soft, warm slippers. Sinking my feet into them, I headed to the bathroom. My neck was aching from sleeping in the wrong position. *Apparently, this is what thirty-five felt like.*

Sunlight poured in through every sliver of the giant oak trees that lined our back yard. North Carolina was a beauty. The lush green everywhere was a sight to see and as autumn came, the tinges of color made it seem like we were in our own haven of nature. I quickly brushed my teeth as I heard Eric and Lola trek downstairs. Her giggle straggled behind her, and no matter how I tired I felt, the sounds of joy that radiated through her made me smile. I turned the shower on, and cold water hit my face as I pressed my eyes closed, pumped a bit of face wash between my hands, and rubbed it on all over.

"Don't forget your neck, that's where the true age shows, and ain't no one wanna see a wrinkly ol' turkey gobbler," my mother's voice chimed in my mind.

I pumped out more face wash, scrubbing my neck upward, as if my fingers had some form of magic Botox in them to ward against gravity. Letting the stream rush down my body, I took a few deep breaths in and out. I had started listening to a new podcast on meditation and mindfulness, and decided I needed to give it a try. I had always dealt with some mild anxiety from a young age, but who wasn't anxious? Life was a wild, chaotic journey—everyone was stressed and overwhelmed. *It was almost as if you were carefree and happy, you mustn't be doing something right, because anything worth caring for meant stressing about it.*

Suddenly, creaking rose near me. I opened my eyes, flinching. *So much for meditation.*

"Ow, damn it." The lingering face wash burned my eyes.

I wiped my eyes with the towel, quickly grabbing my robe that hung behind the door. Wrapping the band across my waist, I peered into our bedroom from the bathroom door.

"Eric? Lola?" My voice echoing lightly in our stark white bathroom.

I could hear their voices downstairs. Opening the door fully, I saw the curtains dance in the wind as cold wind rushed in, stinging my face even more.

"What the hell?" I moaned.

Eric must be crazy to have opened it. Trekking over, I looked out and heard the rustling leaves below. Bending out slightly through, I peered out…. *No one was there.* Yet the rustling leaves seem to trail away as if they were a magnet to *something, or someone,* dancing away in unison. Drawing the curtains tightly together,

I shook my head, laughing lightly. I really needed to start sleeping more. I lectured my patients daily about the value of sleep, yet I never took my own advice.

Chap, our goldendoodle, pranced in, brushing his soft fur against my bare legs.

"Hey, buddy, who's a good boy?" I cooed, running my hand through his soft, teddy bear fur as his tail wagged in appreciation.

Heading back into the bathroom, I wiped the steam from the mirror. Staring back at my reflection, I couldn't help but sigh. Looking at yourself in the mirror was ironic. The girl I saw wasn't the woman that appeared. I still felt like I was eighteen with the world in front of me, but now here I was, an adult in the rat race of life. Stretching the bags under my eyes with my hands and pulling my skin upward, I titled my head and examined myself carefully. *Maybe I needed that Botox after all.* One by one, I lathered on the rows of fancy serums and creams.

Pulling open the drawer, I looked down at the shiny lipstick tubes that were neatly lined up. Reaching for a deep red, I opened it and twisted the creamy stick upward. I paused as I touched it against the pink of my lips.

"Mmm… not today, Dr. Indigo." I smiled at myself, rolling it back down, before grabbing the usual soft pink and gliding it on carefully. Chap came back, shaking his tail excitedly.

"Sorry, buddy, I know you're ready for breakfast."

"Mommy! Daddy making heart-shaped pancakes!" Lola squealed. Chap was already licking up the scraps that Lola had dropped around her chair. We joked he was better than any robotic or fancy cordless vacuum we'd purchased after having a baby.

"Mmm, that smells delicious." I wrapped my hands around Eric's waist from behind. He turned his head and smiled down at me. Eric Hudson. My husband. My college sweetheart. He was handsome as ever. We'd met at UNC Chapel Hill our freshman year. I remember seeing him standing in his doorway down the hall. His shaggy, blonde hair and stunning green eyes stood out to me as I carried a box into my small dorm room.

"Here, let me help you with that." He chivalrously walked up to me, grabbing it out of my hands. He walked as if he were floating; he oozed confidence and zero self-doubt—character traits I believed all men should come equipped with. Women, well, we couldn't be like that since we were wired to be creatures of self-doubt. *Self-doubt that would ultimately consume us and every action we took.*

We spent the next few hours chatting and laughing

away, realizing we were both pre-med and had many classes together. We were inseparable during our freshman year. Eric was far more laid back, whereas I had always been a perfectionist. I knew the unrealistic standards I had set for myself were suffocating, but I had learned to breathe just fine with them. Eric was laid back because he didn't think there was anything he needed to improve. You could see it in the way he walked, the way he spoke… he radiated self-love. I admired that about him, but secretly, I was envious that he was completely pleased with exactly how he was. He didn't feel the need to prove anything to himself or to anyone else.

Late one night when we were studying in the library on campus, Eric leaned in and said, "So, Miss Indigo, I'm going to marry you one day. Then, we're going to have five kids." He said it with full confidence. It wasn't a question, it was a statement, and that was exactly who Eric was. Who Eric is.

"Five kids? I can't imagine what that would do to my body…" I looked down at myself. I was tall and thin. My mother was obsessed with appearances. My entire life was spent weighing myself on the bathroom scale every day to make sure I stayed the same weight. She made me do it, and she did it herself, so I just thought that was *normal.* I even brought the glass scale to college, stashing it away in my closet. Every time my roommate would leave in the morning, I pulled it out, stepping on with my breath stopped. There was no way in hell the freshman fifteen would apply to me.

"Well, that's what the gym is for…" Eric shrugged. He had a way to play on my insecurities. He always did it in a manner where I couldn't necessarily pinpoint what was wrong with his statement, which irked me even more. Part of me knew not to pick him apart— my obsessive need to be perfect didn't mean everyone else had to be.

During our sophomore year of college, Eric proposed at my parents' house in the backyard, just by the pool. We got married six months later. He had rose petals scattered everywhere, and I remember seeing the red tinges splattered across the backyard, thinking it looked so… messy.

My parents were standing by the gazebo proudly when I walked outside. My mother wore a bright yellow tunic dress with her hand clutching the pearls around her neck as she smiled excitedly. I didn't know why it bothered me so much that she was so happy for me. My father was wearing his usual sports coat and puffing a cigar. He wasn't pleased. I knew he thought I was rushing into everything when it came to my relationship with Eric. I think part of me so desperately needed to find someone to lean on that wasn't Daphne and Ian Indigo. I think I also knew it would be near impossible to find someone to marry who didn't mind my extremely type-A personality.

Meanwhile, Eric was down on one knee and held a small black box in his hands, proudly displaying the diamond ring he'd bought for me. It was a large stone, and I knew he must have borrowed money from my father since we were just two college students. If I was obsessed with perfection, Eric was obsessed with making sure everyone thought he was the best. Eric's parents had money and lots of it, but they made it clear to Eric that it wasn't his.

I had only met them once. My parents, on the other hand, were extremely wealthy and more than giving. If I asked them for a golden unicorn, I'm sure they'd go to Earth's end to find one. I was their everything, which also contributed to the immense pressure I placed on myself. I was an only child with unnatural expectations. Sometimes, I wondered what life would have been like if I had a sibling to split the pressure with.

We both went on to medical school and residency. I became an obstetrician-gynecologist, and Eric was an Emergency Room physician. Lola came later on toward the end of residency—we never used birth control after graduating from college, yet it took us years to have her. I thought we'd want more children by now, but we never really talked about it. Our sex life was lacking, and we were both always running in two directions. Besides, with our fertility struggles, I didn't know if I wanted to put my body through that again. Not only was I terrified to put my body through that, I was even more fearful to put my mind through the entire obsessive process. A process no matter how much I tried to control, I couldn't. I had a new sense of sympathy for my patients who went through the struggles to conceive.

CHAPTER TWO

"*S*erena, do you want pancakes?" Eric asked me. His blonde hair was cut shorter now but aging only made him more attractive. The joys of men versus women, I suppose. Gravity didn't even scathe him. Meanwhile, my breasts needed an expensive bra to even resemble the cleavage I had in my twenties, especially after pregnancy and childbirth.

"I think coffee is enough for me right now." I looked down at the steam.

"Yea, you do look like you've gained a few pounds. I'm telling you, stay away from those pharmaceutical sales reps who bring junk to the office. It's complete crap, and a carb overload," he said quietly, without turning.

I felt my face flush and looked down. I didn't gain weight. How did I know this? Because I still stepped on the damn glass scale *every day.* One would think becoming a physician and one who solely saw women, that I'd know better. I'd be better for myself and my daughter, but I guess the scars ran deep and my mother raced through me more than just blood. I'd hold my breath and watched as the blue light would appear, indicating my weight... it would freeze on a number. 135 pounds. I'd been the same weight since I was basically a teenager.

The only time that number went higher was when I was pregnant. I let my hand trace my stomach, looking up at Eric who was humming a tune as if he'd have said something completely normal. People would often comment on how perfect we were together, and we truly were. No marriage is truly without flaw... I think it was just the way he showed care for me. He didn't grow up in a very warm, loving environment, so to a certain degree, it wasn't his fault.

My father never liked Eric after meeting his parents. He sat me down in front of the blazing fire pit in our backyard and told me, "No good apple comes from a rotting tree, baby girl..."

I really needed to compile my parents' quotes into

a goddamn book. As outlandish as they were, they somehow actually made sense.

"Serena, did you hear what I said about the food? It's trash, stay away from it..."

I nodded in agreement, knowing I didn't want to start something with him. Instead, I let my thumb rub the center of my other hand, taking a few deep breaths, while heading over to Lola. She was sopping up a tiny piece of pancake in a generous amount of syrup.

I leaned in. "Honey, let me help you."

"No, I big girl, I do it!" Lola demanded.

I sat next to her with the coffee mug warming my hands. Parenthood was all about choosing your battles. Glancing down at my hand, the nail polish on my thumbnail had been picked at too much. I would have to fix it before work.

"Eric, did you open our bedroom window this morning?" I asked while looking out the breakfast nook windows. The leaves were officially changing from their usual opulent green to a cozy red and orange hue. I had lived here my entire life; there was no better place. I had traveled the world, but home was here. I felt in control here. We were sandwiched between the stunning mountains on one end and the endless Atlantic on the other.

Eric turned to me with the spatula in his hand. "No? Why?"

"I could have sworn I didn't open it, but there it was, wide open after I came out of the bathroom."

"Huh, weird. You probably did leave it open. Serena, don't be paranoid." He turned back to the pan.

"I'm not paranoid… but yea, maybe I did open it or something," I replied, knowing there was no way I'd have opened the window.

"That's what every paranoid person says… that they aren't paranoid." Eric laughed in that condescending way that made my insides curl with fury.

I stood and started to help him make Lola's lunch. Reaching in her monogrammed, pastel pink lunchbox, I took out the bag of chips and replaced them with organic baby carrots and hummus, then plucked out the folded paper towel Eric had crammed in. Taking an autumn-themed cocktail napkin out from the kitchen drawer, I drew a quick picture of a stick figure mom, little girl, and a pie in between.

I always left Lola little notes that made her smile. Since she couldn't read yet, I'd draw sweet images of her favorite things—one of which was baking pies together. I grew up baking the famous Indigo pie with my mother, even though baking with her usually meant having to stand in the kitchen corner and just smile since she hated any mess. I'd watch her mix up a bowl of bright blueberries with sugar and lemon juice, then she'd meticulously cut and craft the top into elegant lattice designs. The aroma would linger in our home, and I'd always feel warm and happy. *Normal.*

I got Lola ready for our nanny to take her to preschool and then went back to our bedroom to get myself ready for what I knew would be a busy day. Pulling out a fitted ivory sheath dress, I tugged off my pajamas and stared at my body. The nude sports bra and matching panties I had on weren't doing me any favors. Maybe I needed to spice things up a bit. Pinching the loose skin around my hips—which never seemed to go back to its original state—I stared at the stretch marks that lingered over my smooth skin. I hated them. The imperfections that decorated my body didn't belong there, they'd dug into me without permission.

I knew most women called them all sorts of names that sounded empowering and wonderful, yet I thought they were hideous markings painted across my hips that prevented me from ever wearing certain lingerie or swimwear for the rest of my life. Irrational? *Maybe.* That's who I was, though. Serena Indigo, the perfect woman, and if something wasn't perfect, I'd die trying to make it happen.

Closing my eyes, a deep breath released from my mouth… it didn't help. I still felt like I was suffocating. Obsessive thoughts induced by anxiety, topped with extreme self-guilt, had always been my own cocktail of hell. I pulled a small matchbox out of the bathroom drawer, sat down on the stool of my vanity, staring back at myself in the mirror.

Leaning all my weight onto one side, I lit the match, held it up, and watched the flame as tears stung my eyes. Eric's earlier words scorching into me. The fire had already rapidly grown far too close to the tips of my fingers. Moving it downward, I let it burn into my hip, tracing one of the stretch marks. Watching as my skin burned, the stench of flesh meeting with heat, I clenched my eyes shut as the pain overcame the racing thoughts that covered my mind. Mind over matter, or some bullshit like that.

Now I felt better. I stood and looked back into the large, gilded mirror. My stretch marks were something I couldn't control, but the flawed scars that embedded in them I could. *Pain.* It isn't constant, nor is it permanent. Pain is variable, changing, and evolving. Coming and going. What isn't variable is grief. Grief is the grim reaper. It'll haunt you until it gets what it wants. Not just a piece of you, but all of you.

Pulling a large bandage out, I slapped it over my

hip. Stepping into my dress, I covered my face with the expensive makeup products that neatly lined my vanity. Down in the South, it was every woman's social responsibility to "put her face on" before appearing in public.

Swiping on more pink lipstick, I tilted my head and examined myself. My long, dark hair cascaded over my shoulders into shiny waves thanks to the luxurious hair serums I had bought from my hair stylist. Running my pointer finger over my eyebrows, I grabbed my tweezers and plucked a stray hair out. *"Prim. Pluck. Pucker up, my perfect buttercup,"* I mumbled the ridiculous saying.

My mother would say it in the mornings when she'd look at me before I headed off to school. She'd pluck a stray hair or insist a woman without lipstick was a woman who didn't care about anything in the world. She'd grab a tube of lipstick, adding to the lip balm that I already had on. Clenching my cheeks together, she'd apply it meticulously as her long, manicured nails dug into my skin. I'd glance in the mirror on the way out the door, seeing the small crescent shapes engrained into my skin.

While other high school students wore hoodies and sweatpants, I wore chic outfits and looked like I walked out a catalog. Appearance was excessively important to my mother. *Check.* Intelligence was extremely important to my father. *Check.* I had to be both, and I was trained to balance it all and never show the world I was overwhelmed. The popular student body president, yet straight 'A' student, I was built to be it all.

I turned out of our expansive closet that was lined with designer clothing, letting my hand graze the rows and rows of money that now hung on our racks before heading down the stairs. Gripping the banister, I looked at our home. I had it all. *We had it all.* I couldn't help but smile. *Everything was and would always be perfect.*

Getting into my car, I saw a young woman from a distance. Her sleek blonde hair was tied in a high ponytail, wearing black fitted shorts that barely covered her butt, and a matching fitted sports bra. She had abs that were carved clearly into her abdomen with impeccable tight, youthful skin. Oversized sunglasses covered her eyes and her lips were brushed in a shade of bold red that stood out against her tanned skin. She smiled and waved at me. I was driving faster than I should have been, so I couldn't tell for sure, but I thought it might be our neighbor. Gorgeous blondes with perfect bodies were a dime a dozen here—it was stay-at-home mom central in our gated community.

They'd spend their mornings working out or having brunch together while their nannies cared for their children. I was a working mom, meaning we relied on our nanny, but if I was home, I was savoring ever second with my daughter. She was my entire world, the calm to my storm. She made the darkness I always felt *light.* I swore there was a permanent hole in my heart that always pained me, yet Lola filled it. She grounded me.

The parking lot was packed to the brim as I pulled into my office.

"Happy Monday," I sighed.

"Morning, Mindy!" I walked past the young, and definitely unqualified, receptionist sitting perched at the front desk. She was flipping through a fashion magazine and blowing a giant pink bubble with her chewing gum. Quickly shutting her magazine as soon as she saw me, she let the bubble pop over her lips. I cringed at the way it stuck to them as she nervously began peeling it off. Her blue-painted nails were chipped up and the scrubs she wore were wrinkled.

"Oh! Hi, Dr. Indigo. How are you?" she replied.

"Good, any messages?" I pointed to a spot of gum she'd miss on her lower lip.

"Thanks, Dr. Indigo. I'm sorry. Uh yeah, messages… yea. Some lady called for you, asking if you could squeeze her in today. Says she's your friend or neighbor, I can't remember. I left the note on your desk."

"What did you say her name was?"

"Crap, I don't remember, Dr. Indigo. It's on the note." Mindy picked at the residual gum that was now all over her fingers.

"Thanks… and Mindy, it goes without saying that you need to come to work perhaps a bit more… put together." I turned and saw the full waiting room. Some of them with burgeoning bellies holding hands with partners, others scrolling through their phones, probably dreading the infamous white sheet and annual checks.

Walking into my office, swinging my purse behind the desk, I sat in the hot pink chair and went through the bubbly-lettered notes Mindy left for me.

"Macy Callahan." I tapped my painted fingers against the sticky note. Just as I was about to call her, my cell phone rang. Reaching down into my purse, I saw Eric was video chatting me.

"Baby…" He smiled softly, tilting his head.

"Hey… everything okay?" I looked into the camera but stared at myself rather than him. *Shit, I didn't blend my makeup in enough.* I rubbed the foundation line from my jaw.

"Baby, I'm sorry if I hurt you this morning. I love you, you know that. I just want you to be healthy for me. For Lola. For yourself. You know you're gorgeous." He winked.

I couldn't help but feel my cheeks grow warm. Something about him always had that effect on me. He could break me down, yet piece me back together faster than anyone. In many ways, I resented him for that... I also resented myself for giving him that power, that control over me.

"I love you, too. I really have to go, Eric. Waiting room is packed and I need to call a patient."

"See you at home, beautiful. Maybe we can pick up where we left off in bed..." He smiled again. This time, a young nurse behind him began rubbing his shoulders, not realizing he was on a video call. His eyes instantly widened, turning toward her slightly and shaking his head. My heart pounded faster.

"Eric... who is—""

The call ended.

I looked at the time, I didn't have a chance to call back. I began to peel the rest of the nail polish off my thumbnail and reminded myself that Eric was always adored by women. It didn't mean I needed to panic every time some young woman flirted with him. We were good. Everything was good. I leaned back in my chair and took a few deep breaths with my eyes closed.

"He's a pot of honey, and dirty ol' flies are gonna stick to him," my mother told me after I called her crying, shortly after we were engaged, when I saw him wrapped in the arms of another student. He swore they were friends; I swore I wouldn't be that dumb, ignorant woman. So, I had him followed, and he was clean as the crisp, white Oxford shirt he wore when he got down on one knee and asked me to be his forever. *Forever.* He didn't ask me to be his wife, he asked me to promise eternity to him.

Lifting the sticky note up from my desk, I quickly picked up my work phone and dialed the number.

"Hello?" a sharp voice answered that made me cringe.

"Hey, Macy, this is Dr. Serena Indigo. I got a note from my receptionist about you needing an appointment. Is everything alright?"

"Hello, darling! Oh, my goodness. This is great. I saw you drive by just a few minutes ago and wanted to grab you then, but you seemed to be in a rush. Anyway, yes, I'm in desperate need to have my current IUD replaced. I don't have an OB here in town... Can you please squeeze me in? I leave for St. Bart's tomorrow," Macy pleaded.

"Macy, we are pretty packed today, especially for a new patient visit. Dr. Sully and I are the only physicians here. I might be able to work you in after four. I'll have to connect you to Mindy, my receptionist, and see what she can do," I offered, annoyed. This was typical. People with money loved to think if they knew someone who was a doctor, they could just weasel their way into appointments or concierge service and expect to not have to pay. If there was one thing rich people loved the most, it was saving their money and not spending it.

Macy Callahan lived in the house directly beside ours. She was a trophy wife to a big-time lawyer, James Callahan. He was easily more than a decade older than her. We'd occasionally run into them briefly at neighborhood dinner parties. James seemed quiet and reserved, whereas Macy preyed on the attention of everyone around her. Giddy all the time. She was a thin, blonde woman with her face painted in layers of makeup and no movement in her forehead. Her lips were always stained with that signature red lipstick.

They had a son who we barely had seen. He was probably no older than fourteen and always had his headphones on—typical teenager shadowed by a successful father and an attention-seeking mom. Macy was definitely younger than me, but rumor had it, she had plotted the surprise pregnancy to force James into marrying her. Apparently, she was only eighteen when they'd met, and she lied to him that she was older. Every stereotype women fought against, she was basically just that. Secretly, I couldn't help but envy her, though. She seemed carefree, confident, and most of all, easily unflawed. She just seemed so happy all the time. I wondered how a human could be that stress free, that genuinely happy? Then again, I'm sure her husband didn't make snide comments about her body every damn day, and she spent her mornings with iced coffee and Pilates while I delivered babies and performed surgeries.

"Dr. Indigo, your next patient is here." My nurse's voice broke my thoughts.

I quickly stood and headed to the room across from my office. Knocking lightly, I took a deep breath after grabbing the folder that was sitting right outside the door. I plastered on my signature smile and glided in.

"Hello, Cameron!" I cheerily let out. *The other side of me.* It always fascinated me how it was human nature to mask who were and how we felt at the drop of a hat. Or maybe I just was too good at that because I had Daphne and Ian Indigo as parents. The mirage of perfection, yet they were probably some of the most flawed people I knew. Well, not my dad, but definitely my mother, and what made him flawed was letting her get away with her madness.

"Hi, Dr. Indigo! I'm so glad I got to see you for this appointment." She smiled back at me.

"Aw, thanks, hun. How are you feeling today? Getting closer to baby day." I scanned through her folder and sat on the small circular stool, rolling closer to the patient table she was already laying on.

"To be honest, I didn't want Dr. Sully swabbing my rear end. I mean, I'm already feeling unattractive and swollen at seven months pregnant, but then you have basically a male model sticking your nether regions with a Q-Tip... can you say humiliating?" She nervously laughed, her cheeks bright red.

"Oh, trust me, we've seen it all. Dr. Sully is incredibly professional, you never have to worry about looking a certain way. You're pregnant, and we care that you and baby are healthy and in capable hands," I assured her, paging my nurse to come in before beginning the Group B strep test. It was a quick swabbing of the vagina and anus. My patients dreaded it. Most of them were first time moms, and I didn't have the heart to tell them that during delivery, all modesty would fly out the window significantly quicker than the birth of their child.

"Dr. Indigo, do you have children?" Cameron asked me quietly.

"Yes, a daughter," I replied while putting the swab in its small vial. "You can sit up, Cameron." I smiled at her, turning back away so she could feel more comfortable adjusting her gown.

"Aww... what's her name?"

"Lola, she's a wild one but also the sweetest. Oh, I wish I had my phone; I'd have shown you a picture." I watched Cameron as she looked down at her belly.

"We don't have a name yet for her..." she cooed, glowing with admiration of the growing life inside of her.

"I'm sure you guys will find the perfect one before you know it. I have patients who don't decide until they meet their little one," I offered back.

"I actually was thinking about naming her Serena... but didn't want you to think that was... I don't know stalker-like." Cameron looked at me, her cheeks were flushed again.

"You're the reason I'm even pregnant. I went to ten different doctors, and they all turned me away, saying there was no way I'd ever carry my own child. You were the only one who cared enough. I just can't thank you enough, Dr. Indigo."

Her eyes filled with tears. After peeling off my gloves and washing my hands, I walked up to her, reaching my arms around her as she softly cried into my white coat. This is what I loved about my career. Most of the time, I could fix the problem. I could help someone find the missing piece to their puzzle. *After all, that's what life was. A giant puzzle, and each of us eagerly wanted all the pieces to fit together, to complete the greater picture. The picture we have high hopes and antici-pation for.*

"I think Cameron is a great name, too. She'd be named after a woman, her mother, who fought for her and never gave up hope to bring her here." I pulled away and rubbed her arm. She smiled back at me with tears racing down her cheeks.

After getting through a morning of a whirlwind of ultrasounds, annual exams, and pregnancy appoint-ments, it was finally lunch time. I walked into the workroom. Being an OB-GYN was a marathon. I loved everything about it, but that didn't mean it wasn't exhausting.

"There she is!" Parker's voice boomed. *Dr. Parker Sully.* The other obstetrician-gynecologist who worked with me and also my closest friend since residency training. We had our own private practice together, Indigo-Sully Women's Health Clinic.

"Hey, Parker, how was your weekend?" I smiled at him. His short brown hair was neatly brushed; he was wearing a full suit, but instead of a jacket, he had his white coat on. He was also the reason we had a surge of patients. He truly could be a GQ model, and every single day ladies came in donning strong perfume with plastered faces full of makeup. They would trickle in with some Googled ailment that would amount to nothing just to have an appointment with Parker. His creamy, tanned skin had a glow to it, probably from all the working out and clean eating he was adamant about.

There was a time I thought Parker and I may have had a future together if things were different, but Eric and I were already married when I met him. Parker was still single and always joked that I was the one who got away and that he wished he'd met me earlier. He cycled through women, but nothing was ever serious. He was looking for another version of me, but I didn't know why. I looked at my reflection in the mirror hanging on the workroom wall. The stresses of medicine and parenting had weighed on me.

The bags under my eyes were more sunken in and harder to conceal. My long, wavy hair wasn't as full as it used to be thanks to postpartum hormones and a diet that wasn't one to be proud of. I was thankful that my mother's metabolism had passed on to me, and I could get away without the gym combined with my height. Compared to the other women here, my body wasn't tight and fit. Days and nights blurred together with deliveries and early mornings with Lola. I was trying to balance being it all and doing it all. *I had to.*

The perfect doctor, wife, mother, friend, and daughter. Something had to give and, of course, that something was *me*. I was attractive and only thirty-five, but the tiredness lingered on my face. Designer makeup and clothes were a simple façade, but inside I felt like I was crumbling.

"What are you up to tonight?" Parker asked while we sat together scrolling through our phones and eating our lunches.

"On a raging Monday night? Take out and Lola duties. You?"

"Come with me to the pharmaceutical dinner. It's at Topper's," Parker said while poking at his pre-made, overpriced salad.

"Eric's working tonight and leaves for an emergency department conference in Charleston tomorrow. I don't even know if our nanny is free tonight." I bit into my sandwich that Eric made for me using the same cookie cutters he used on Lola's. I guess he'd taken portion control seriously, considering that the majority of the sandwich was missing with the floral-shaped cut.

"Well, how about after the dinner, I'll bring you dessert and come help you with Lola. It's been a while since I've seen that cute little goddaughter of mine." Parker leaned back in his chair. The way he looked at me made goosebumps appear across my arms. I broke our stare and sipped my water, wiping my face with a napkin.

"Damn. It's already one? I'll see you tonight, Sully." I pulled my glasses out and slid them on my face.

"See you tonight, Seri," he replied with a grin that could make a rock melt.

A few patients later, I knocked on the wooden door and opened it, revealing Mrs. Macy Callahan. She was sitting carefully on the white-papered patient table in four-inch black heels and a tight, black revealing dress. She looked like she belonged at a Vegas casino serving cocktails, not a Charlotte, North Carolina doctor's office. Her shiny, blonde hair was pin straight and her thick lips were covered in the same bright red lipstick I'd seen her wear earlier.

I glanced over my clipboard at her records.

Nothing unusual. One completed pregnancy. A past abortion. There weren't any notes about either, which was particularly strange. I didn't really have any previous history to discuss.

"Hello, darling! Oh, you are gorgeous! Look at you all doctor-y in your white coat and glasses. How cute are you?" Macy's shrill voice pierced my ears.

I fidgeted with my oversized, tortoiseshell glasses. I barely wore them, but in the morning rush I sometimes didn't have a chance to put in my contacts. I looked down at my ivory sheath dress and nude heels.

"Thanks, Macy. How are you doing today?"

"Fabulous as ever. Thank you for getting me in today. Perks of being friends with the doctor." She smiled as her red lips highlighted her bright white teeth.

"Well then, let's get straight to business. I'm going to need you to pull your dress up, and you can cover yourself with this." I placed a paper sheet in her hands.

"Spread your legs and scoot down for me."

"Ooh, Dr. Hudson, buy me a drink first!" She laughed, tossing her head back.

Something about her just aggravated me and I didn't know why. Maybe she was everything I wanted to be, minus the whole bimbo act she had going on.

"Macy, I really have a jam-packed afternoon. Also, it's Dr. Indigo."

"Wow, yea, modern woman. Got it. Even though I can't believe you wouldn't want to take claim to Eric's last name. That man is stunning. I mean goodness, he reminds me of my high school dreams... you know, the adult version of those stunning All-American Sweetheart models. You need to mark your territory. It's a vicious world out there," Macy chimed.

"Scoot as far as you can for me." I redirected the absurd conversation and quickly checked Macy.

"How are James and...." I paused, unable to think of her son's name.

"Brooks. They're good. You know teenagers. He's just busy with his music and friends," Macy replied.

"Yea, luckily I have a way to go with Lola. However, she's a real three-nager." I squinted while inserting the speculum.

"Lola? I didn't think you and Eric had children." Macy pulled slightly upright to look at me with a raised eyebrow. Her forehead remained smooth, unlike the creases that formed on my own. I really needed to check out Botox.

"Macy, of course, we do. You live next door; have you not seen her out playing on the driveway with her chalk? She's always wanting to play outside." I chuckled, trying to hide my shock. It shouldn't have surprised me considering how self-absorbed she was with herself. Why would she notice a neighborhood kid?

"I'll have to meet this Lola." Macy laid back on the table. She intertwined her long red nails together over her chest and stared up at the ceiling. There was a silly photo of a koala bear holding a sign that said, *"At your cervix."*

After measuring her uterus, inserting her IUD, and being badgered with her extravagant details on her upcoming trip to St. Bart's, there was a knock on the door, freeing me from my rambling neighbor.

"Dr. Indigo, there's a call for you," Lindsey, my nurse, said.

"Great. Macy, Lindsey here will take you to check-out. Have a safe and fun trip to St. Bart's."

Lindsey stood with the door opened, waiting for Macy.

"Dr. Indigo, you are just so pretty, you know that." Macy was close to my face, I could smell her minty, cold breath against my skin. She carefully lifted her hand and traced a finger against my cheek. Chills ran up my spine. Her face was so smooth, there weren't under eye bags or fatigue plastered on her face. Her finger was soft. She was truly... *flawless.*

"Oh, um… thank you, Macy. It was nice seeing you." I stepped back from her, offering a small smile before quickly turning away. *What a strange woman.* I let my hand touch my face where she grazed it. Shuddering, I quickly picked up my pace and got to the workroom.

CHAPTER THREE

*T*he rest of the afternoon flew by. After dictation and answering a few more emails, I felt drained. Some days I'd stare at the clock from my desk chair and think how life was so peculiar. It was a hasty cycle of the same thing every single day. Wake up, get ready, work, go home, dinner, bath, bed, and repeat. *How was that normal?* Is that what living was? Doing the same things over and over again until we all just died. I grabbed my bag and headed home, but just before I got to my car, I felt as if someone was watching me. I turned around and looked over my shoulder. There was a loud crunch. My heart jolted as I looked down. Softly laughing, I stared at the red leaf that had trapped itself under my heel. I began shaking my foot to get it off while walking.

"Hello, darling..."

I just barely stopped in time before running right into her. My hand jerked to my chest, the soft ivory wool of my pea coat firmly gripped under my nails.

"Macy? Oh goodness, you startled me. Is everything alright?" I looked around the quiet, empty parking lot.

"Serena... you don't mind me calling you that, right?" She moved closer to me, again trailing her finger on my cheek. She slowly twirled a single red rose, as the cool, fall wind rustled the leaves around us.

"Um, no, I don't mind... Serena is fine. Is everything okay?" I felt frozen in place, quickly stepping back, and anxiously brushing my hand over my hair.

After studying my face carefully, Macy smiled brightly. "Can we grab a drink?"

"Oh, Macy, I'm so sorry. I'd love to, but I really have to get home to Eric and Lola." I grabbed my keys out of my pocket. Looking around, I noticed there weren't any other cars parked.

"Well, would you mind giving me a ride home?" She drew closer again.

"Have you been here since your appointment?

Macy, you do know car services exist, right?" I chuckled awkwardly.

"No, no. I was just around the corner handling some business and thought I'd stroll over to see if my neighbor would like to get drink with me. I mean, I feel as if we barely know one another…"

I glanced down at my watch. Around the corner? The only thing around the corner was a luxury hotel and restaurants. Dressed like that, I wondered if she was meeting someone other than her husband.

"I'm really sorry, Macy. I have to get home. We will definitely get something in the books though… maybe on a weekend night?" I didn't know why, but I felt guilty.

"How about that ride, then?" Macy smiled cheerily, continuing to spin the rose round and round.

"Sure." I began walking to my car as she followed me. I looked over my shoulder and saw her face light up again with a smile.

We both sat down in the car.

"Ouch! Damnit," Macy yelped.

I looked over at her just as my key slid into the ignition. Her finger was bleeding and the blood dripped slowly onto her exposed thigh. I reached for a tissue in my console, but just as I was about to hand it over to her, she smiled slightly and placed her finger slowly into her mouth, sucking off the blood. She wiped the residual blood from her thigh with the hem of her dress. My eyes froze on her as she stared back at me and raised her eyebrow ever-so-slightly. Clearing my throat, I broke the awkward glare.

"Are you alright? I have band aids..." I reached back into the console and lifted one up to her. She smiled eerily at me. It was almost as if she weren't looking at me, but through me. I could feel chills rising across my arms.

"You know why I simply hate roses?" She pulled her finger out of her mouth and looked at me as if I had the answer she wanted.

"Um… no? I didn't think anyone could hate roses," I whispered back with hesitation. I wasn't sure I wanted to hear what she was about to say.

"They are so beautiful, yet deceitful. You're drawn to their beauty, yet when you get close, they inflict pain." She lightly laughed and lifted her finger in the air while shaking her head.

"Well, maybe that's because they have to protect themselves from all the pests in the world who just want to relish in their beauty, but don't want to respect the fact that they are the ones having to live with their thorns," I fired back.

A moment of silence radiated through my car as I

gripped my steering wheel.

"Well then, Dr. Indigo, I do think this belongs to you. You seem to understand it more than I do." Macy dropped the rose into my lap and sunk back into the passenger seat.

Letting the rose lay exactly where she placed it, I began to drive home. The rest of the ride was silent. I felt extremely uncomfortable, but Macy looked as carefree as always. Her head was pressed slightly against the cold window, and she seemed to be engrossed watching the buildings and trees dance past us. I couldn't help but glance over at her. I wanted her to say something, but she didn't. Something about the way she spoke, the way she carried herself, made me want more of *her*. We were about to be in the neighborhood when the silence was finally broken.

"Oh, sorry, darling, you wouldn't mind dropping me off just around the corner before the gate, would you? I need to swing by a friend's house. Also, this is going to sound completely strange, but can we not tell James or Eric about this? I know it's ridiculous, but I'm supposed to be on an evening run and I don't want James to know I skipped it today." She looked out the window. Suddenly, I realized Macy Callahan had demons that taunted her in her home like I did. Maybe we really could be friends.

"Of course, Macy." I stopped my car just before needing to punch in our gate code. Macy opened the door, letting her legs swing out. The sound of her heels clicking against the concrete below. She slowly turned her head and looked at me. Her eyes were filled with desolation as she began to open her red-painted lips. She paused and arched her eyebrow.

"Thank you, Dr. Indigo. I do hope we can get to know one another more. I think you'll be surprised to find we have plenty in common. You and I both have quite a few thorns under all this beauty." She smiled at me and climbed out carefully.

I paused as I watched her. She didn't go through the gates; instead, she walked away from them. *Where was she going?* The loud buzz brought me back to reality. I drove through the gates wondering if maybe Macy was just as tired of living a life of a caged bird as I was.

Pulling into our driveway, I saw Eric outside with Lola on his back as he stood in his blue scrubs, barefoot, talking to James, who was standing next to his Mercedes in a dapper navy-blue suit. Eric was so untroubled. Sometimes I felt pangs of envy race through my body as I watched Eric. He had it all, too. We shared everything. Except he wasn't self-critical. Really, he had the god complex that many doctors had. I never felt that. Being a doctor seemed to be the most out-of-control element of myself. Patients wouldn't always listen to my advice, and I couldn't guarantee anything with them. Everyone was different. It was also why I think I needed this career to keep myself stable. *Balanced.*

"Mommy, my mommy, she home!" Lola screeched and kicked her feet indicating to be let down.

She raced toward me as her white dress floated around her while her curls bounced. She had her dad's blonde hair but my deep blue eyes. Her curly ringlets were my favorite, making her seem eternally young. I wanted to relish in her youth as much as I could since I knew time was fleeting whenever we were together. She leaped into my arms and we nuzzled our noses together.

"Hi, babe!" Eric called out.

"Hey, sweetie. Hi, James. How are you?" I said, turning toward him.

"Doing well, thanks. I was telling Eric that you both should come over next weekend for dinner with Brooks and I. Macy will be out of town in South Carolina visiting her parents this week."

"South Carolina?" I squinted my eyes as my forehead crinkled. Lola was squirming in my arms, so I placed her down. She busied herself with a lingering piece of chalk on our driveway.

"Yea. Her folks live in Goose Creek. I can't stand to go to their dump of a house to be quite frank... bunch of backward rednecks." He arrogantly laughed.

I let out a half smile feeling uncomfortable. *Why would she say St. Bart's?*

"Eric's actually heading to Charleston tomorrow for an ER conference, but when he's back, we would love to get together," I replied kindly.

"Well then, let's get something on the calendar. Enjoy your conference. Have a goodnight, y'all." James turned away, spinning his car keys around his finger. I looked down at his free hand and saw he was clutching a worn cognac leather notebook.

"Night..." I trailed. *Who wrote in notebooks anymore?*

"Come on, Miss Lola. Time for dinner. Dad picked up your favorite!"

"Boodles?!" Lola exclaimed.

"Yep, *noodles!*" I laughed.

Eric put his arm around my waist as the three of us went inside. I turned back around, feeling an eerie sense I was being watched. I looked at the Callahan's house and saw the curtain shift from upstairs. I could have sworn I saw bright red lips just as the curtain closed. We walked inside and I double locked the door behind us.

"4-1-9-2-0 Arla Drive," Lola sang as she slurped her buttered noodles.

"Good job, Lola!" I said proudly. We'd been teaching her basic things like our phone numbers and address after watching too many crime documentaries at night.

"I have to be out of here in thirty minutes for my shift and won't be back until tomorrow morning. My flight to Charleston is at noon, so I'm going to need to crash for a few hours as soon as I get home in the guest room," Eric said while cutting into the eggplant parmesan.

"Yea, sounds good. My mom said she'll take her to the P-A-R-K when she wakes up." I spelled the words out so she wouldn't demand a visit right now. I pushed the spinach leaves around on my plate. The aroma of eggplant parmesan grazed my nose. It was my favorite, and he knew it. But after this morning's comments, I chose to have the salad for dinner. Or rather, he chose the salad for me. I looked at my husband.

"I feel like we never see each other…"

"I know it's been fucking crazy at work…" He

stared at his plate, meticulously slicing through the soft yet fibrous eggplant.

"Eric… language, please." I widened my eyes, pacing them between Lola and him.

"Right, sorry." He looked at Lola, who was happily watching her tablet. I swore we wouldn't be that family—the one who had the television or tablets on to get through a meal—but here we were.

Eric worked four, twelve-hour shifts each week, but he always added more shifts. Sometimes I wondered if he even wanted to have time with me. I'd always imply we should take time off for a vacation together, but there was always an excuse. We lived an extraordinary life and that came at a price. We had to work to maintain this. I just never realized *this* came with a price tag that was more than money.

The doorbell rang, making me jump. I quickly took a deep breath, remembering Parker was coming over. He was earlier than expected. Walking over to our foyer, I opened one of the two giant doors that protected our home. My chest felt tight; I really needed to start taking melatonin again to sleep better since my anxiety had been off the charts lately.

"Hey, Parker, you're early," I said tipping my head, knowing he did that on purpose.

Parker and Eric didn't really care to be in each

other's company but knew their places in my life were equally important, so they didn't discuss one another and tried to stay clear of each other's paths. Parker enjoyed how much he got under Eric's skin, and he also disliked Eric immensely and thought he was an ass to me. I didn't see it that way. I knew the truth was that we were just exhausted from the chaos and busy lifestyle we led. Marriage, two demanding careers, and parenthood were hard. Of course, Eric and I were on edge often; he just didn't know how to handle it all. He didn't have to since he had me to do that.

He had to release it somewhere; I was just better at concealing how overwhelmed I felt. I knew it sounded pathetic, that I knew I was essentially his scapegoat, but one day, things would get better. Lola would be older and we'd have enough savings, and when that happens, both of us swore we would cut back on work and travel the world. *Things would get better.* We were just in the trenches of life. If there was one thing I was certain of, it was that divorce was something I'd never accept. I could handle broken… I thrived off repairing things.

"Hey, man." Parker nodded at Eric, who had a stoic face seeing him. Eric forced the fakest smile he could at him while Lola jumped out of her booster seat shrieking, "Uncle Parker!"

Lifting her into the air, Parker spun her around as her giggles lit the room. "There's my favorite girl in the whole world. You're as beautiful as your mom. Thank God." Parker grinned with a twinkle in his eye, purposefully poking at Eric's irritation.

"Well, I hate to do it, but I have to go to work now. You guys be good. Love my girls. Serena, throw the rest of my eggplant parmesan away so it's not tempting to you." Eric pulled me close, kissing me deeply, staring over in Parker's direction. His hand slid over my butt as he grabbed it.

I pulled away and pushed his hand off. It annoyed me that he kissed and touched me only out of spite because of Parker. I usually got a small peck on the cheek and a side hug, *if that.* I watched as he picked up his bag and headed out the door.

"Can we go one visit without you and Eric having some kind of weird interaction?" I whispered, looking at Parker. My thumb swiping my smudged lipstick from the passive-aggressive kiss, Eric painted on me.

"What? He started it. He thinks I'm going to bang his wife and steal you from him. I mean, not that I haven't thought about it, but Seri, you know he's just bitter. I don't get what you see in him anyway. What's up with the food restriction bullshit he's still doing?

God, he's such an asshole," Parker's voice laced with irritation.

"He's my husband, he's Lola's dad, so please, just cut it out, Parker. He's... looking out for me. I need to eat healthier, and you are definitely not helping. Speaking of, where is that dessert you promised me? There's a ton of Italian food on the table, so help yourself." I nodded toward the dining table that was covered in takeout containers.

"One chocolate triple mousse cake for you, and one strawberry cake with pink icing and sprinkles for my favorite girl," he replied, putting the brown bag on the counter. Parker studied me carefully. "You know that kind of shit gives people eating disorders. I'll talk to him if you want me to. Seriously, he did this back in residency, too. You know it's messed up."

"Sully, I'm fine. *We're* fine. Everything's fine." Waving my hands around me, knowing I didn't need to be saved.

Lola cheered in delight and raced to her stool. I quickly went to help her as Parker followed behind and sat beside her at the large marble kitchen island.

I pulled Lola's cake out, setting in front of her with a cup of milk and reached for two wineglasses. Pouring a hefty amount into each glass, I slid one across to Parker.

"Damn, woman, trying to get me drunk and take advantage of me?" He laughed. I looked over at him, rolling my eyes with a small giggle. I tossed the hand towel over at him, knowing my cheeks were probably flushed.

"Lola, honey, finish up, then it's bath and bed." I winced at the pink icing mess covering my daughter's mouth and dress.

"So, where's your doting husband headed to tomorrow?" Parker took a sip of his wine and eyed me while I stood across the island from him.

"Charleston for an emergency department conference." I took a large sip of wine. I gently swirled the deep red liquid around the glass. Watching it crash against the sides of the delicate glass without spilling brought me some form of odd satisfaction.

Parker squinted at me. "Don't you think he goes on a ridiculous amount of conferences for a physician? I mean, when was the last time we got invited to an obstetrics and gynecology conference?"

"I dunno. I guess he enjoys learning about the new..." For the first time, I thought about how Eric had truly been at many conferences this past year. Every day, I felt as if I were barely keeping my head above water with life. I was never one of those women who analyzed everything their husbands did. I was too busy over-analyzing everything I did. Sometimes, I often thought we moved too quickly. I didn't really experience college life, because before I blinked, I was engaged and married to Eric. For the most part, we were happy. I mean, people would kill to have the life we did. I didn't want to be the ungrateful snob— my mother held that title already.

CHAPTER FOUR

*E*ric Hudson and Serena Indigo, *inseparable*. In college, we were the couple everyone wanted to be. Medical school was the same. We did everything together. Once we started residency, I spent so much time with Parker since we were in the same program, yet I always thought it was slightly odd that Eric didn't mind as much. I had seen him flirt with other women before, but we were stronger than that. I didn't worry, and he didn't, either. In the end, we were meant to be together. I wasn't the jealous type and didn't have time to dissect everything everyone else did. I already had more than enough going on in my own life.

"Done, Mommy!" Lola broke me out of my thoughts. It was officially bedtime for her.

Lola was fast asleep after what felt like thirty books and ten songs by Parker and me. He was great with her, and she adored him. As we walked downstairs together, I watched him, thinking how he would make such a great husband and father one day.

Eric was a wonderful dad but lacked patience most of time and was short-tempered easily. When he was irritated, he'd yell so loudly, my hands would shake. He always made it seem as if we were a burden on a life of freedom he seemingly wished he had. I guess we were a ball and chain. I didn't quite understand why he proposed so quickly when we were clearly young and had plenty of time, especially if he didn't want such a commitment. Parker was always optimistic, comforting, and gentle. I hated how my mind compared them, almost as if deep down, I regretted not being with Parker.

Then again, Parker was single and had no stress of marriage or parenthood. That may make anyone more optimistic. Life had a funny way of making humans desire things we think will make it better, but really those things—marriage, parenthood, careers, money— all complicate the simplicity of what you're accustomed to. Eric was safe and stable; he was laid back and driven. *He was my husband.*

Parker was always the life of the party and women

adored his charm to the point I'd have spent years worrying he'd leave me for a newer, better edition. When we were younger, I felt so self-aware of myself. He was just too good to be true. *The whole deal.* Once I got to know him, I realized he really was the entire deal, but the unexpected part being he had a selfless heart of gold. Parker understood me in ways I didn't understand myself. He'd say something to reassure my anxieties before I even mentioned it.

The one thing that Eric and Parker shared was their confidence. The only difference was that Eric used his as a vehicle to manipulate and condescend, whereas Parker used it in the complete opposite way.

We sat down on the sofa and I curled into the over-sized statement chair, draping a blanket across me, chucking Parker another.

He loosened his tie, pulling it off and tossing it aside on the couch. He slowly unbuttoned the top of his dress shirt and suddenly, I felt nervous. Reaching over, I grabbed the remote control and quickly turned on some TV to break the silence. Looking back at him, he had settled into the chair and pulled the cozy blanket around him. His eyes were on me. Both of us just staring at each other, as if there were a million things to say, but both knowing those things should remain unsaid.

I remember years ago one of our mutual friends from residency couldn't believe we hadn't had sex or dated. She swore Parker and I had an undeniable chemistry. I remember Parker smiling at me while she said it to us, pulling me closer. He lifted my hand, showing the ring that lived on my finger. "If it wasn't for this finger handcuff, I'd have made her mine on day one." I remember in that moment wishing I had never met Eric. That made me feel like the worst person ever, and I knew that definitely made me the worst wife.

"Serena, you know you're beautiful, right? If you ever felt like you were restricting food or... and you know, I'm here for you in general to talk about—"

"Oh God, Sully. Don't doctor me."

"Don't you think it's toxic, though? Your marriage? I mean, Serena, it's not normal what he does. He's just such a fucking asshole. You could have done so much better..." Parker sounded angry. He never got angry.

"Like you?" I whispered back softly, staring into the eyes of the man who would have moved all the stars in the sky for me.

"Seri..."

The chime of the doorbell sliced through the tension that was built like a wall between Parker and me.

"Let me go check who it is..." I smiled and got up, thankful the doorbell rang because I wasn't sure what would have come from that conversation.

Walking to the door, I could see an outline of a woman holding something in her hands and tapping her foot rapidly. Opening the door, my eyes widened.

"Hello, darling!" Macy sang. She was now wearing a fitted white jumpsuit, her blonde hair in a sleek ponytail, and her long nails matched the bright cherry red that seemingly always stained her lips. I couldn't help but look down at my leggings and oversized UNC alumni T-shirt. There were chocolate cake crumbs lingering on the shirt and damp patches from where Lola splashed me during bath time.

"Macy... hi." I looked over my shoulder, praying under my breath that Parker wouldn't come over to meet her. There I was, looking like a complete frump, as she was standing in my doorway with a fucking pie, looking like she was about to be crowned in a pageant.

"I wanted to thank you for squeezing me in with the last-minute appointment and giving me a ride today." She lifted the pie toward me, flashing the rows of her perfect white teeth.

"Oh, Macy, you don't have to thank me. We're neighbors after all." I smiled and looked at the pie in

front of me. "I didn't take you to be the baking type…"
I laughed, glancing her over with my eyes.

"Oh, I'm definitely not. I got this from Sonali's Bakery. I'm a terrible cook." She smiled as her cheeks flushed.

"I'd invite you in but… I'm a little busy." I glanced back again.

"No, it's fine. I actually have to get home and pack for St. Bart's…"

There she went again, lying about her extravagant trip when she was apparently going to Goose Creek, South Carolina. I felt somewhat sorry for her. Why did she feel the need to lie to me? Then again, my parents were the epitome of Southern charm and wealth. I didn't know what it was like to have parents to be embarrassed of since mine were perfection in the public eye.

"Have the best time… 'Night, Macy!" I reached for the door and slowly began to close it when her long red nails gripped the door and pressed it back open.

"Thank you again, Serena. I really appreciate you being… nice to me. I don't have many friends here that aren't basically… well, like me."

For some odd reason, I took offense to her statement. Was I not like her? Beautiful, charismatic, personable? *Bitch.*

"Well, thanks for the pie. I've got company and it's late. Bye, Macy." I quickly shut the door, annoyed.

I walked into the kitchen and placed the pie on the counter. Grabbing a fork, I dug into it, taking a heaping forkful into my mouth. I continued to hungrily shovel pieces down my throat. *Who the fuck did she think she was?*

"Seri?" I froze, ashamed, wiping the corners of mouth with my sleeve. My face grew warm as I stared at Parker.

"You gonna share that?" He smiled at me and grabbed another fork, spooning some into his mouth.

"This isn't as good as your blueberry pie… What is this, some weird peach?" he said with a mouthful.

"I dunno… my neighbor who looks like a goddamn Barbie brought it over… You'd love her." I snickered while pushing more pie into my mouth.

"Nah, Barbie's not my type. The sexy, smart doctor with long, dark hair is." He winked at me, and I immediately put my fork down. Parker always knew how to make me feel better. I don't know what it was, but it wasn't the flattery or flirtation… he just understood me. He knew what I needed and when I needed it.

"Parker Sully, you really need to find a girlfriend, or I might have to report you to HR." I laughed and shoved his shoulder.

"Well, luckily for me, I am actually head of human resources, cause my best friend and I opened up our own clinic like crazy people."

I smiled back at him. "You're my best friend, too, Sully."

"But seriously, why don't you join that dating site I told you my friend is on?"

"Serena—" Before he could finish, there was crashing noise.

"Did you hear that?" I jolted, looking at Parker as he sat back up, furrowing his dark brows.

"Yea. What the hell? Lola up?"

I pointed to the baby monitor showing her in bed. "No, she's asleep."

"Stay here, I'll go upstairs and check," Parker's voice grew lower

I nodded gratefully while grabbing my phone tightly. "I'm going to check on Lola behind you," I whispered back.

Moments later, we were upstairs and I was sitting on Lola's bed brushing the loose curls away from her face. Parker appeared in her doorway. He mouthed *nothing* and shrugged. I walked over, shutting Lola's door tightly behind me.

"You left your window open in your bedroom, so I shut it. Must have been the wind or something."

Parker looked over at me.

"What the hell? I closed it. It was open this morning, too." We sat back on the couch, and I pulled the blanket around me. I sat directly next to Parker while we watched the baby monitor like hawks.

"Maybe Eric did?" Parker shrugged again.

"I don't think so... I swear, this house is haunted. I know that sounds ridiculous. I just hate how much Lola and I are alone here. I swear I can hear the thoughts in my mind out loud. Eric won't be back until the morning, and I'm... actually scared."

"Seri, don't worry... I can stay the night." He pulled me closer, wrapping me in his arms. I felt safe and didn't want to move. I knew it was odd how much I relied on him since he wasn't my husband, he wasn't even blood. In the end, he was always the one who was there. He was always there for me. *For us.*

Seri. The nickname Parker called me from day one of residency. I remember standing with the other five co-residents. He waltzed through the doors, and I could have sworn every woman's eyes were frozen on him. Over six feet tall, a buff frame, perfect hair, and piercing eyes, he looked like he belonged in some hospital drama on television rather than in real life. His scrubs were tied tightly around his waist and the white coat framed his body. He confidently walked past the other residents and came to stand right next to me, where I was standing farther away and alone.

I was always the shy one of the groups. I wondered if people like me—the overly self-aware perfectionists were always introverts. I was also already married at that point, unlike the rest of my co-residents. I felt older, lost, and just always... *different.*

"Hey, I'm Parker Sully." He reached his hand out to me and smiled. I remember tucking my left hand— that was adorned with my wedding band—into my white coat.

I nervously smiled back at him. "Serena Indigo."

"That's the coolest name ever." He looked into my eyes in a way that made me feel vulnerable. "Why'd you choose obstetrics and gynecology, Dr. Indigo?" Parker asked.

"Um...well, I... I had... Well, you know, I just love how a woman's body can start from this to that. It's just... a miracle." I pointed to myself and then toward a fully pregnant patient across the room. "What about you, why did you choose it?" I asked curiously.

"I love being a piece of bringing new life into the world. There's something so surreal knowing you are holding this baby in your hands as they take their first breath. That's a good reason, don't you think?"

"It sure is and besides, I also don't think I could deal with men all day long." I smiled.

"Well, Seri, you're gonna have to deal with me now." He grinned at me as my heart pounded.

"I don't think I'll mind that too much, Sully." I laughed.

"Seri and Sully... the dynamic duo. Can you just imagine we're gonna have our own office one day? I just know it. But maybe we'll have to go with Indigo and Sully." He threw his arm around my shoulder as if we'd known each other our entire lives.

"Count me in," I added while following the rest of our resident group down the hall.

A few weeks later, Parker came over to our apartment to study with me. He sat in my desk chair and pulled open the drawer in search of a pen, instead he saw the wooden box my father had given me. I remember my heart throbbing as he pulled it out and set it on top of the small, white desk. He ran his fingers across the top, opening it with care. His eyes widened as he lifted the dagger into his hands. The light reflected against the steel.

"Be the hunter or the prey," he whispered, tracing the carved verbiage that was displayed on the handle. His finger glossed over the indigo blue velvet as he turned toward me. "That's some dark shit, Serena." He cracked a small yet inquisitive smile at me.

"My grandpa and dad. They're just crazy. It's a family tradition... I know it's insane." I laughed awkwardly. I couldn't believe he had found the damn dagger my dad gifted me years before.

"Nah, I think you are darker than you give off, Dr. Indigo... and I'm diggin' it." Parker stood and walked up to me. I could feel his warm breath against my face as he leaned in and whispered in my ear, "We all have darkness inside of us, some just hide it better."

I remember looking up at him, his brown eyes looked into mine as if they knew who I really was. *What I really was.* I didn't even know who that was, but he sure as hell seemed to know.

I opened my eyes slowly and found myself wrapped in Parker's arms on the couch. We fell asleep after talking for hours, reminiscing about residency days. I slowly pushed his arm off me and looked at him. We'd fall asleep in the call room after excruciatingly long shifts, and I remember some days just wanting to stay there as long as I could. He opened his deep brown eyes and slowly sat upright.

"Seri, it's creepy that you're watching me sleep. I know you're dreaming about me, but damn woman, stalker much?"

"Ha, very funny. You better not say anything about us falling asleep on the couch together to Eric. I just know you'll make it sound worse than it really is," I sternly warned him.

The last thing I needed was Eric screaming at me over something silly and giving Lola anxiety. She hated when we fought. I hated it, too. I just wanted to give her the childhood I had craved. My parents were busy making sure I was everything and anything they wanted me to be. I don't even remember a childhood, more so seven days a week filled with seven different activities or extracurriculars. *Most days, all I felt like was a pile of clay they were busy sculpting into whatever they saw to be the best fit. The perfect fit for their perfect lives.*

Parker pretended to zip his mouth and smiled at me. Lola's footsteps pitter-pattered down the stairs and her sleepy eyes brightened as soon as she saw him. He seemed to have that effect on every lady around him. After a quick breakfast, our nanny had Lola off for preschool. Parker had left to get home before we had to be at the office, and I desperately needed a shower before heading out for another busy work-day. Starting our own private practice was over-whelming, but exhilarating. We got to be our own bosses and care for our patients as we saw fit. We didn't have to meet certain quotas and treat patients as a numbers game; we got to take our time and really connect with them. That was valuable to both Parker and me.

I turned the knob on and looked up at our giant rain shower head, the hot water poured out, washing away the impending neck pain I was feeling after falling asleep on the couch upright. This was definitely my thirties; neck pain from sleeping in the wrong position. There was a time my body could go into any position with no pain, but pleasure. My mind trailed to Parker's sultry eyes and morning tousled hair.

I grabbed the shower attachment and turned the water pressure higher, trailing it down in between my legs. My empty palm connected with the cold shower door as my head tossed back. I envisioned his strong arms tracing my wet body. Eric and I rarely had sex and when we did, it felt so cold, so goal-oriented. He never really even looked at me. He'd keep his eyes closed or put me in a position where the back of my head was seen instead of my face. It made me feel unseen, unattractive, and most of all, I could never find the release my body begged for.

I learned to moan at the perfect time to prove I had an orgasm, just to give Eric the satisfaction he needed. My clenched eyes quickly opened as a sudden crash rose from my bedroom. I dropped the shower attachment as the metal clanked against the glass door. Quickly wiping the steam from the door, I peered through. My chest was heaving rapidly as terror seemed to drain down my body rather than the water droplets.

I took a deep breath and gently opened the shower door. The creaking wasn't discreet; I felt the sound of my pounding heart collide with the steam around me.

Wrapping my towel around me as my hair dripped, leaving a trail behind, I tip-toed toward the noise. I scanned my bathroom, hoping to find something that would potentially provide protection, knowing it was a useless endeavor. My phone was in the bedroom, and I had nothing more than an electric toothbrush. I grabbed the toothbrush and pried off the head, revealing the sharp metal attachment. It would do.

"Hello?" I whispered, my voice was spiked with panic.

I swung the door open, jerking my head around when I heard Chap bark viciously downstairs.

I ran to my nightstand and grabbed my phone. Fear coursed inside of me as I kept entering my passcode incorrectly.

"Fuck, fuck..." I hissed at the screen, finally unlocking it.

9-1-…I began typing as my fingers shook and slid across the sleek glass screen.

"Dr. Indigo?"

I froze and listened closely, hoping it was a familiar voice.

"Dr. Indigo?" It was a male voice, but I couldn't recognize it from the closed door I was huddled behind upstairs. I clenched my eyes together tightly and began to pray. I didn't even know for sure if I truly believed in God, but in that moment, I prayed so quickly, it brought me back to the church pews in the bigoted and backwards conservative church I grew up in.

Footsteps echoed and grew louder. I bit my bottom lip and held my breath. Counting, I felt nauseated. A light knock grazed my door. My trembling legs lagged behind as my arms reached to the doorknob, lifting my body upright. I turned the knob, grasping my toothbrush handle as I exhaled and saw the soft face and creased forehead of James Callahan.

"Dr. Indigo, are you okay? Your front door was wide open, and I saw your dog barking…" His face was lined with concern as his eyes trailed down to my shaking legs and the wet puddle around my legs from my sopping hair.

"Oh my gosh, Dr… I mean, James, there was a loud

crash. I was terrified." I breathed out and immediately hid the toothbrush behind my back. The last thing I needed was James Callahan thinking I was some kind of psychopath.

I opened the door fully, tightly holding my towel in place.

James was in another debonair suit with his worn leather notebook gripped in his hand.

"Do you want me to check around?" Apprehension was still embedded on his face.

"I think I'll be fine. Maybe the nanny left the door slightly ajar, and you know the wind...Perhaps it pushed it open." I knew I was reassuring myself more than James.

"Alright. Are you sure, Dr. Indigo? You look quite frightened... maybe, just breathe?"

"Oh, please, call me Serena. I'm absolutely sure. Thank you for coming by." I felt silly and overdramatic, especially after he basically told me to calm the fuck down and breathe.

"Well, if you are certain, I must get to work. Have a good day, Serena. You might want to close your window." James paused, pointing at the open window behind me. I shuddered. *How?*

"Yes, must have left it open... Thanks again. Have a

good day!" I painted a smile across my face, even though underneath it, I felt sheer terror.

I quickly closed the window, sealing the curtains tightly together. Walking over to my dresser, I opened the small jewelry box and pulled out my go-to pearl earrings my parents had gifted me. They were my most cherished piece of jewelry, and I wore them regularly. I think I cherished them so much because they gave them to me the day I graduated from college. I had been accepted to medical school and graduated top of my class, all while having gone through one of the hardest times of my life.

They were both glowing with pride. When they handed me the box, I was thankful it wasn't something abnormal, like a dagger. It was a beautiful pair of pearls in a Carolina-blue box. The pearls were taken from the necklace my mother wore around her neck, which was a family heirloom. At that moment, we were a family. A real, normal family. I took a deep breath and turned to check the time on the small crystal clock that sat atop a stack of decorative books on our dresser.

"Shit." I would definitely be late to the clinic, and it would result in a domino effect of late appointments, meaning the day would end later than expected.

I quickly dried my hair and applied light makeup,

choosing a silk, emerald-green blouse and fitted trousers. I put my earrings on and the gold necklace that had two small birds—Eric had bought it for me as a 'push' present.

"Hello?" Eric's voice answered on the other side of the phone. I was balancing my phone between my chin and shoulder as I pulled my heels on.

"Eric, I'm running late to the office. Long story short, but our front door was wide open, and I heard something, so James came over and—"

"James? Who is James?" Eric questioned.

"Callahan. James Callahan. Our neighbor." I replied, slightly annoyed.

"Oh, are you alright?"

"Yea, I guess. I swear, something is off here but I don't know... Maybe we should downsize?" I walked out to my car and looked back at our home. It was a gorgeous, brick three-story house in Charlotte's best gated neighborhood. I sounded ridiculous, I knew that.

"You're just paranoid, Serena. We are not downsizing. Just stop being so—"

"I'm not fucking paranoid. Don't do that. You always do that. The window is opened one day and the next, it's the damn front door," I hissed. I dropped my keys on the driveway as I balanced my phone, bag, and coffee thermos in one hand.

"Damn it. Hold on, Eric." I leaned down and swiftly grabbed my keys and looked up.

Brooks Callahan was staring straight at me from his driveway. His eyes were a deep shade of blue that neither parent had. Wearing his polo Oxford and khaki pants made him blend in with the rest of the neighborhood teens. His backpack was slung over his shoulder.

"Oh, hey, Brooks." I smiled and waved the hand that was now gripping my keys, jingling with the movement of my fingers.

Without smiling back, he walked toward the end of the driveway and climbed into a black town car that came to pick him up for school. He looked at me as if he didn't know who I was. I saw him turn his head and look through the back window. *Teenagers.*

"Poor kid." I sighed.

"Who? Serena? Are you still there?" Eric sounded agitated.

I climbed into my car and put on my Bluetooth.

"Yea, Eric? Sorry, Brooks was outside. Isn't it weird that a driver picks him up? I mean, what the hell? His mom stays at home but is more concerned about vacations and Botox than her own child," I replied while backing out of our driveway and heading toward my office.

"I mean, our nanny takes Lola to preschool. Who cares, I guess," Eric said.

"Yea, but we both work crazy hours. Look, I'm not saying stay-at-home-moms don't work. Shit, their job is harder than any other, but not taking your kid to school is just ridiculous to me."

"Yea, whatever, not our business. Anyway, I'm almost home and gonna crash for a bit, then head out for the conference in Savannah. I'll see you and Lola in a few days." Eric yawned.

"Savannah? I thought it was in Charleston?" My voice grew louder as I thought back to my conversation with Parker last night when he questioned Eric and his conferences. I suddenly felt a pit in my stomach.

"Yea, that's what I meant. Charleston. I'm exhausted, Serena, don't put me on trial. This fucking gated mansion you were so adamant about us buying costs money. So, excuse me while I work my ass off to pay these excessive bills."

Before I had a chance to pry and push more, my work phone buzzed. The one thing that pissed me off was when Eric acted like he was the sole earner. If anything, I made more money through my private practice with Parker than he did as a hospital-employed emergency medicine doctor. Along with my trust fund, there was no justification for him badgering me about expenses.

"I gotta go. Have a safe trip to wherever the hell you're going, Eric." I hung up the phone, shaking with anger.

"This is Dr. Indigo," I answered my work phone. My voice instantly changed, making me wince.

"Dr. Indigo, it's Mindy. Where are you? Dr. Sully is having to see your patients and his. It's so crowded and backed up here. Patients are pissed," she whispered into the phone.

"I'm turning in now." I hung up the call.

I raced inside, my heels slipping across the rain-slicked, dark concrete parking lot. I pushed away my many questions I had for Eric. It would have to wait. My marriage was always going to have to wait when it came to work or Lola. I rushed through my first few patients and felt guilty for how crass I was with them. There was no room for a bad day when it came to private practice. Patients who didn't like me would leave the practice and give us poor ratings, and I couldn't do that to Parker, who only increased our patient load.

I put my best Serena Indigo face on and pushed

through the rest of my morning appointments. Before I knew it, it was finally lunch time. My stomach had been churning from skipping breakfast while I had a pounding headache from forgetting my coffee in the car. Today was a shitshow. *It was that kind of day where when one thing goes wrong, everything goes down with it, and nothing can go right.*

CHAPTER FIVE

"*I* think Eric is having an affair." I picked at the overrated salad in front of me.

Parker and I were at the new, hipster, health food café across from our office that he frequented. This was the last kind of food I wanted. I just wanted a plate of fried okra, mashed potatoes, and macaroni and cheese—comfort food. Who was I kidding? When did I ever eat comfort food? I was from the South, yet comfort food in the Indigo house was some reduced fat bullshit.

"What makes you think that? His many conferences?" Parker asked casually, while sipping his green smoothie.

"You think so too, don't you?" I felt like such an idiot. The signs were all there. We were rarely intimate—which I blamed on our opposite schedules and having a toddler in the house. We never went out on dates; he went to work conferences and worked hours that didn't align with his salary.

I dropped my fork into the large plastic bowl and sighed.

"Shit, I'm so stupid." I locked eyes with Parker while I rubbed my head, the headache from this morning still lingering. The sun was shining on Parker's face, making his chocolate brown eyes glow, and his gray, fitted suit framed him perfectly.

"Now aren't you just a tall glass of handsome..." my mother said to him the first time she met him back during residency when Parker came with Eric and me to my parents for Thanksgiving. My dad was so taken with him that they shared cigars and stories in his study—something my dad never did with anyone. Eric was fuming. Parker's family lived in California, so he often came home with Eric and me for holidays. I didn't care that people thought it was strange. Parker was my best friend and if he was a girl, no one would have second guessed it. I hated the old-fashioned ideals. Men and women could be friends... *just friends.*

"Serena, you're not stupid. He's a moron. If he really is cheating on you, that makes him the world's greatest fool and idiot." Parker leaned in and opened his palms upward.

I placed my hands in his as he closed his around mine. I sighed. What would I do if he really was cheating on me? I shuddered at the thought of my daughter bouncing between two homes, not seeing her every day, and splitting holidays. She was the greatest piece of my life, no matter what happened between Eric and I, she would always be worth any ounce of what we shared. I didn't want to lose any more time with her—I barely had enough time with her as is. Sometimes, all I wanted was to just stay home with her. Envy paced through me when I'd see the stay-at-home-moms pushing strollers or meeting at the park, laughing and gossiping while their children played together.

"Who do you think he's seeing?" Parker broke through my racing thoughts.

"I bet it's that damn redhead he works with all the time. She has giant, fake boobs and wears an extra small scrub top so they look like they're gonna explode. She's a tech or something."

Parker smiled mischievously. "Can I see a picture?"

"Not funny. You're a shit best friend, and you're even shittier for bringing me to this place." I rolled my eyes, throwing my napkin at him. I felt like I had just consumed a meal intended for a small, domesticated bunny.

"Look, I know a guy who's a private investigator. Let me know if you want me to put y'all in touch." I realized we were still holding hands and I quickly pulled away.

"This is crazy. He's my husband for God's sake. I just need to talk to him. Maybe he's running off to play golf or drink? I mean, our lives are chaotic. It doesn't have to mean he's screwing another woman and ruining our family... right?" I wondered out loud, knowing I didn't want an honest response from Parker.

"Sure, Seri. Just let me know if you need help with anything. You know I love you and Lola." Parker smiled softly and tilted his wrist upward, revealing his shiny Rolex. "We gotta get going. I'm here for you, always," he added before grabbing both our bowls to toss in the trash.

"Do you remember taking a multiple-choice test in school and erasing an answer for a different option? It's as if no matter how hard you tried to erase it, there would still be residual pencil marks left behind from your original answer. Isn't that how life is? No matter how much you try to move on to the next answer or the next question... the original choice will linger and trail behind you." I looked at Sully as we crossed the street.

"So, you're worried if you leave Eric, he'll still be around?"

"Even if he is cheating on me. We have a child together... he'll always be the smudge on my perfect sheet of paper."

After what felt like an eternity of patients and notes, I finally got home. Lola was spending the weekend at my parents' house, and Eric was supposedly in Charleston. He had texted me multiple times and there were some missed calls from him. I texted him once about Lola, but ignored the rest. The irony of guilt is that a person feels so terrible about what they are lying about that they end up wasting their efforts, proving they really aren't doing what they are guilty about in the first place. *So why even do it?*

Our home felt quiet and empty without Lola. I was on-call this weekend and with Eric out of town, if I got called in for a delivery, there would be no point in dragging her out of bed and dropping her off at my parents' house in the middle of the night. I checked my phone, scrolling through pictures and videos my mom sent of Lola. She really was an amazing grandmother, which was odd because she really didn't win any awards as a mother. Chap came up to me and flopped over on his belly. Crouching to the floor, I gave him a good scratch and his tail slapped against the floor excitedly.

"Hey, buddy… wanna split some cereal for dinner?" I smiled at him and made way to the kitchen. He pranced after me.

My heart began to race faster because even from a distance, I could see red. On top of our sleek, white counters sat a single, red rose. I walked toward it, lifted it into my hand, then turned and looked around me. Suddenly, the unnerving silence felt louder than noise. Chills permeated my skin.

"Ouch." A thick thorn became tinged with red as blood dripped into droplets onto the counters. I stared down at the puddle that was quickly building. Just as I was about to reach for a napkin, I paused and pushed my finger into my mouth. The taste of my blood made me cringe. I stared down at the droplets that were lingering on the counter—the white and hints of gold from the marble looked almost beautiful with the red. With the tip of the rose stem, I traced the blood, smearing it on the surface, watching it fade into a lighter shade as it spread. My phone vibrated. Holding it up, I saw a text from an unknown number.

Hello, darling...

I leaned against the counter and instantly looked

around. I could feel my body turn cold. Some reason in that moment, I felt as if a pair of eyes were watching me and knew what I was doing. Grabbing the paper towel, I quickly wiped the messy counter.

Macy? Hey... how'd you get my number?

She replied immediately.

I got it from Eric. I saw him outside the other day. Hope you enjoyed the pie.

Oh, I'm so sorry. I should have come by. Thank you so much. It was delicious....

I'm glad you enjoyed it...

Macy, did you happen to come by my house today? I hoped my message wouldn't seem accusatory, but I had to know.

Darling, I'm not in town. Anyway, I'll need my pie dish back sometime soon. You can drop it off with my maid, Jasmine.

Right. So sorry, again. I'll drop it off tomorrow. Night, Macy.

Goodnight, darling...

I re-read the text messages. Who even talked like that? Macy Callahan was unlike anyone I'd ever met before, that was for sure. She even put a bakery bought pie in her own crystal dish.

After work, I had picked up a box of the sweetest cereal I could find. Eric never let us have this kind of stuff at home. I curled up on the couch with a bowl of cereal for dinner. The rose sat in front of me on the coffee table, taunting me. *How in the world did it get inside our house, and most of all, who was inside our home?* Flipping through the channels, I settled on some reality dating show, even though I wanted to watch the new crime documentary. Though I couldn't because I knew I wouldn't be able to sleep.

My phone rang and I looked down at the screen. *Can a girl not get a minute to eat cereal in peace? Damn.*

"Yea?" I replied hastily.

"Babe? Look, I swear, I'm just in Charleston at a conference. I sent you the link and information in an email. What else would I be doing? I love you so much, Serena. I always have and always will. We just need to getaway together… it's been a long year. Let's just go to dinner at The Jewel when I get back." He was pleading with me.

"Okay. Let's just talk when you're home. I'm tired. I have to get some sleep. I'm guessing there'll be a few deliveries this weekend. Goodnight."

"I love you, Serena… goodnight. We're good right?"

"Yea. Super. Bye." I hung up the phone, my eyes trailed to the large, black-and-white wedding portrait that was displayed next to my favorite picture of Lola. We looked so happy and in love. Sometimes I wondered if we were just posing and pretending or did we really feel that way? I could remember the photographer telling us to look into one another's eyes and smile. Then, she directed us to hold each other in a specific way. It was so staged. Is that what our life was? *A staged series of events just to seem perfect? If perfection was what we chased, why was imperfection the only thing that found us?*

I was about to head upstairs, but not before arming the security system that covered the entire downstairs. I told Eric I wanted to add security to our upstairs but as usual, we were living in a rat race and couldn't get things done quickly. The turnaround time to accomplish anything was always months later.

I peered outside from the floor-to-ceiling glass windows that lined our living room. I could see the Callahan's upstairs windows with one dim light still beaming. A shadow appeared and I leaned over the couch to see clearly. The thin figure slowly peeled back one curtain. Squinting as best as I could, I saw fingers move in a slow wave. I immediately hid behind the couch, feeling warmth in my face.

Our house was on more of a hill than the Callahan's, and with the glass windows encompassing the entire living room, we could see a good amount through theirs. It was one thing I really disliked about this house, but the windows emitted an incredible amount of natural light, so the benefits outweighed the negatives when we came to see it. *If I could see so much of the inside of their home, what could they see in ours?*

Making it to our room, I opened our closet doors and traced my hand across Eric's side of neatly lined dress shirts. Stopping at his coat, I leaned in and inhaled. The soft wool was embedded with the scent of cologne he only wore when he went out to nice places. It seemed fresh, I ran my finger against it and noticed a single thin strand of blonde hair teasing me. My heart sank. I plucked it off, lifting it above me. I watched the light glisten against it. Tears filled with fear as deceit lined my lids.

Oh, Eric. What have you done? Who was she? Where did you meet her? What was better about her than me?

I'd given Eric everything. *Everything.* Tears flooded my cheeks. How could one single strand of hair be the culprit of my entire marriage crumbling, falling, and drowning. It showcased how weak we were. That the woman behind this hair held enough power to sink our entire marriage.

Pulling off my clothes, I looked over at my nightstand. I knew I shouldn't, I had been doing so well lately. But the pain I felt was too much to carry, and I needed a release—a release that helped me breathe through the thick air that suffocated my lungs. I slid the drawer open and pulled out the wooden box. The dagger stared at me as I lifted it out and walked to the bathroom. Leaning down, I turned the faucet to our large, standalone tub. The water echoed against the sides as it rapidly filled. I slowly unscrewed one of the golden bottles that lined the small wooden tray, slowly dribbling some of the purple liquid into it.

The smell of lavender rose into the steam, coiling around me. Pulling my clothes off, I stepped into the hot water and submerged my head underneath. Feeling as if I were in a different world, I slowly counted. I felt safe, like no one could hurt me here. I was weightless and free. Opening my eyes, I froze. There was a lingering dark shadow above me, reaching for me. Trying to save me? *Was there even anyone to save?*

Forcing myself out, I exhaled a loud breath, choking on the water I had consumed. The steam pricked against my arms, as I glanced around the open space like a deer in headlights, I sunk back into the tub. Staring at the shiny sharp steel, I saw a reflection filled with disappointment. *A reflection of nothing more than a broken, shattered girl. I was drowning in life. I didn't know if I could swim to shore... it seemed so much easier to give in and float away. Forever.*

My perfect life was being shred apart, piece by piece. *I had lost control.* I had given him the world. How was I still not enough for him? Taking the dagger into my hand, I gripped the wood tightly. Touching the sharp, shiny tip carefully, as if I weren't trying to get hurt. My skin creased inward while I watched the blade puncture my smooth flesh. Holding it against my wrist, I could feel fear embed into my veins. Tears rolled against my cheek as a hint of salty liquid hit my parted, trembling lips. My body shook as I watched the steel deepen into my wrist.

Lola.

She needed me.

Choking on my tears, I let my body roll slightly to the side as water splashed out onto the shiny, marble floor. Sliding the cold, wet steel against my skin, and with my eyes clenched shut, I let it carve into the groove right above my hip. Lines, well... scars decorated the place where a couple unsightly stretch marks laid. They blended together, just as the pain did from both events that crafted the lasting wounds.

I looked down as the clear, steamy water became tinged with blood that raced around. It was a picture painted, a statement without words, but more than anything, it was a release. A release I had full control over. The pain that lingered against my open flesh reminded me to just breathe. I was only human. The physical pain I felt released the mental torture within. Questions swarmed in my head as I stared at my naked body. I was fucking perfect. Beyond the hidden scars that told a story of their own, I was more than Eric Hudson deserved.

Grabbing the dainty black chemise out of my drawer, I pulled it over my head and towel dried my hair while looking into the mirror again. Leaning in, I traced my face with my damp, prune-like fingertips. I couldn't help but feel tears brewing. The wrinkles near my eyes were growing clearer, the elasticity of my skin was no longer the same as my roaring twenties. Looking down, there were bottles and bottles of expensive skincare. Slamming my hand against the marble counter, one swift motion wiped the counter clean of the products. The glass bottles crashed onto the floor around my feet. What was the fucking point? Stepping over the shards of glass, I walked to my bed. The soft, white comforter felt warm against my cold body. The crisp, fall air was starting to get cooler, and all I wished for in that moment was for the world to swallow me whole, to put me out of the misery and pain I still felt.

I closed my eyes and drifted into a state of deep sleep, letting my dreams wash over the harshness of my reality. Except I knew that was far from the truth of what would happen, because it wouldn't be a dream. It would be a nightmare, in which I would be drowning on the water that would fill my lungs and all I would beg for is to breathe. Finally, a wave of gratitude would eventually wash over me because I'd wake up. I'm given another chance to live my normal, perfect life. Every night this happens.

My dreams become nightmares, and nightmares turn into opportunities that remind me how much my life is and will be perfect. The only issue is when you close your eyes to fall asleep, you lose control and when you do that, bad things happen—after all, that is why we have nightmares. So, I've learned the key is to grip onto control and make sure you can and will keep your reality the way you want it to be... just make sure you know it isn't a dream.

CHAPTER SIX

"Dr. Indigo, Julia Burke is in labor." The nurse's voice trickled through my phone. I felt a cape of grogginess cover me, and it took me a minute to realize I was actually awake. Feeling trapped in my own body, I didn't want to open my eyes.

"Put me through to the triage nurse." I yawned and sat up in my bed. It was four in the morning.

"This is Reese," the nurse replied.

"Hey, Reese, it's Dr. Indigo. What's going on with Mrs. Burke?"

"She's five centimeters dilated, contractions every six to eight minutes," Reese replied.

"Okay, get a room ready for her. I'm on my way." I hung up and saw a text from Parker.

Hey, just checking in. Hope you're okay. Did you talk to Eric?

Heading in for a delivery now. Sorry, I fell asleep before I got your text. I'm okay. I may take you up on that private investigator. Talk to you in the morning.

I threw my glasses on, tied my hair into a neat ponytail, and pulled on a pair of scrubs.

I walked over to my nightstand, habitually sliding on my wedding band but leaving my engagement ring behind. Grabbing my pearl earrings, I realized they weren't there.

"What the hell?" I muttered.

Frantically, I searched my nightstand and the floor around it. I knew with certainty I had taken them off only a few hours ago, leaving them in the small bowl. I paced around my bedroom as if the earrings would magically appear. Rubbing my head, I tried to recollect my memory and pictured taking them off before bed. My phone buzzed with Nurse Reese's updates on my patient.

I had to go. Running down the stairs, my mind was obsessing over my earrings throughout my entire drive. Once I got to the parking lot, I pulled out a tube of lipstick and swiped it over my otherwise chapped lips. *Old habits die hard.* I slowly counted and took some deep breaths. I needed to focus. A pair of earrings weren't worth screwing up bringing a baby into the world. After all, if something happened during delivery, it could potentially wreck and alter the course of those parents' lives forever. As always, the delivery and adrenaline paired together into a blur, helping me concentrate and complete another flawless delivery.

"Mommy!" Lola's pink lips and nostrils were displayed on my screen.

"Hi, baby, can you flip the screen around so I can see you better?" I laughed.

"Dis better?" she asked sweetly with the screen now showing me the floor.

"Sure, baby. How are you? Did you eat breakfast?" I asked with a yawn.

"Gigi is making me armlet, but I want pancakes!" she whined.

"Armlet? Oh, an omelet?"

"Baby, you be a good girl and eat what Gigi makes you. Let me talk to her. I love you so much and will see you soon." I blew her a kiss.

"Hi, Mom. I hope Lola is behaving for you guys."

"She's doing great. How's work? Honey, you look tired. Maybe a bit more concealer..." She pointed to her face, which was meticulously painted in heavy makeup.

"Work is good. Had a delivery that just finished. I can't find my earrings anywhere... I had them on last night and now they are missing." I ignored her snide comment, which was a skill that was excessively necessary as Daphne Indigo's daughter.

"The pearls we had made for you?" Her voice rose.

"Yea, Mom. I mean, I wear them daily and had them on my nightstand. This morning, they were gone." I rubbed my head, feeling like I was sixteen all over again. My mother would intimidate me even if I were sixty.

"Well, you better find them, just backtrack. This is exactly why I waited to give you anything of such value. You should be a bit more responsible, Serena... I mean, just look at yourself, honey. Drink more fluids and take care of yourself. You have a husband... he doesn't wanna bite into a sweet watermelon and find seeds."

"Yea, Mom. Thanks for watching Lola." I hung up and let my face fall into my palms.

"Seri?" I looked up and my eyes met Parker's. He was standing with two coffees, wearing a pair of blue scrubs with messy hair and tired eyes.

"What are you doing here? It's my weekend on-call," I questioned as he approached the table, sliding a coffee to me.

"You know that patient I did the complete hysterectomy on last week? She had some complications overnight. ER paged me and I had to come in." He leaned back into the cafeteria chair, stretching his arms over his head.

"Oh, sorry. Is she okay?" I sipped the hot liquid gratefully. He knew exactly how I took my coffee—one sugar with oat milk.

"She's great. How was your night?" he asked, taking a sip of his own.

"It was fine. Except my pearl earrings are missing, and I swore I had them on my nightstand. Weird things keep happening, and I'm starting to freak out." I blinked quickly, looking around our table. Brushing my hand against my exposed neck, I realized my hair was still tied up. Eric hated when I put my hair in messy buns or ponytails. He told me I looked like I didn't care, and every time he said that it reminded me of my mother. While he lectured me on my appearance all this time, he saw it fit to care for someone else besides his wife.

"The ones you always wear? The ones your parents gave you?" Parker furrowed his eyebrows.

"Yea. I mean, I've had them for over a decade and have never lost them... I swear they were on my nightstand, and by four this morning, they were gone." I rubbed my face against my palms.

"That's odd. Let me come over and help you look," he offered.

"Really? I just don't want to go home and be alone, so that would be nice." I smiled but exhaustion was creeping through and dizziness set in. The caffeine didn't help; instead, it made my heart race as my body begged for real rest.

"Yea, let's go. I'll drive, and if you get paged, just take my car." He stood and held his arm out for me to take. I laughed, intertwining my arm in his as he led us to his sleek, black Porsche.

Inhaling the sweet leather scent, there weren't any lingering Cheerios or coffee cups. It was clean and sexy. *Just like him.* I glanced over at Parker. He had pulled on a pair of black aviators and his jaw was slightly clenched. Rubbing my head, I snapped out of my romantic fantasy. *Still married, Serena.*

"Well, in other news, my mom just compared me to a watermelon with seeds…" I broke the silence.

"Huh, is that so? Oh, Daphne." He let out a small sigh of solidarity.

"Yep… good ol' Daphne Indigo's famous words. I guess she'll be thrilled to know my husband is probably screwing a seedless watermelon…" I said, as I chipped away at my nail polish.

Parker shook his head with disgust. "Ugh… that's a really gross image, Seri."

"Welcome to my life." I turned away and looked out the window. My right hand habitually touched my left ring finger while I spun my thick diamond wedding band around. Suddenly, it felt so forced sitting on my finger. I didn't even know the man behind it.

Parker and I spent some time scouring through the house. We flipped everything inside and out, searching for my beloved pearls. They were *gone.*

"Parker, I am serious. Someone has been in my house. I just feel… I just feel like I'm being watched." I crossed my arms over my chest and sunk into the couch.

"Why don't you get some security cameras?" Parker offered.

"We have them. Eric said the tapes were clean. Nothing's on them." I kept my eyes on the orange and red trees that were lush and full outside the windows. The leaves were swaying ever so gently in the wind.

"You can always stay with me…"

"Parker, you want me to bring Eric and Lola?" I smirked at him.

"Well, you, yes. Lola, yes. Your cheating husband

who is screwing a seedless watermelon… no." He shrugged, following my gaze to the windows. A moment later, we both erupted into laughter.

"Oh, Sully… what's my life become? Remember when we'd walk back to our apartments late at night after studying and you'd give me piggyback rides because I'd complain about my aching feet." I laughed while reminiscing.

"Oh, yea. Except, some reason when my feet ached, you never returned the favor." Parker winked.

"I remember one fall night, we had grabbed tacos at that small hole in the wall, the leaves had completely covered the sidewalk. I slipped because it had rained the night before and you caught me. You have always been there." The smiled faded from our faces and our eyes met. I could feel my palms growing warm.

"Serena…" Parker's gaze lingered on my lips. My heart was pounding, and I swore it'd burst through my chest cavity. Parker slid closer to me, lifting his warm, masculine hands to my face. Heat rose inside me, and I felt as if I was losing control over myself.

This time the loss of control was invigorating. *Freeing.*

He leaned in closer, and I could feel the grazing of his minty breath on my face. Our mouths met and my knees instantly clenched together. Parker used his tongue to part my lips while his hands entangled in my hair, gently guiding me closer.

My phone rang, slicing through the heat of the room and the moment.

"I have to get that… it could be Lola." My breath was heavy.

Parker's mouth was still pacing down my neck.

"Hello?" I answered without checking the caller ID. "Hello? Who is this?" I glanced at my screen and saw *private caller* displayed. I could hear light breathing on the phone that sent chills up my spine.

"Hello?" I slid off Parker as he straightened himself upright, looking at me with concern.

I could feel the lines in my forehead creasing as I put the phone on speaker. Parker's eyes grew wide when he heard the sinister heavy breathing on the other end.

"Hello? Who the fuck is this? If you call this number again, I'll track you down and you'll regret ever calling," Parker shouted in the phone.

The call ended. My hands trembled as I stared at the screen.

"I told you something is off. I'm so scared. I don't want Lola coming here until I figure out what the hell is going on." Tears stung my eyes.

"Come here. It's probably some stupid kid messing

with you, Seri. Why don't I stay the night?" Parker pulled me closer.

"Parker, we can't do this. I'm married. I think you've stayed the night more than my husband. I know he's up to something, but I'm still married and the vows I took... they mean something." I looked up at him.

"I know, and that's why I... Look, I'll sleep on the couch. Let me be here for you. You've gotten too good at taking care of yourself, Seri. It's not the way things should be." Parker rested his chin on my head, gently placing a kiss on top.

"Okay." I closed my eyes, inhaling the cologne that emitted from his shirt. It was different from Eric's—light and comforting. Eric's always seemed like a mask. I guess that was fitting considering that is what he was doing all along, *wearing a mask.*

CHAPTER SEVEN

woke up to the windows darkened by the setting sun with humming coming from the kitchen. Sitting up, I turned and checked my phone. How had I slept so deeply? I had four missed calls from Eric and texts from my mom. I called Eric back, even though I didn't know what to say to him. How was that possible when he was my husband? I married a stranger—a stranger who seemingly found joy in making a fool out of me.

"Serena? Hey, were you at the hospital?" Eric sounded apprehensive.

"Seri! Dinners ready!" Parker's voice boasted loudly in the background. I instantly covered the speaker of my phone, squeezing my eyes shut.

"What the hell is Parker doing at our house? You have the audacity to fucking accuse me of having an affair, but the second I leave my house, you have him over?" Eric bellowed so loudly, my neck and hand jerked in opposite directions.

"Eric, I checked the guest list of the Emergency Medicine Conference. Your name wasn't on it, you lying asshole. You sent me an old one. I'm done," I hissed and immediately hung up, feeling my heart race through my shirt.

I hadn't told Parker I had found that out. I hadn't told him about the blonde hair on my husband's coat. I was still processing everything. I knew my husband was with another woman. I checked our credit card statements and found expensive dinners at the nicest restaurants, charges at a luxury spa and inn. I even scrolled, backdating to "conferences" Eric had supposedly gone to and found flower deliveries and jewelry purchases instead. None of which I had received. I felt so naïve and foolish.

Eric knew I never checked our statements. They were on auto pay, with fraud alert set up, so there really was no need. He took advantage of my trust in more ways than one. My phone rang out of control as I hit ignore, shutting it off after texting my mom one more time about Lola. Unlike Eric, I couldn't just run off into the sunset with a lover; I had to be a parent 24/7.

I got up and made my way to the kitchen. Parker was standing there with takeout neatly placed on dishes with two wineglasses. His was filled with wine, while mine was filled with sparkling water. There was no drinking when on-call over the weekend.

"Thanks for letting me nap and having dinner set up. It smells divine." I inhaled the spices and warmth emitting from our plates.

"Golden Taj, your favorite." Parker smiled at me, raising his glass.

"What are we toasting to?" I asked.

"*You.* The strongest, smartest, most perfect woman and doctor I know." Parker tilted his glass toward mine.

"I'm not perfect..." I scooped a generous amount of chicken tikka masala on a piece of naan.

He looked away. "You are to me."

"Sometimes being perfect is exhausting..." I pushed the curry around.

We spent the next few minutes devouring the delicious Indian takeout when suddenly, a loud bang echoed from upstairs.

I jerked upright, glaring at Parker. He squinted, looking at the ceiling above us. Quickly walking over to the butcher block filled with knives, he revealed the sharpest and longest one.

"Oh my god…" I whispered. I felt my body grow cold as fear took over, yet I felt frozen in my seat.

"Serena, call 9-1-1 and go to your car. I'm going upstairs," Parker whispered.

"No! Please don't go, come with me!" I begged.

Parker put his finger over my lips to silence me, then he walked upstairs with the large knife in his hand. A few moments later, I could hear multiple footsteps running. I gasped and rattled off my address and information to the emergency responder who seemed to take eternity to answer. Running outside, tears streaked down my face as I prayed Parker would be alright. My trembling hands could barely unlock the car, and once I finally did, I climbed in quickly then hit the lock button multiple times while peering up at my home. I thought a security system and locks would keep the monsters out. Yet, for some reason, as much as I tried to keep them away, all the monsters were inside my house, *always inside my house.*

The sun had set, and the dark sky provided a backdrop for even more terror and fear that coursed through my body. The cold fall air felt haunting, and I didn't know what to do. I didn't want to leave Parker, but I didn't want to die. I had Lola to live for. Inhaling the dry heat that pumped in from my car vents, I counted slowly.

"1-2-3... ...4..." I whispered softly, but the tremor in my hands matched the one that lingered in my voice.

Pulling out of my driveway, I headed for the cul-de-sac, driving around until the flashing red and blue lights appeared. Swiftly turning the car around, the shrill sound of rubber against the cold pavement echoed into my ears.

Two police officers jumped out with their hands on their guns. I pulled over, watching what seemed to be a movie scene and not my life or home.

Before they could even go through the large double doors I had left opened, Parker appeared, holding a shadow by the collar. I squinted, not being able to make the person out. My heart was racing so fast that I didn't realize my knuckles were turning white from the grip I had around my steering wheel.

The police officers grabbed and pinned the man against their car door as I slowly creeped up to my home. Tears poured out of my eyes as I thought of Lola.

What if she had been home?

"Parker?" My voice sounded meek and hoarse. He turned away from the officers and raced toward me. His hair was a mess and his face had clear scratches. One scratch was slowly dribbling blood out on his otherwise smooth skin.

"Oh my god! Parker!" I cried out, throwing my arms around him.

One of the officers strolled up to me. "Serena Hudson?"

"Um, yes? I'm Serena Indigo." My body shook with panic as I held on to Parker tightly.

"Ma'am, is anyone else home?" the officer asked with a clear southern drawl.

"No, it was just us." I looked up toward Parker. He had his hand pressed against the swelling on his face, while his other arm protectively held me.

The officer turned to Parker with a raised brow. "Are you Eric Hudson, sir?"

"No, I'm Parker Sully. We are friends and work together," he calmly stated.

The officer looked between us with clear judgment and nodded while writing something on his small notepad.

"Officer, who in the world is that? What did he

want?" I was irritated that it felt like Parker and I were being interrogated rather than given answers.

"Kid's name is Brooks Callahan. Know 'em?" The officer was balancing a toothpick in his mouth and was obnoxiously chewing it. I couldn't help but want to rip it out of his dried-out lips. "Ma'am?"

"Brooks? Oh my god, yes, he lives right there." I pointed to the Callahan house. "What did he want?"

"Not sure yet. My buddy, Officer Lopez, is questioning him, but really waitin' for his folks to answer their phone. He's a minor, so we can't do much without 'em."

"His mom is out of town and his dad is an attorney. James Callahan," I added without being asked.

Suddenly it crossed my mind that Macy Callahan and Eric were both out of town in the Charleston area. *Blonde hair.* I felt stomach acid rise into my throat as I recalled inserting a fresh IUD for her so she could basically go fuck my husband.

I pulled away from Parker, bent over in the grass, and vomited with tears purging from my eyes as my stomach emptied itself in disgust.

"Hey, Serena, hey. You're okay. I'm here. You're

safe." Parker rubbed my back gently as I choked on the thick saliva lingering in my mouth.

Collapsing into Parker's arms, I prayed that magically I'd wake up from this nightmare and we'd all be back to normal. Well, whatever the hell I apparently thought normal was.

"Serena?" I opened my eyes, quickly sitting up and realizing what had unfolded the night before. Looking down, I noticed the gray bedding and glanced around at the stunning modern furniture and décor. There I was, in Parker Sully's bed. This was something I fantasized about, but blinking my sticky, dry eyes, I realized waking up didn't let me escape my nightmares. There stood Eric, directly in front of me, through the haze of my vision. It didn't feel like I was looking at my husband; instead, I felt like I was looking at my worst enemy—the man who betrayed me, who betrayed us.

"Baby, Parker called me last night and told me everything. I swung by your parents and checked in on Lola and told them everything. They are keeping her there until we figure out everything. Your mom sent this."

He lifted the blueberry pie in the air. Of course, my mother would bake a pie when she found out someone broke into my house—as if a baked good could alleviate a world of pain and anxiety I felt that my parents never saw.

"What did Brooks want from our house?" My voice sounded raspy from a full night of crying and waking up in sheer terror. I kept reminding myself that a teenager would be highly unlikely to come and try to kill me. But then again, why would he be stupid enough to break-in?

"They don't know yet. James isn't letting them question him. He's going to meet with us later today if you are up for it." Eric sat down on the bed. He pushed the straggling hair away from my face, which made me flinch in repulsion.

"Baby? Are you okay?" He leaned in to kiss me, but I quickly turned my head, knowing I had nothing left in my stomach to throw up.

My eyes stung with tears. "No, I'm not fucking okay. You li—"

"Hey, man, I think she should get some rest. How about you go home and rest, and I'll bring her later when she's ready to meet with the Callahans." Parker leaned against the doorframe.

Eric sighed. I knew this was humiliating, finding me in Parker's *bed*. He deserved it, though. I was terrified to be alone, so Parker slept next to me all night, but he didn't lay a finger on me. After helping me change into his oversized T-shirt—since my clothes reeked of sweat and vomit—he held me while I cried. He wasn't just a great partner at work, he was a great partner in life. Except, I had married a complete prick and had a child with him. You couldn't turn back from that. I would be connected to Eric Hudson for all of eternity, and that alone was the greatest punishment to me in this moment.

Hours later, I finally showered and got dressed. It took me double the time to paint makeup all over my face—my mother didn't care if an apocalypse broke out, a woman should have her face on and a proper one at all times. I left Parker's and headed to my parents to spend some time with Lola before meeting Eric at the police station with the Callahans. Guilt panged me knowing I'd been such a bad mom lately, either busy working or handling the never-ending drama that seemed to follow me. Did fathers ever feel "dad guilt"? Why is it that as women, we drown ourselves in shame and guilt, yet men can be completely content with doing and being the bare minimum? The joys of societal pressure and expectations burned deep.

Pulling up to their house, I paused. Well, more so their estate, *our estate.* Perched on endless land before Charlotte boomed and became a big city, it had a gothic feel to it. It didn't fit with my mother at all. She was a beautiful Southern belle, always donning beautiful outfits, shiny dark hair, and pink lips. The house she created into a home was a façade, just like the one she constantly had on. I parked my car and closed my eyes, rolling the window down.

I could hear my laughter when I was just a girl—a girl with the world at her disposal, dancing in circles and laughing away. Everyone knew my parents growing up, and we were untouchable. Boys wanted to date me and girls wanted to be me. I could be whoever I wanted to be. Well, as long as Ian and Daphne Indigo approved.

"Serena!" My mother stood on the front porch, smiling widely. She was wearing an elegant two-piece suit that was most definitely designer, with oversized sunglasses covering her eyes. Her dark hair was pinned neatly, while pearls lined her neck and ears. The epitome of a lady. She was truly beautiful. I looked just like her, and maybe that's why I hated my reflection so much. My whole life, I was terrified I'd become her.

"Hi mom…" I looked at her. Thankfully, I had chosen the hot pink sheath dress.

"Oh sweetie, you look so absolutely tired. Come on in. I'm simply terrified for my girls." She opened her arms wide and swallowed me in her signature hug with a gentle pat on my back—the pat that made you feel like she really didn't want to be giving you the hug in the first place.

"I'm not tired. I'm just drained. Cut me a fucking break, Mama." I pushed out of her arms. Her eyes widened as her pink-lined lips parted, but she pasted them back together just as quickly.

Lola was happily playing with her new toys she had conned my parents into buying as usual, as my mom sat down in the chair nearby and began crying with concern, holding a monogrammed handkerchief at her nose.

"Serena, I think it's best you and Lola come stay with us until things are sorted. Your home was broken into, and I don't know why you'd even think to go back there right now," my dad said to me. Ian Indigo, my dad. He was so different from my mom. Warm and loving. He didn't care what I looked like; he just wanted to watch me succeed. He was what they called "old money." He wanted to become a doctor, too, but his dad—my grandfather, an abusive, rich drunk would never have allowed that. Family business or nothing. My dad devoured books and self-taught himself a world of knowledge. My great-grandfather owned a chain of hotels and through the generations, it got passed along. My dad made me swear I would go make something of my own. He told me it would be my decision whether to keep the hotels or sell them off. Either way, for generations to come, no one would ever have to worry about money.

My mother, dramatic as always, was gently dabbing at her eyes with a monogrammed handkerchief.

"Mom, can you please just stop for once? We don't need to make this all about you." I rolled my eyes, sinking back into the sofa.

Lola had gone off to the kitchen with the nanny to get a snack after barely even giving me a hug. Sometimes I missed her as a baby, when all she wanted was to be held by me, when she was completely dependent on me and needed me for every little thing. Now, new toys and snacks meant more. I knew I was being irrational but, in the moment, it felt as if no one needed me.

My mother began to cry harder. "Ian, look at how she's speaking to me."

"Baby girl, please, you know your mother is just worried to the moon and back about you and Lola." As soon as my mother looked away, he winked at me. I shook my head, laughing under my breath, concealing it with a cough as my mother glared between us.

"Bella!" my mother called out.

A woman with deep, beautiful caramel skin wearing a bright yellow sundress came out immediately. Her hair was neatly pinned in a bun, and she looked to be barely forty.

"Yes, Mrs. Indigo?" she said meekly.

"Bella, go on and get Serena some sweet tea with a slice of lemon and one of them tomato mayo sandwiches."

She immediately turned and walked back to the kitchen with urgency.

I stood, going into the kitchen after her. I needed a break from Daphne's melodramatic performance.

"Hey... Bella, is it? You must be new since we haven't met yet." I could see Lola and a nanny my mother had hired to watch her own granddaughter outside, swinging.

"Well, it's actually Isabella, but Mrs. Indigo says it's to... ethnic?" She suppressed a snicker and turned away. Her accent was smooth and beautiful.

"Wow, I'm so sorry, Isabella. My mother... Well, she's just... insane." I sighed with embarrassment. *How the fuck is the name Isabella too ethnic?*

She slid the sweet tea over to me, and I plucked the lemon off the glass.

"I hate lemon. I mean, I actually despise it, and my

mother knows that." I smiled at Isabella, who began to laugh with me, hoping it would offer her a slice of solace.

"Would you like a tomato mayo sandwich, Dr. Indigo?"

"Definitely not. I'll never get the appeal of white bread saturated in mayo, salt, pepper, and tomato being a southern delicacy."

Turning away, I walked toward the window, watching Lola's young face burst into giggles as she went higher and higher on the swing. The Carolina blue skies met the grass and for a moment, I almost felt as if she were flying away from me. *Far, far away.* My hand planted against the cold glass and I kept my gaze on her. One... two... three... I begin slowly counting my breaths. My heart rate increased, and I felt panic rush into me, turning my body cold.

"Dr. Indigo, are you alright?" Isabella's voice broke my count, and I inhaled one last breath before plastering a smile on my face and turned back toward her.

"Of course. I'm just in awe how children are just so free and live in oblivion. You don't even realize it when you're young. You wish away your youth, wanting the freedom and autonomy of adulthood, yet I've never felt less free in my entire life than as an adult." I looked away, setting my sweet tea on the table. I could feel Isabella staring at me curiously.

"Take care, Isabella." I waved at her and went back to my parents. Standing in the archway, I studied them. My mom was on her phone, smiling at probably some group chat with her conservative, two-faced friends. My father was puffing a cigar, sipping tea while flipping through a book. They had been married for an eternity. My mom was only eighteen when she married my father. I didn't remember them ever fighting, or even bickering. They just meshed together well, even as complete opposites. How could two people love one another even when their flaws were always on full display?

"Well, I really have to head out. We are meeting the Callahans at the police station," I said softly.

My mom sniffled, tucking her phone away. "Serena, honey, I really wish you'd let our lawyer come with you…"

"Mom… Brooks Callahan is a teenage kid who happens to be my neighbor. What on earth is a lawyer going to do?"

"Serena Indigo, you best mind your manners next time you're here," my mother called out after me.

Just before my hand hit the brass handle, I went back to the doorway.

"I'm so sorry, Mother." I gave her a curtsy, rolling my eyes as if I truly regressed to a sixteen-year-old. My father eyed me in shock and began to laugh loudly as my mother's jaw dropped, shooting a look of discontent to my dad.

CHAPTER EIGHT

*L*eaving my parents' house, I thought about my mom. Her southern accent always annoyed me. She was born and raised in a small town on the outskirts of South Carolina. I had a slight southern drawl, but thankfully, not even close to hers. Going to college, especially a liberal one, had helped dissipate it even more. I just couldn't stand to be any more like my mother. I pulled up and saw Eric's car, he was standing beside it, looking down at his phone.

"Hey," I shot in his direction.

"Serena, I wish you had let me drive you here. How are you feeling? I'll have to thank Parker for taking care of you and everything he did last night. I know

I'm such an asshole to him. I owe him big time." He looped his arm around me.

I inhaled his scent. He didn't smell comforting or like the man I fell in love with. He had changed and maybe I had, too. I looked up into his green eyes, which no longer had an effect on me. The eyes that once sent chills through my body and heat between my legs now seemed cold and filled with secrets and deceit.

I pulled away from him. "We should go in."

"Yea, we can talk more when we get home." He reached and grabbed my hand, holding it tightly as we walked inside the station.

"Home? Where would that be, Eric?" I shot at him, pushing through the glass police station doors.

I looked across the table and saw James and Macy Callahan, but Brooks was nowhere to be seen. James was wearing a suit, the bags under his eyes more apparent. He had that same cognac leather notebook neatly placed in front of him, tapping a shiny silver pen against it. Macy had makeup plastered on her face and sunglasses covering her eyes. Her red lips were pursed together while her blonde hair didn't have a piece out of place. I wanted to reach over and slap the shit out of her, but until I confirmed my suspicions, I couldn't go around making accusations. Especially since it not only involved my family, it also involved my ego.

"Dr. Indigo, we would like to extend our sincerest apologizes for what occurred at your residence last night. I am ashamed and embarrassed at the behavior Brooks displayed, and I want you to know that ramifications are in process." James had his hands folded neatly on the table. I tilted my head, examining him. No wonder he was one of Charlotte's best attorneys. I cleared my throat. It felt sticky and dry.

"Hey, Lopez, let's get water and coffees in here," James shouted at the open conference door as if he could read my mine with ease. I forgot he knew the inside and out of the police department, too.

"What was he doing in our house? What did he want? Things have been going missing, so I'm realizing how it could have been him all this time." I leaned in, starting into the serious face of James Callahan while Macy fidgeted with her enormous diamond ring showing zero emotion.

"Dr. Hudson—"

"Indigo."

"Right, Dr. Indigo. I can assure you this was a one-time occurrence. Brooks was dared into entering your home and taking a photo of himself to show his friends. A simple teenage foolish game," James replied.

"What?" I questioned him.

"It was a dumb game of truth or dare. Can we let this shit go now?" Macy cut in.

"I have my own assumption, actually. How about he knows something connected between our families and is lashing out?" I glared between Eric and Macy.

"Serena... please, let's just go." Eric sounded nervous and started to stand.

"Go? I'm not going anywhere. I'm pressing charges!" I yelled out.

"Serena! You will not press charges against my fourteen-year-old. James, say something!" Macy cried out.

"Dr. Indigo, please reconsider. You'll end up wasting your time. A first-time break-in, that was a prank by a minor with no property damage or personal injury, will amount to nothing but community service, if that. Not trying to boast but being friends with every judge in this city means they will chuck this case to the side," James said monotonously, glancing at his watch. He made me feel irrelevant.

Eric hunched over, his hands intertwined as if he were praying, "Serena, please, babe. Let's just go home."

I wanted to demand answers from him and rip the sunglasses off Macy's face—the bitch couldn't even look me in the eyes—but I needed to talk to Eric privately first before creating havoc.

"Tell your son to stay the fuck off my property. Or else next time, a body bag will be leaving my home." I pointed at both of them and stood. I could hear Macy breathe out in shock and say something to James, but I didn't care. It felt good. I felt alive. I wasn't going to take anyone's shit anymore. It was time to get control over *my life.*

Eric and I didn't speak, both going to our own cars, supposedly driving back home. I was grateful that we didn't ride together. I couldn't stand to sit next to him while he criticized me and my behavior. I looked in the backseat of my car and saw the two suitcases I had packed—one for Lola and one for me. I didn't tell Eric, but I wasn't heading home with him. I was going to my parents' house and would stay there. I didn't want to be anywhere near the supposed place I called home, not after the traumatic night before and having to pretend things were okay with Eric. Even though staying with my parents would be a special kind of hell, it was worth it to be safe.

Parker, I need the information on your private investigator. I texted him quickly before driving.

Carlos Garcia. Parker shared the contact link with me.

Let me know if you need anything else, Seri.
Thanks, Sully. 'Night.

I pressed my head back against the seat, once again recollecting memories of residency days when I'd call Parker "Sully," and we would laugh our way through study sessions or hospital shifts. It was my happy place. The place I tried to get lost in when the world around me grew darker, and colder. I couldn't believe this was my life. If Eric was really having an affair with Macy, what would I do? I thought we were planning a second baby before I turned forty. I thought we'd buy a vacation house, watch our kids grow as we grew older together. He broke us and broke me. *Everything that was once perfect was now shattered. The glass was everywhere, and I didn't know how I'd ever be able to piece it together.*

It was late by the time I got to my parents' house, and I had a few missed calls from Eric.

Staying at my parents for a few days with Lola. I texted him before turning my phone off.

The next day I woke to the laughter of Lola and Eric's voice. *Was I at home?* I looked around and saw posters plastered on my pale pink walls. No, definitely in my childhood bedroom. I pulled the cream comforter over to under my chin, just like I did all those nights when I'd see shadows on the wall and was terrified of the dark. The first night I was scared, I remember going to my parents' bedroom. I was shaking, in tears. The dark frightened me and the shadows haunted me, but what I was most terrified of was that it made me feel as if someone was there, *watching me.*

I climbed in between my parents. My father turned over, kissed my head, and went back to sleep. My mother sat up and shook her head. She led me back to my room and told me, "Serena, the only thing you have to fear isn't out there, it's right here," she tapped my shoulder. Then she abruptly turned and left me alone. That was the night I became terrified of *myself.*

"Mommy, Dada here!" Lola trickled in and jumped on the foot of my bed.

"Good morning, my love. That's nice." I reached over, pulling her close to me. She smelled sweet, like vanilla and cinnamon. Her soft cheeks gently glazed with sticky maple syrup.

"Hey, sleepy head." Eric leaned against my doorway. He was wearing a fitted V-neck and jeans that hugged him perfectly. He looked just like he did when we were in college, even his hair was growing back out. The subtle wrinkles were growing near his eyes, but I knew why I had fallen in love with him. Eric Hudson came from a chaotic family. His mom was a certified narcissist, and his dad was an addict. Eric relied on me in ways no one had ever needed to. I loved being able to take a piece of clay and form him into exactly what I wanted.

He tried to form me into his own flawless woman, too. It was a thrilling, revolting game that drove our relationship. We fed off each other's weaknesses and loved the competition. *It wasn't a marriage, it was a puzzle. A puzzle where we both desperately wanted perfection, but when a piece is missing, it'll never be beautiful, it'll always be incomplete.* Just like us.

I looked down at Lola, who was observing our interaction intently. My hand was habitually stroking her curls.

"Good morning, Eric," I replied, forcing a smile on my tired face.

"Your parents offered to watch Lola so you and I could go meet with the new security company and grab lunch before coming home this evening," Eric said sternly. He didn't ask me... he was warning me.

I didn't have the energy to start a fight, especially not in front of Lola. She was too little to even begin to understand what was happening and what was going to happen.

"Sure. Let me go shower and get ready, then we can head out."

"Lola, come on, let Mommy get ready." Eric opened

his arms up, squatting down. Lola squealed, leaping into his open arms, and I quickly got out of bed. Parker was covering for me today with patients. I needed to get our life pieced back together or else my professional life would sink, too.

An hour later, Eric and I were in his Tesla, headed to what I knew was our favorite brunch spot in the city. Once we arrived and were seated, the waitress came and asked for our order.

"I'll have the chicken and waffles, with a side of hash browns, and she'll have the egg white omelet with grilled vegetables." He handed the waitress our menus without a second thought.

I cleared my throat. "Actually, I'd like the French toast with strawberries, add extra whipped cream and a side of grits please." I stared straight back at Eric.

The waitress took our menus and turned around.

Eric sighed loudly. "Babe, let's just start over and clear everything up."

"Start over? Okay, how about you start off by telling me why you're fucking our neighbor and spending our money on lavish trips and gifts for her?" I said through clenched teeth.

Eric surveyed the tables around us and leaned in, reaching for my hands. I shook my head, placing my hands in my lap. He took a melodramatic, deep

breath. "Serena, you're right. I have been seeing someone. I am so sorry, baby. It's over. It's not our neighbor, though. It was just meaningless sex with a girl
from work."

"Meaningless sex? With a girl from work?" I hated
how pain seeped through the rage that erupted
from me.

"Then why did you and Macy magically have the
same bullshit Charleston trip? I'm not an idiot, Eric!"

"Baby, please, lower your voice. It's not Macy, I
swear. I don't even know her. She seems like such a
bitch. You really think I would be that dumb to get
involved with Charlotte's most prestigious attorney's
wife and our neighbor? You know me, I'd never. It's
just a new nurse at work, and I got caught up in the
mess. I ended it, I swear. She's even transferring out of
the emergency department. Just forgive me, baby. We
have Lola and a beautiful life together. It was just sex,"
he pleaded with me with his palms open in the middle
of the table and for a brief moment, all I wanted was
this all to be some cruel joke and to melt into them,
into him. That made me pathetic, and I knew it.

"No, Eric. I don't even know who you are anymore.
This isn't something you just bounce back from. I
fucking cannot believe you?" My voice cracked like a
leather whip against the air.

"Who is she?" I asked in the weakest way, making me hate myself.

"Does it matter?"

"Yes, it does."

"Tessa," he replied while staring at his hands.

"Sex is never meaningless, Eric. You know how many times I could have…"

The waitress brought our food out. I looked down at it, devouring it without a care in the world. Shoveling the piping, hot grits in my mouth, I could feel the roof of my mouth peeling while Eric's eyes lasered through me.

"What? Fucked Parker Sully? Why didn't you? Doesn't he fit in your seamless life better than I ever do, or ever did? Do you know how fucking hard it is to be *this* for you…? I can't breathe. I'm suffocating in this life. Do you know what it feels like to know if your wife met her best friend, the fucking perfect man, before you, you'd never have been chosen? I can't keep up. You're this manic roadrunner." He waved his hands aggressively around him.

"There he is. The apple doesn't fall from the tree, does it, Eric? Your mother's narcissism always comes out at the best time. You think I suffocate you? How about I'm too fat? My wrinkles are showing too much? I'm the same damn weight as college, yet I shouldn't eat this and that. You are sleeping with a nurse at work... but no, please, let's dive into how this is all my damn fault." I leaned back into my chair, crossing my arms against my chest. I wasn't staring at my husband, I was staring at an imposter, a stranger. The rose-colored glasses were off, along with the desperation for the perfect marriage.

"Damnit, Serena, will you not wipe your fucking plate clean, it's disgusting." I was scraping away the whipped cream and syrup from my plate. Lifting the fork in front of my mouth, I could see my reflection—one I didn't feel proud of, but one I didn't resent, either. I looked back at Eric and licked the fork, leaving nothing behind. My tongue bending through the crevices of the cold, metal.

"Would you both care for anything else? Boxes, perhaps?" Our waitress was looking at Eric's untouched food. The tension between Eric and I could have been cut with a knife. Her manager probably sent her over after our heated charade in the middle of a nice restaurant.

I smiled up at her. "We are good. Just the check please."

The waitress eyed us carefully. "Together or separate?"

"Definitely separate." I stared at Eric, his cheeks

reddened as his fist clenched against the table. I knew he would have loved to plant that fist against my jaw. He had once. Years ago—shortly after Lola was born—we had been fighting. I was in a dark, deep fog. Postpartum depression didn't seem to fit the description of the gloomy cloud that stalked me. I would muffle sobs into my pillow every night whenever he tried to touch me. Finally, after months, he slid the strap of my chemise off my shoulder and kissed my flesh. I cringed at his touch, and I knew he could see the resentment dripping down my face.

That's when I sat up to leave, but instead he pulled me back, and when my eyes met his, the strength of his clenched fist met with my jaw. I'll never forget that feeling. Hearing a crack and the taste of blood filling my mouth as my teeth dug into my tongue from the impact. We didn't talk for two weeks after that. I took care of Lola, and he slept in the guest room. I couldn't believe I was the woman who I warned my patients to not be, the woman who was defenseless. *The victim.*

After spending the day with the security company and Eric, I was ready to go back to normal life where I spent my day at work and my nights home to my beautiful Lola. The security company put alarms on every window and cameras all around our house. I downloaded the app on my phone where I could constantly watch the cameras. Yes, I felt paranoid and over the top, but I needed this. I couldn't risk Lola's life. After all, she was the only thing I had left to keep me from drowning.

Parker was with a patient when I got to work the next day. I was hoping to talk to him before seeing my own, but he was basically pulling the patient load for the both of us. I really needed to focus on maintaining my career and not getting comfortable with Parker dealing with the weight of the world just because my life was a mess.

"Dr. Indigo, there's a man in your office. He's been waiting for you. Dr. Sully let him in." Mindy raised an eyebrow at me.

"Um, okay? Thanks." I approached the door and saw a man with hair that was once black but was now mostly streaked in silver. He was spinning my paperweight that had glitter in it. Lola picked it out and loved playing with it when she was in my office. I cleared my throat.

"Oh shit, sorry. Hi. Dr. Indigo?" The man stood, placing the paperweight down.

"It's okay. Please, call me Serena. How can I help you, Mr...?" I turned to walk behind my desk to take a seat. I pointed to the navy, suede chair he was standing in front of while the matching one beside him held a worn briefcase.

"Carlos." He stretched his hand out. "Carlos Garcia."

I looked down at his opened hand and reached out to shake it. "Nice to meet you, Mr. Garcia."

"Carlos is fine. Mr. Garcia is my angry, drunk father. Dr. Sully asked me to swing by and chat with you," he replied as he crossed his leg over the other. I sunk into my chair while inconspicuously glancing at the time. Thanks to a cancellation, I had an hour before my next patient.

"Yes, Parker highly recommended you. Mr. Garcia, um… Carlos. Okay, where do I begin? My husband is having an affair. Our house was recently broken into, and I just…" I tapped my pen anxiously against my desk. "I just don't know if I recognize the life I am living. Suddenly, it's as if I'm watching my life shatter in front of me and spiral out of control with no means to do anything about it."

Carlos was examining me vigilantly, not giving away much emotion as I spoke. Suddenly, it felt as if I were the one being investigated.

"Okay, well, that's what I'm here for. I can find out anything and everything in about two days' time, and most of it will be things you will probably wish I hadn't found out. You give me names and information, and I'll do the rest."

"How does payment work?" I questioned, wondering how I'd manage to withdraw the kind of money Carlos would require without Eric realizing. I kicked myself, wishing we had separate accounts like I had wanted from the beginning.

"Parker Sully has paid me in full already. You just give me names and questions. I'll have information and answers for you before you know it, doc." He smiled at me.

I noticed the worn, gold wedding band that was wrapped around his finger. *I bet he never cheated on his spouse.*

"All I have is that my husband, Eric Hudson, claims he is cheating with his coworker, a nurse named Tessa, yet I am still convinced he's sleeping with our neighbor, Macy Callahan. I just need to know the truth."

"If you don't mind me asking, what is it that you want to do with this truth?" Carlos questioned.

"Mr. Garcia, I need to know if I am married to a cheating sociopath and to what extent of an asshole he really is. That way, at least I'll know to what extent I should tear his fucking life apart as he has done to mine." I stared into the dark brown eyes of Carlos, who smiled at me.

"I like you, doc. I'll have your information by the end of the week. If you think of anything else, here's my card." He slid a slightly bent cream-colored business card over to me.

I nodded back. "Have a nice day."

Moments later, there was a gentle knock on my door.

"Come in," I answered.

Parker strolled in.

"It's actually unnatural for you to look like that at work..." I leaned back into my chair, staring at Parker. He was dressed in a three-piece suit with a stethoscope flung around his neck.

"Well, my partner has been busy, so I'm having to hustle harder. How'd your meeting go?" He grinned at me.

"It went great. Sully, I'll pay you back, I promise. I just have to do it discreetly, so Eric doesn't catch on."

"Serena, come on, I'm not taking your money. I just want you to get whatever you need out of this."

"Anyway, I've got to head to the hospital for a delivery, but I'll see you later. Let me know if you need anything." He gripped the door handle, about to leave just as fast as he came in.

"Sully?" I called out.

He looked at me over his shoulder. "Yea, Seri?"

"I'm okay right? What happened to me... before... It isn't happening again, right?"

"Seri, you're perfect. It isn't happening again." He smiled before he left the room.

I looked at the gold frames neatly displayed on my desk. One was Lola in a field of flowers—she was laughing and her eyes were filled with excitement. The other was a photo of Eric and I on our honeymoon in Turks and Caicos. The photo showed us posing on the beach, smiling and holding each other tightly. My hair was in waves and blowing in the salty wind along with my maxi dress. Eric was wearing a white button-down with the sleeves rolled to his elbows and swim shorts. We were genuinely happy, or at least, I thought we were. I flipped the photo down and slid it into my desk drawer. I centered the one of Lola.

"Dr. Indigo? May I come in?" Mindy's voice was muffled behind the door.

I cleared my throat. "Sure, Mindy."

She walked in with a stack of papers in her hands. "I just need you to sign these."

My eyes remained fixed on the photo of Lola.

"She's so perfect, isn't she, Mindy?" I looked up and held the golden frame in my hands, turning it to her.

Mindy's forehead creased as her lips feigned a smile. "Mm-hmm..." She placed the papers in my hands and turned away to leave, peering over her shoulder to look at me with squinted eyes.

"Everything okay, Mindy?"

She quickly widened her eyes and smiled again. "Oh yea, of course. Have a good day, Dr. Indigo." She opened the door and carefully closed it behind her.

I guess I didn't care about other people's kids when I was younger, either. Leaning back into my chair, I closed my eyes.

CHAPTER NINE

*E*ric and I knew we wanted children immediately after getting married. I remember throwing away my last plastic packet of birth control pills. Just like many of my patients, I, too was in the state of oblivion, assuming we'd get pregnant as soon as we had unprotected intercourse. Month after month, my period would come as a brutal reminder that there wasn't a baby. The blood was always a ruthless reminder of what could have been, what should have been. It was the first thing in my life that was out of my control, it was the first thing in my life that embarrassed me. I often saw teenagers get pregnant after having sex once, yet here I was a married OB-GYN who was infertile and for the first time in my life, I couldn't fix it.

The physician in me who specialized in women's medicine knew to be rational and patient. After one year, I finally had ultrasounds and tests done. There were no issues detected. Eric and I were both completely healthy. After two more endless years of tears and trying, we finally came to the diagnosis of unexplained infertility. By that point, we had begun our tumultuous IVF journey.

Soon enough, we'd had already grown resentful of the mere touch of each other. Foreplay had become Eric massaging my thigh before injecting me, and sex had become a business transaction of every other day during my ovulation week. One night, I turned away from Eric's soft snore beside me, and wrapped myself in the blanket I had grown to hate. Tears streamed out of my closed eyes as I adjusted my hips on the pillow to keep them elevated.

I was still in residency, and each day, I would show up and deliver healthy, beautiful, crying babies into the arms of ecstatic parents. During the day, I'd reassure pregnant women with large bellies cradled in their protective arms. Eventually, the sound of a heartbeat that radiated countless times in the office through my handheld doppler began to haunt my dreams. The swooshing sound consumed me.

One cold winter morning, I sat over the toilet and

peed on a pregnancy test. It had become as common as someone drinking coffee in the morning, a part of my morning routine, an obsession. Brush teeth, wash face, pee on pregnancy stick. I set it on our stark white counter and didn't think twice. Walking away from it, I got ready for another day of work. As soon as I was about to put my pearls on, I glanced down and saw two thick pink lines. My heart paced as my stomach churned. Holding the plastic test in my shaking hands, I stared at it, blinking so quickly, in hopes I wasn't hallucinating. I called Eric.

In that moment, he snapped at me, demanding I take another test and not to be so emotional. He could hear my voice shaking with excitement, but he stole that away from me with his realism. I suppose that was the physician in him, or maybe the narcissist I never wanted to see. Four tests later, I went into work and pulled my attending physician, Dr. Nix, to the side. Her round, wrinkled face lit up with a smile. She took me to an empty patient room and had me lay down. I could feel my heart beating outside of my body as she placed the cold, lubricated transvaginal ultrasound probe inside of me. I clung to my rolled-up scrub top as she checked. Sure enough, the small amniotic sac appeared—a sign of hope.

I clutched the slick, rectangular, black and white

image against my chest and tucked it safely into my pocket, carrying it around with me as if it were treasure. It was treasure. Our baby. *My baby.* Everything I could have ever wanted was inside of me. Life was perfect. Eric and I would finally be the family we dreamt of. The missing piece of our puzzle was finally complete.

I got home that day and Eric had a giant bouquet of pink roses. His green eyes were tired but filled with light. There were no words exchanged, there was no need. Walking up to him, he opened his hands and I placed mine inside of them. We'd be okay. Our baby would help us get through any hardship we had faced.

"I thought you were mad this morning," I whispered as he pulled me closer and let his hand fall to my stomach.

"Oh, baby, I wasn't mad. I was terrified it would be false hope. I ran into Dr. Nix, and she told me about your ultrasound. I just… I'm just so happy, Serena. I love you. I love our daughter…" He kissed down the side of my neck, finally kneeling in front of me, lifting my scrub top. His lips connected with my cold skin and I exhaled, letting my fingers graze through his soft hair. *This was love.*

"We don't know if it's a girl or a boy, yet…" I smiled

down at him with his cheek brushing the inside of my open palm.

He grinned back at me. "It's definitely a girl…"

"Lola Indigo Hudson," He whispered as he stared up at me. Eric Hudson was genuinely happy. Part of me knew he wanted to prove he could be a better parent than his were. I knew he would, especially since they had set the bar so low. After what we endured in college, he had to be the best parent, or this would shatter us both completely.

"Lola? I love it."

Every day I stared at the black and white picture on our fridge that was proudly displayed. The image of just an amniotic sac was replaced with our growing baby often. I was lucky to get weekly ultrasounds because I had become close to every tech at the hospital through work. It was a breath of fresh air getting to hear our baby's heartbeat and eventually, see her move around. The swooshing sound of a fetal heartbeat no longer haunted me in nightmares; it had become the music of my sweetest dreams.

"Dr. Indigo, your nine a.m. is here." Mindy's voice echoed through my phone speaker. I headed out of my office and walked into the patient room.

"Hi, Gaby! How are you doing today?" I smiled at my young patient who was fidgeting with her wedding ring while wearing the thin paper right under her waistline. She and her husband had been trying to get pregnant for a year now.

"Hey, Dr. Indigo…" Defeat lingered in her voice. I recognized so much of myself in her. I knew what it was like to have to sit in a waiting room amongst women with perfect protruding bellies, glowing with excitement, even the women who were battling morning sickness became a source of envy. I desperately wanted to have to carry salty crackers and ginger ale in my bag because waves of nausea would only mean there was a healthy baby flourishing inside of me.

"So, your urine test came back negative for pregnancy, but I think now is a good time where we can finally discuss fertility options. I'm thinking we start with Ovo. It's a new medication that essentially helps increase the surge of hormones that support ovulation. The side effects can be somewhat daunting, but it's a great place for us to try before potentially discussing IUI or IVF. Basically, Gaby, you guys have lots of options to help you conceive." I rolled over to her and patted her knee. She smiled at me with a sigh.

Days went on. Lola and I were back home. Staying with my parents was exactly what I knew it would be like with my mother hovering, analyzing and critiquing every little thing I did. Eric was extra upbeat, trying excessively to keep us both happy. He was overcompensating through flowers and chocolate. I'd throw the chocolate away, I loved anything sweet and the temptation was too much, so into the trash it went. He was buying Lola toys and books. I didn't know who he was anymore, but I tried my best to pretend things were okay since I needed solidified answers rather than assumptions. I hadn't heard from Carlos yet, but I knew I would by Friday. While Eric swore he and his mistress, Tessa, were no longer having any form of communication or a relationship, the mere sight of him made my stomach curl.

One evening, when Eric took Lola up for her bath and bedtime routine, I peered at his keys that were sitting in the blue decorative bowl on our foyer console table. Quickly, I glanced around the corner, looking up at the stairs that led to an open balcony. I could hear the echoes of Lola splashing and Eric making funny sounds at her. She'd be in there for at least thirty minutes, and getting her ready for bed would take another twenty minutes. I hesitated but grabbed his keys and opened the garage door.

His Tesla was parked next to my SUV. With my hands trembling, I unlocked his doors and slid into the driver seat. I inhaled the intense smell of cologne that lingered. *Son of a bitch.* There was no way in hell he'd wear cologne to work, especially in the emergency room. This was all after-hours. The scented air smothered me.

Checking inside of the arm rest, I found nothing but lingering fast-food napkins and his hospital badge. I unhinged the glove box and dug around. There was the car manual and random knick-knacks, nothing else. I leaned back into his seat and stared at the garage opener clipped above my face.

I slid it off slowly, noticing that it looked cracked. Turning it over and back again, there was nothing else. I sighed, pushing the garage opener back onto the visor but I heard a jingle and pulled it off again. I shook it next to my ear and the clinking taunted me. My heart began pounding quickly as I fingered at the groove that was embedded in a slight crack. Pulling the cover off, I saw a small silver key.

"What the hell?" My hand hit the key fob and suddenly, the car alarm sounded. The piercing alarm radiated all around me, and a cold sweat washed over my body as I fumbled. I grabbed the keys and pressed the button to disarm the shrill noise, praying under my breath that Eric didn't hear it. The tiny silver key was secured in my palm as I pieced the garage opener back together and put everything back as it was.

I have something else for you. I found a key in his car.
I texted Carlos as soon as I made it up to my bedroom.
Luckily, Lola had Eric hostage in her bedroom,
reading possibly the hundredth princess book.

Carlos texted me back immediately. *Make a copy
tonight. Then put the original back where you found it
right after. Chances are he'll notice it went missing
tomorrow morning and have whatever it fits changed.
Can't risk that. Do it tonight.*

*Also, make sure I'm not listed as Carlos Garcia or
Private Investigator in your contacts. Don't be a fool.
Put me under as Nurse Carla.*

I looked down at my contact and sure enough, I did
have him listed as Carlos Garcia, P.I. I shook my head,
realizing how much of an amateur I was at this. But
then again, I didn't think in a million years that the
man I married would be someone I needed to have
investigated. Why did I need a private investigator?
Did our vows not mean anything?

I thought back to our wedding day when Eric held
my shaking hands in his as he promised the world
to me.

"I promise to protect your heart, to honor your
soul, and to keep our love ignited every day, for the
rest of our lives..." he said with sheer confidence.

I heard Eric's footsteps approach, and tucking my phone under the blanket, I closed my eyes to feign sleep.

"Serena? You up?" he gently whispered. The minty scent of his mouthwash hit my nose as his cool breath hit my face...

"Mmm..." I hummed back.

"Goodnight, sweetheart." He kissed my cheek and suddenly, my eyes felt wet underneath my lids. The man I fell in love with, and the father of my only child, was now a man I didn't know, but so desperately wanted to cling to. My emotions were everywhere. *What was the key to? Why would he have hidden one away like that.*

As much as my body craved sleep and rest, I needed to go to the local hardware store before ten to make a copy of it and put it back in his car before he woke up in the morning for work.

As soon as Eric was lightly snoring next to me, I looked over at my phone under the blanket. I felt like I was a small child, again, hiding from the dark with a flashlight praying nothing would come to hurt me. Nine-thirty. I had thirty minutes to make it to the store. I slid out the bed and trekked down our stairs as quietly as I could. My hand grazed the banister and every creak in the steps made my heart jolt. Pulling on my ivory coat, I climbed into my car.

I was thankful that we had the quietest garage door installed since Lola's room was right above it, especially since we were in and out at odd hours for work. I sped to the hardware store and turned in. The parking lot was empty except for one red truck parked in the spot directly in front of the door.

I went inside and offered a small wave to the old man standing behind the cash register. He nodded back at me curiously as he folded things on the counter.

I turned and saw the *make your key machine* in the corner. Peering over my shoulder at him, I pointed over to the machine. He nodded again, this time with a reassured smile. I pulled the silver key out of my pocket and inserted it into the slot, and within seconds, a loud click followed by a duplicate key but in a brushed gold color came out. Staring at it, I saw a reflection, but for some reason, I couldn't recognize her. She wasn't the woman I wanted to be, but instead, the woman I had to be. I pulled cash out of my wallet, handing it to the older man.

"Keep the change." The key was fifty cents and I handed him a twenty. I didn't have time to have him count out all the change.

"You sure, ma'am?" He looked at me again with a raised eyebrow. He seemed like the kind of man who had been married to the same woman for forty years and sat around a wraparound porch sipping sweet tea, watching his grandchildren play in the grass.

"Yep, sorry for coming in so close to closing. Have a good night."

"Thank you, honey. You be good."

I drove through the darkness and couldn't believe this was what my life had turned into—a game of cat and mouse with my own husband. The stillness surrounding me on the empty roads made me recollect my wedding day. We were so young and in love. Or at least, I thought we were. My parents hosted an elaborate garden wedding. I remember walking down the aisle, gripping my father's arm, as smiles erupted in the sea of people, most of whom I barely knew. There he stood, gorgeous and charming as ever in a gray suit and Carolina blue tie. I remember his teeth looked like small pearls neatly lined from a distance. *Aren't weddings such a paradox to marriage?*

A wedding is a giant show in which we depict our absolute and most perfect self to the world around us, yet it sets such an abnormal high standard to what marriage encompasses. Marriage is when the curtains open and you can clearly see the person you have

145

committed yourself to. With no place to hide, your ugliest bits are on full display.

Pulling into our driveway, I found the garage was still opened. I looked near the side of Eric's car and a shadow seemed to appear. My heart sprinted as I reached for my phone. Grabbing my pepper spray canister, I squinted, trying to make out the figure. It started growing closer to me, and I considered backing out of my driveway, but my sweet Lola was in our home, sound asleep. I wasn't going to leave and let someone break in and take her from me. *No one would ever take her from me. No one would take my baby from me. Never again.*

There he was. Brooks Callahan. He was wearing baggy sweatpants and a Charlotte high school hoodie. My headlights caused him to squint as he placed his hand protectively in front of his eyes, shielding them from the high beam blasting from my car.

I sighed and turned my car off. Still holding my pepper spray and keys, I slowly opened the door.

Serena, he's just a kid.

"Brooks? What the hell do you think you're doing?" I hissed as quietly as I could, looking up at our home. The lights were still all off.

"Dr. Indigo. I'm so sorry. I shouldn't be here, but you should know..." Brooks was trembling. He was tall and scrawny, just a teenage boy. I knew he played baseball for his school since he was always wearing the hoodie with the team name displayed.

"Know what, Brooks? Why do you keep coming to my house?" I approached him carefully. "Are you okay?"

He raised his hands and turned away. "I shouldn't be here or be speaking to you. Please be careful, Dr. Indigo. Nothing is as it seems..." His voice was shaking. The motion lights went on over at the Callahan house and his deep blue eyes widened.

"I gotta go." He looked back at me and ran to the back of his house.

"Brooks, wait," I called out, yet he sprinted away with his hands in the front pocket of his hoodie.

My head was pounding. I had so many questions. I walked into the garage and hurriedly shut it. Opening Eric's car, I slid the original key into its secret spot and went inside as fast as I could. Climbing into bed, still wearing my coat, I shut my eyes and let myself fall into oblivion.

The sun was shining through the giant red leaf tree just outside our bedroom window, creating an eerie reflection throughout. I sat up, reaching for my phone, and one text from Nurse Carla was displayed.

Did you get the surgery done? I need the sample for

the lab by ten a.m. if you want results by Friday. I
smiled at the discreet message Carlos had sent
me. Not a moment later, the smile I felt on my face fell
and was replaced with embarrassment. This wasn't a
fun game... this was my life. My pathetic life being
paraded around amongst private investigators, neighbors, family, and friends. My life's downfalls being
showcased without hesitation. I shuddered as anger
boiled inside of me.

Surgery done. 10 a.m. today. Thanks. I sent the
message and heard a throat clear. I shook my head and
saw Eric sitting in the corner of our room, intently
watching me. The red reflection covered him as he
squinted his eyes and studied me.

"Oh my god. Eric, what the hell?" I gasped.

"Serena, is everything okay?" He spoke in that low,
calm way that sent chills racing inside me.

"Yea? Why wouldn't it be?" I replied cautiously.

"Well, for starters, you're sleeping in your coat. You
left our house at nine-thirty last night, and then you
were having a conversation with Brooks Callahan at
ten-fifteen in our driveway," he replied, lifting his
phone to show our new security camera screens
pop up.

I swallowed as my heart thumped under my coat.
"Oh. Yea. I didn't want to worry you. I got called in for

a patient emergency. I pulled in and Brooks was standing there. He apologized about the dumb dare and breaking into our house." I paced my words as slowly as I could, hoping they were believable. One thing I realized was when someone was lying to you, they often spoke faster—a natural human response to talk faster and speak too much to cover up something. It shows the fact that you are second guessing yourself and the words that are seeping out from your deceitful mouth are all a lie.

"Oh really? I knew he wasn't a bad kid. God, I remember being fourteen. Tough shit." Eric was soaking in everything I laid out. I guess I was just as good a liar as he was.

"I can't believe I fell asleep in my coat though." I offered a forced laugh. "Where's Lola?"

"Brooklyn took her to school." Eric smiled. Brooklyn was our back up nanny. She was twenty years old and a local college student. She was always reading a new book or doing something interactive with Lola. I appreciated the fact that her face wasn't buried in an iPhone. She was studying to be an elementary school teacher, which was appropriate considering she had an amazing level of patience with our rowdy three-year-old who could definitely test anyone's limits. Her mom was an emergency medicine doctor with Eric, so I had less hesitation with Lola being with her.

I struggled for months to find the right nanny. I had immense trust issues and deep-rooted anxiety with Lola being taken from me. I didn't know why, but I always had this feeling inside that would arise and make me feel nauseated at the thought of Lola not being in our lives. I blamed years of infertility and then a challenging delivery, followed by severe post-partum depression. All in all, I was thankful we were all here, alive and well.

"Wow, I slept in." I glanced down at my phone and noticed it was already seven forty-five. I needed to be at work by nine to drop off the key for Carlos since I had surgery at eleven back at the hospital.

"Well, since we won't be interrupted, I was thinking I could have some quality time with my gorgeous wife." Eric walked over to the bed and my stomach churned. It had been so long since we had last been intimate. I considered lying about being on my period, but I also knew I couldn't not sleep with my husband for months until I figured everything out.

"I have to be at work soon," I whispered.

He smiled seductively at me. "I do, too."

I hated how I felt desire rise inside of me. Physically, my body still craved his.

"Eric, you cheated on me with a nurse. You slept with her. I don't think I can..."

"Baby, please. Everything will be better now. I love you more than anything. Please, let me fix what I broke. Let me fix *us*. People have affairs, people fall off. It doesn't mean that is the end of something so... *perfect.*" He spoke slowly as he unbuttoned my coat revealing the lacy camisole underneath.

I sighed and laid back. I wanted to be with my husband, but I also hated him. This wasn't fair. He gently parted my legs and dropped his pajama bottoms. Pulling my panties down my cold, bare legs, he pulled me close to the edge of the bed and leaned in. I thought back to our happier days. Opening my eyes abruptly, I watched Eric hover over me. My eyes met his, and I realized it hurt too much to look at him when all I could see was him on top of another woman. I could see him wrapped around and engulfed in... *her.*

I closed them again and thought about our wedding night. The false perfection it was; the false perfection we were. In that moment, I didn't feel pleasure, I felt rage.

Yet, in some way, the rage made me feel all that more satisfied.

CHAPTER TEN

I dropped the key off at work and went to the hospital to perform a couple of scheduled surgeries and deliveries. It would be a long few days playing catch-up from my time off after the break-in. I replayed what Brooks had said to me in my head.

"Nothing is as it seems..." What did he mean by that? I wish I could have asked him, but I had no business interrogating a teenager.

Eric was on the nightshift, so we saw each other for thirty minutes a day when I came home and he was on his way out, basically just swapping shifts with Lola. I was thankful I didn't have to forge insincere feelings around him. I could barely look at him. My body cringed at the thought of sleeping with him. How stupid could I have been?

Yet, day after day, I smiled at my husband as he assumed we were on the mend. I needed to keep him close. I needed to make sure he paid for wrecking me. For wrecking us. I was Serena Indigo. I deserved better. *I was better.*

Friday morning finally arrived. My meeting with Carlos was at my office at eight a.m., Brooklyn was back at our house to help with Lola so I could get in early. I hated how little time I had with my daughter. This was nothing new, though. I had cut back hours originally, but I had brought them back on after everything that had been happening. I needed my full salary back. I hoped that one day she'd grow up knowing how everything I did was for her. Parker had been more than generous to pull so much of the weight of our private practice, and I felt immense guilt, hoping he didn't think I was using our friendship to my advantage. *Wasn't I though?*

I arrived at my office and Carlos was already seated. He was wearing a button-down tucked into dress pants, the wrinkles on his face creased upward with a smile when he saw me walk in.

"I got good stuff for you, doc." His smile faded quickly while he added, "I hate that good stuff is actually what tears my clients lives apart, but you should know the man you're married to."

I handed him the second latte I picked up on my way to the office. He gratefully nodded, taking a sip.

"So, here's the deal. Everything you *want* to know is *not* in this envelope. Everything you *need* to know is." He looked at me intently.

"Thank you, Carlos. May I?" I reached my hand out and he handed me the heavy envelope. I could feel my hands stick to the paper as they began to sweat. Anxiety was nothing new to me since I suffered from it my entire life. I resented that this physical and emotional reaction my body crafted had such a major impact on me. Sitting down in my chair and crossing my legs at the ankles, I reached the flap of the envelope that was tightly sealed, taking a deep breath in and exhaling slowly.

Placing it cautiously on my desk, I reached down to grab my purse. Carlos was studying me carefully. Opening my bag, I pulled out the infamous Indigo dagger. Holding it up to the envelope, I sliced it open. The sound of paper shredding against the blade ignited something within me. Something, indescribable. Something I knew with certainty was far from normal. Carlos's eyes widened, and I could have sworn that there were sweat beads building at his hair line. I smiled, hoping to reassure him without words, as I placed the dagger back inside my purse.

I slid the contents out onto the slippery marble surface of my desk. My pink nails began pacing through a stack of black and white images while nausea trickled into my stomach and acid teased my esophagus as I felt waves of hatred and disgust.

Lifting an image up, I saw my husband, intertwined, shirtless with a very naked, very stunning Macy Callahan. Our fucking neighbor. They were in bed with sheets draped around them. Her body was flawless. In another image, Eric's lips were parted against hers. With my heart frozen, I flipped through the stack. They were eating breakfast together at a local restaurant, laughing and holding hands. They were pictured in a kitchen someplace with Macy in lingerie on the counter while Eric gripped her tiny waist. He was looking at her like a hungry predator looking at his delicious prey. She was glowing with the attention my husband was painting on her.

I tilted my head and looked at a piece of paper with nothing but a single line, *1108 Rio Drive, Apt. 4.* The copy of the key I had made was taped on the paper.

"What's this?" I turned the sheet over to Carlos. I could feel tears brimming in my eyes. I wasn't sure I was ready to hear his response.

"It's a sort of love nest, I suppose. The apartment is leased under Eric Hudson," Carlos added. "Look, if I were you, I'd go over there when he isn't there. I'd take pictures and do whatever you want to in order to compile evidence for a divorce and custody case. Clearly, you're married to a complete asshole."

"Why can't you go in?" I questioned.

"Because if I'm caught, or my men are caught, it's considered breaking and entering, which means charges and jail time. If you're caught, it's a concerned wife looking for her husband in his secret apartment."

"Right. That makes sense. God, he's such a bastard. Fuck," I moaned, slamming my fists against my desk.

"Sorry, doc. Is there anything else I can do for ya?" Carlos began to collect his things.

"No, I think I've learned enough. Can I ask you a question though?" I looked up at him.

"Sure. Shoot. Well in your case... *slice?*" He looked back at me, and his eyes wandered to my purse. He must be wondering why someone like me would carry a dagger in her designer purse?

"Why do you do this job? I mean, you're essentially the messenger of breaking marriages and revealing brutal details. *Heartbreak.*"

"Doc, my job is to reveal the truth behind the illusion you all create. No one is as they seem. Nothing is.

It's a mirage. My job is to take that mirage and hose it off. You know when lightning hits sand, it creates glass?" Carlos asked me.

"Yea? I think I have heard that."

"Well, my job is to take the sand off and reveal the delicate clear glass underneath all of it. Then, you can hold it up and see what you need to." He smiled down at me and turned to leave. "Plus, the pay is great. Not many people enjoy digging for glass, it's just too delicate and once it shatters, it can be extremely painful to touch, let alone clean up. Take care, doc." He nodded at me and left.

I looked down at the stacks of pictures and bronze key lingering on my desk. Spreading them out, I lined them carefully, creating a perfect eight by eight square. He made the perfect puzzle with her, there was nothing missing. Hot tears dribbled down my cheeks. Eric would be on nightshift tonight, so this would be the only chance to go over to the apartment and scope it out myself. I needed to know to what caliber I'd be forced to have retribution.

Hey Brooklyn, can you stay the night tonight? I texted quickly.

Of course, Dr. Indigo.

Thank you. I'll order pizza and cake. Lola will be

happier than ever, and you can just turn a movie on. I'll be home around ten.

I then texted Parker. *Sully, you free tonight?* I needed to take someone with me. I was terrified to go alone, and I didn't know if I'd be able to handle what I could possibly find.

You finally asking me out on a date, Seri?

If you consider going to my husband's love nest that he takes his mistress to, in order to find shit, I can use against him when I leave his ass, then sure, it's a date.

Well damn. Carlos did good, huh?

A little too good. You up for it?

Of course. Let's ride over there together after work, and Seri, I'm sorry. No matter how I feel about Eric, I'm really sorry for you.

I leaned back in my chair and stared at the images that were splayed out on my desk. My heart felt as if there were a million daggers inside of it. *Dagger.* I reached back into my bag and felt the cool steel in my palm. Lifting it up, I pushed the sleeve of my dress up and allowed the blade to mark its territory right under my forearm. The pain from the cut burned, but I watched it seep out. Draping it over the black and white images, I watched as the red droplets decorated the joyous faces of two people who were going to burn. *No one was going to ruin me.* I was too damn perfect, and if anyone was going to hurt me, it would be on my terms.

Hours later, we pulled up to a swanky apartment complex. My breath quickened as we approached security, who asked for our pin. I looked over at Parker, who raised his eyebrow at me.

"Security code?" the guard asked again.

"Um, 602?" I meekly answered.

"Great. Have a good day, y'all." The guard smiled.

It was Lola's birthday. My asshole husband was using our child's birthday as a passcode to his love shack, except this was far from a love shack. I pushed the shiny key into the lock and turned it carefully. Entering the posh apartment, I wondered how the hell I didn't know he was pouring money into a monthly lease. Parker stayed close behind me.

"Damn. Serena, how did he get away with renting this place under the radar. It's ridiculously nice. You can see the entire skyline from here." Parker walked up to the window that proudly displayed the Charlotte skyline. It was true. I had been so consumed by my own worries and obsessions that I couldn't see what was clearly in front of me.

I looked around and put my purse down on the barstool. Trailing my fingers on the cold, smooth counter, I felt envy pooling inside of me. One of the pictures Carlos had given me was taken right here. The cabinets were all empty, except one, which housed two wineglasses. There was no food, no snacks, no dishes. I closed my eyes envisioning Macy and my husband dining on takeout and laughing together while I was at home with our child all those nights thinking he was at some conference or working an extra shift.

I turned out of the kitchen and saw Parker, who looked worried. Tears began to pool in my eyes and I shook my head at him, signaling no words could be said for they'd make the budding tears escape. He knew I hated being pitied. Pity was for people who had messy, imperfect lives, and as much as mine was disheveled, I'd quickly clean up the mess and then tie a perfect, pink fucking bow around it.

I headed down a small hallway and opened the closed door. The bed was unmade, and discarded lingerie trailed on the floor. A crumpled Carolina football T-shirt stared back at me next to a lacy, red thong. I swallowed the thick saliva that lingered in my mouth, hoping it would coat the dryness that scaled my throat. Picking up the lacy bra with my index finger, I lifted it in the air. I could picture Eric peeling it off Macy, with her perfect, smooth, unmarked body grazed by his hungry lips. The moans that probably seeped from her haunted me.

I walked toward the small trash bin and leaned over, wrappers and used condoms decorated the inside carelessly. I was suffocating. Except it wasn't my fault. The sins of the man I married were tightly wrapped around my throat, ceasing the air around me. Sinking onto the floor, I pulled my legs inward to my chest, counting my breaths while rocking back and forth.

"Serena, let's go home. This… it's just too much. Come on," Parker said softly as he gently rubbed my shoulder.

I felt embarrassed. Humiliated. *Destroyed.* I needed to feel pain. Here I was in person and pain covered me in its black veil, sinking me. Taunting me. I wanted to wake up from this dream. No, not a dream. This was a nightmare.

"No, I need to do this. Can you take pictures of all this? Please, Sully. Carlos said it would help," I replied, wiping the tears that were racing furiously down my cheeks.

There was a bottle of some fancy massage oil displayed on the nightstand. I opened the drawer, which was empty except for a box of opened condoms. The second drawer was jammed, but pulling at it as hard as I could, it opened to reveal a small, pale pink box inside. I reached in and pulled it out. Tossing the flimsy lid off, there was a single row of ultrasound photos. I could feel stomach acid rise in my throat, meeting my dry mouth. It burned, but not nearly as bad as the burn from what laid in front of me.

"Oh, fuck..." Parker whispered, easily able to recognize what my eyes were frozen to.

"Parker..." I whispered as the room spun and I collapsed onto the shaggy white rug underneath me.

"Serena!" Parker leapt beside me and held me tightly, prying the ultrasound images out of my hands. I pressed my forehead against his chest. I could feel his heart racing. I knew it ached for me. Tears consumed me. I hoped they would drown me and take me away from the pain I felt I couldn't handle.

"Serena..." Parker lifted the ultrasound image and pointed to the small date in the corner.

"Oh my god. She had a terminated pregnancy listed on her records. I put her goddamn IUD in... They made a fool out of me." I was sobbing hysterically, soaking Parker's shirt. They'd been together for so long... long enough to get pregnant and terminate it.

"Serena, come on we have to go. You're going to be okay. You will be okay... Come on." Parker lifted me up and basically had to carry me away from the love nest. My legs felt weak. I felt like I was choking on the deceit that floated around me. I had never felt weaker than this moment in years. Walking past the hall mirror, my cheeks had imprinted black streaks from my tears and eye makeup mixing. The circles around my eyes looked significantly worse and my hair was disheveled.

I was disheveled.

CHAPTER ELEVEN

I stayed silent for the rest of the car ride as numbness radiated through me. Parker had his free hand holding mine tightly. It felt so warm and strong against mine, while my entire body felt frozen and weak, trembling with panic, fear, and anger. We pulled into my driveway. It was such a gorgeous home. Leaves were scattered through the otherwise well-kept lawn. It cost us a fortune, but we envisioned filling this large home with the giggles of our children, growing old together, and having our grandchildren come here. We envisioned Christmases in the living room around our decorated tree, and Thanksgivings sitting around our custom-crafted dining table, laughing amongst our closest friends and family. Right here… we dreamt of forever. Together.

But now... the only thing this house felt like was a mausoleum for our marriage and unkept promises.

"Serena?" Parker whispered softly. "I'll go in and get Lola packed up. You need to just stay with me until things cool off. Your parents will be a mess if they know everything that is going on, and with your dad's heart condition, I don't think it's a good idea for them to see you this way."

He was right. My parents would be wrecked. I didn't even want to think of what my mother would say, though I was certain she'd make sure I knew I had failed somehow. I just stared at the house in front of me that was no longer a home for my daughter and me. My phone buzzed as Parker got out the car and went inside our house. I could see Brooklyn greet him, then she smiled and waved at me. Looking down at my phone, I saw it was Eric.

Hey, babe, I was thinking we could plan a fun trip with Lola for Halloween weekend. We both could take an extra day off and head to the beach or even the mountains?

Tears blurred against the bright phone screen as I typed out my text.

Lola is going to stay with Parker tonight. We need to talk.

My phone immediately rang endlessly, followed by

multiple text messages. Wiping the tears from my face with the sleeve of my blouse, I unfolded the mirror in the visor above me and quickly matted my hair into a ponytail. I didn't want Lola to be frightened, especially since her life was about to be flipped upside down. One parent being a screw up was more than enough. I hated that Eric always made me be the strong one in our relationship and as parents. He always made me be the one who kept it all together. I didn't get a free pass from parenting or marriage like he decided he deserved. If he had a long day at work, he'd go into the guestroom and lay on the bed while staring at whatever or whoever on his phone.

Lola came running out donning a huge smile. The setting sun surrounded her and she looked... *angelic*. It frightened me. Parker was right behind her, carrying two duffel bags. I saw him take some cash out and handed it to Brooklyn as she followed behind him.

Pulling my sunglasses over my swollen red eyes and rolling my window down, Brooklyn came closer.

"Hey, Dr. Indigo, let me know the next time you need me!"

"Thank you so much for everything, Brooklyn. We aren't going to stay here for a bit, but I'd love your help over at Parker's or my parents eventually. Eric and I are going through some stuff," I quickly said, trying my hardest to disguise my sniffling.

"Oh, I'm so sorry, Dr. Indigo. Just text me. I'm going to be on Thanksgiving break in a month, and Christmas is just after, so I'll have a lot more flexibility without classes. You know I love Lola." She smiled and waved before heading to her car.

"Mommy!" Lola exclaimed. She could barely be seen through the window, so I reached and rubbed her hair. Parker was moving the extra car seat from our garage into his car—the car seat that should have been in Eric's, but he hated how it made his perfect car look.

"Okay, princess, let's hop in." Parker buckled her in.

"Sully, I'm going to actually stay back to talk to him. I'll head over to your place right after."

Parker's dark eyebrows furrowed. "Serena, are you sure that's a good idea?"

I reached my hand over to his face, gently stroking the small bit of scruff that lingered on his jawline. "I'll see you tonight. Don't worry." I whispered. Tears stung my already pained eyes.

"Seri, I love you. You are the strongest person I know." Parker leaned in and placed his forehead against mine. I felt his warm breath pick up and inhaled his gentle scent.

"Sully, I love you, too." I pulled away, batting the tears that were begging to stream out. His warm hug provided the surge of strength I knew I desperately needed. Whereas Eric ripped me to shreds, Parker lifted me up. Always. I thought back to whenever I'd fall into a panic or fear, and Eric would stand there, staring at me as if I were damaged goods. He'd never give me a hug or comfort me; he'd simply roll his eyes, forcing me to pull myself together. That was the start of when I began to hurt myself. It helped me find some emotion from something besides myself. I married a narcissistic monster and had become one myself.

"Mommy!" Lola's sweet voice broke me out of my thoughts.

"You be a good girl, Miss Lola. I heard that Uncle Parker has an impressive stash of ice cream…"

She giggled sweetly with excitement. I unbuckled my seatbelt and got out of the car. There I stood, watching Parker pull out of our driveway and waved with a valiant face, though it didn't match how I felt inside, betrayed and flawed. But if there was one thing I was good at, it was pretending everything was okay.

The front door creaked open. I heard his footsteps slowly come in and then his keys chimed against the small glass bowl that sat atop the foyer console table. The sound of his keys echoing once provided excitement that he was home to us, had now become a symbol of doom and dread. I took a deep breath, watching as he looked around.

The low light from the lamp outlined him. He was wearing his scrubs, running his hand through his hair. How could someone do this to another person? How could you stand in front of another human and promise them the world, yet shatter it to pieces because of your inability to control your need to be with someone else? I fantasized about Parker more than I cared to admit. Hell, when my husband slept with me, there were nights I closed my eyes and imagined Parker on top of me and not Eric. But I never betrayed Eric. I was in control. I controlled my urges, my feelings. I kept my vows and promises. I would have kept them forever. We were supposed to be the perfect family. We could have been.

Eric Hudson and I had lost so much together. We'd been through hell and back, and not by choice. Now, he was choosing to drag us through the flames yet again, by choice.

"Fuck, Serena." He jumped back as his eyes caught mine in the dark. His hand jerked to his chest. I was sitting in the oversized leather chair in our living room facing him. It was his favorite piece of furniture in our home.

"Hi, honey…" My voice sounded hoarse from hours spent crying.

"Serena! What the hell are you doing?" I followed his green eyes to the giant cut that was fresh in the armrest of the chair I sat in. He was staring at my hand. I looked down at the small dagger that was half sunken into the expensive leather.

"Oh… it sucks, doesn't it, Eric? When someone you trust rips open something you love…" I stood up slowly and walked toward him. He took a step back with his eyes fixed on the dagger that I spun between my fingers.

"All the bright precious things fade so fast and they don't come back…" I tapped the sharp pointed end of the dagger against his chest, trailing it up to his chin. Eric's eyes pierced into mine with terror.

"You know that was always my favorite Great Gatsby quote. Fitting, isn't it? For this life of hell, you gave me. I could have done so much better than you. You're a pathetic piece of shit."

"Serena, what are you talking about? What is going on?" Eric whispered, backing away carefully.

"I want a divorce, you lying, cheating asshole." The fear in his eyes fueled something inside of me. He had humiliated me, but now it felt thrilling to have this *power.*

"Serena, I thought we were fixing this." Eric reached the end table and tightly gripped it.

"Fixing what?" I walked closer to him. "I can't fix you, you're a damaged man. You've always been damaged. I should have known better. You are fucking flawed. And if there is one thing you know about me, is that I don't do flawed. I can't fix you…"

I turned and walked to the expensive decorative mirror that sat perched on top of a table in the living room. It was a wedding gift—one that Eric loved. I lifted it up, looking back at Eric, and slowly allowed each finger to loosen until it slipped from my hands.

"Serena!" Eric ran toward the shattered mirror. Eric dropped in front of me on his knees, trying to piece the mirror together.

"Oh, you sad, pitiful excuse of a man. Don't you see, sweetheart? Even if you try to piece it together, it'll never be the same. *Your reflection will always be broken. Just like you.*"

I watched Eric as he stared at me without words. He looked like a deer in headlights. The fear that covered his face ignited a fire inside of me. He always knew what to say, how to make anything and everything a fight. Tonight, he had no words. The man who always had a speech was finally left speechless.

I drove to Parker's house and pulled into the driveway. I decided to stay with him for a bit so I could cool off from everything before having to live with my parents and handle the wrath of my mother on her own stomping grounds. Parker's house was a large, equally beautiful home, but in more of a young professional neighborhood over the family-friendly one we lived in. It was also significantly closer to our office. We had picked our house because it was close to Eric's hospital.

I could feel my stomach rumbling, since it was already ten. I couldn't help but smile thinking of the expression on Eric's face. It wasn't heartbreak or sadness, it was sheer fear. *Of me.*

Parker had carried Lola upstairs; she had fallen asleep on the car ride over. I was grateful for the resilience and ignorance of young children. Our lives were completely crumbling around us, but Lola was in the perfect state of oblivion.

Walking into Parker's kitchen, it was spotless. It reminded me of something I'd see in a magazine. There were no colorful silly cups lingering on the counters, no crumbs lonely on the floor, no dishes in the sink. It was bright and sleek. His entire house was modern, but also cozy. He had whites and blues coordinated throughout with gray furniture. I opened his pantry and was thankful the man actually kept snacks and cereal stocked. Grabbing a box of Choco Puffs, I pulled out a bowl and spoon.

"Well, looks like you found my secret stash." Parker turned in with a smile, running his hand through his hair. He had changed into a fitted white shirt with navy joggers and his deep brown eyes were filled with care.

"She asleep?" I looked up at the ceiling.

"Yep, I put her in the guestroom and tucked some rolled blankets under the sheets so she won't fall off."

He came closer, and for a moment, I thought he moved to be next to me, but he reached over, opened the fridge, and pulled out a carton of milk. I quickly moved under his arm and grabbed another bowl and spoon out.

We sat at the kitchen island eating the sweet cereal together in silence. I was thankful Parker wasn't trying to counsel or console me. He was just letting me eat. Whenever I was distraught, Eric would always yell, which only added to my anxiety. When I was already on edge, he'd give me the push off, rather than pull me back. I shuddered at the thought of the time I almost had let myself... *go.*

"Parker, thank..." Tears pricked at my already swollen and tired eyes.

"Serena, please don't do that. You know how much

I love you and Lola. You both can stay as long as you want. I have the space, and it'll make me feel better knowing you both are safe while you sort through everything."

"I'm hiring Landon Hills." I leaned back into the stool, dropping my spoon against the empty bowl.

"Damn. Really? He's going to cost a pretty penny, but he is the best."

Landon Hills went to UNC with us. North Carolina's best, most sought-after lawyer specializing in divorce, but we had worked with him a handful of times for malpractice suits. He was an absolute shark, and just what I needed. When playing with fire, I didn't want to be burned. I needed to be prepared for a fucking, blazing wildfire.

"I want full custody of Lola. She's worth every ounce of money, and if I need to, I'll ask my dad." I sighed.

"Seri, just ask me." Parker took another bite of cereal and a bit of milk dribbled to his chin. I reached over, wiping it with my finger, and without thinking, I licked it off my finger. Parker's eyes widened.

"I should head to bed. We both have an early morning at the clinic, and I need to call Landon during lunch. Thanks for everything, Parker." I moved to leave the kitchen but paused and glanced over my shoulder. "And Sully?"

He spun around in his stool. "Yea, Seri?".

"I would never have guessed that you eat Choco Puffs." I grinned at him and walked away.

Crawling into the plush bed that Lola laid in, I finally didn't feel overwhelmed. Parker offered me the other guestroom, but I didn't want Lola waking up in a new room without me. I looked at her and gently tucked a straggling curl behind her ear. My lips grazed her forehead. No matter how much I filled my heart with regret over wasting so many years of my life with Eric, she was the greatest gift that rose from the ashes of what our marriage had become.

I closed my eyes and began to drift into sleep when a light shimmered through the window. Sitting up abruptly, I waited for the light to pass, assuming it was a car driving by. The light grew larger and closer. My heart began to pulse quickly as my breath hitched. Creeping to the window slowly, I hid behind one panel in hopes my shadow wouldn't be seen. I peeked out, letting my head fall forward, but the rest of my body hidden away. A woman stood outside of her car holding what seemed to be her phone, taking photos, and was staring directly at Parker's house. My body felt ice cold again as goosebumps appeared on my arms. I squinted, trying to make out the car or even figure. *Who was it? Macy?*

I stared through the window, still mostly covered by the curtain. Suddenly, chills shot up my spine, my palms grew moist, and my heart felt like it was pounding outside of my body. The shadowed figure slowly lifted her hand in the air and waved at me, her fingers crinkled like synchronized swimmers one by one. My hand flung to my beating chest. I rushed to grab my phone off the nightstand and texted Parker, praying he was still awake. Within seconds, he appeared at the door and silently walked to the window, peering outside. The car immediately sped off. Parker reached over and held me. His soft breath was a welcome warmth on my cold face. He guided me outside the bedroom, with his finger over his lips. Lola was deep asleep, thankfully.

Reaching Parker's room, I realized my nails had been digging into his bare chest. I glanced down and saw his exposed skin was indented in small crescent shapes.

"She was just... standing there, taking pictures. Parker, no one even knows I'm here." My voice shook with fear.

"I didn't see anyone, Seri. I'll check the security cameras tomorrow. I promise you are safe here." Parker yawned, his hair was messy.

I felt guilty that I was continually disrupting his life.

"She waved at me Parker... She knows I'm here," I whispered into his chest.

"What? She waved? Are you sure? Want me to check the cameras now?"

"No, it's fine. I just don't want to sleep in there with Lola alone..." I looked at the floor, knowing I sounded so childish.

"Look, Serena, I'm going to bring Lola to my bed and you both just sleep here. I'll sleep on the floor next to it." He let go of me and walked over to where Lola was sleeping.

Moments later, he appeared with her draped in his arms and quietly carried her into his bedroom and carefully placed her in the middle of the large bed. I walked in as he placed a spare blanket and pillow on the floor next to the bed and climbed under the sheet.

"Parker, will you just sleep in the bed with us?" I whispered.

"Are you sure?" His eyebrow lifted slightly as he questioned me.

"Yes, I would feel so much safer."

"Anything you want, Seri." He got back up and climbed in his bed on one side of Lola. She was sprawled out like a starfish, so Parker hovered on the edge. I crawled into the other side and closed my eyes. All I could think of was the way the woman waved at me. The calmness of her gesture was the eeriest part.

Who the hell was she?

Before I knew it, exhaustion took over and carried me into my dreams that I was certain would become nightmares. It couldn't have been Macy. *Why would she stalk me?*

CHAPTER TWELVE

L andon Hills. I was sitting across from him, a large sleek desk separating us. His office overlooked the Charlotte skyline. It was on the top floor of a high rise in the center of downtown. He wore thick black glasses, had an expensive suit on, and his silver cufflinks were monogrammed with his initials. He was carefully studying the documents and laptop on his desk, his thumb and index finger rubbing his chin slowly. I brought him everything from the private investigator and my finances. Behind him there were wall-to-wall bookcases filled with law textbooks, along with his neatly hung diplomas.

Looking up from his laptop, he leaned back into his chair and clasped his hands together. "Okay, Serena, we will crush him."

"Yea? I mean, I keep thinking if this is the right thing to do… He is the father of my child," I hesitated, playing with the hem of my skirt.

"Serena, he's a narcissistic, cheating piece of shit who single-handedly destroyed your life. You came to me because you want to chew him up and spit him out. That's what I do. I don't sip cocktails and dab my face. I tear every ounce of perpetrators apart. If you play with dirt, you'll get dirty. Save your manicure and let me pull the gloves on to clean up the mess for you." He pretended to pull gloves over his hands.

I swallowed and reached for the glass of water that his assistant had placed in front of me. "Right. Well then, I suppose I'd like to proceed. The most important thing is my daughter. I want full custody and limited visitation." I stared at Landon.

He bent over, jotting something down with his fancy pen while nodding. "Right. Anything else you can think of make sure to let me know and keep me in the loop. It's a $250,000 retainer fee and my assistant will provide all the documents. Anything else you want to add?"

I hesitated, then leaned forward. "Actually yea. So, for a while now, I've had this feeling I'm being watching or followed. You know about Brooks Callahan and all, but I just feel like there's someone else... *stalking me.* I mean, I mentioned the woman waving at me last night, but I just don't know what to do. I swear it's his mistress. That bitch Macy is trying to make me crazy." I stared at Landon as he rubbed his chin, clasping his hands together again.

"Look, Serena, maybe this Brooks kid knows about Eric and his mom having an affair and he's just pissed off. I mean, think about it, wouldn't you be? He just wants some form of harmless revenge, so to speak. Do I think he's going to be a concern? *No.* Do I think it's some risk-free teenage nonsense? *Sure.* If it persists and you really think someone else is stalking you, then we can look into a restraining order. I'll be honest, until you have visible evidence, it's going to be a challenge having cops or a judge take you seriously. Why don't you try to figure out where Macy was last night?" *Apparently, you can't get a restraining order on a ghost.*

"I mean, but what about my earrings? Can't I file a robbery report?" I asked eagerly.

"Sure, but again, what evidence is there to say you didn't just loose the earrings?" Landon glanced at his watch. "Serena, if there's any form of evidence, send it over to my assistant Everly."

"Okay. Thanks, Landon." I stood up quickly, grabbing my bag and sunglasses.

"And, Serena... one more thing."

"Yea?" I answered, looking over my shoulder.

"I always knew you should have chosen Parker Sully. Eric Hudson was a conniving asshole from the beginning." He was looking at his phone nonchalantly.

"Tell me about it." Granted I was already married when I met Parker, the difference was I could have saved myself a huge mess and a lifetime of pain if I had left him years ago.

I walked outside of the tall building and looked up. The windows were all reflective. You couldn't see what was on the inside, just the outside. *How ironic.*

I cannot believe you had Landon Hills serve me divorce papers. Eric texted me a week later.

I successfully had ignored his calls and texts. He showed no interest in even seeing Lola, which pained my heart for her as she asked about him, but at the same time, it was a relief for me. I didn't care to share the one person who would never leave me. My sweet Lola.

And I can't believe I married a lying, cheating prick. If you need to discuss anything further, please contact my attorney, Mr. Hills.

A few weeks had come and gone. Eric met with Lola at the neighborhood park with my parents, which was fine since I couldn't stomach seeing him yet. He had agreed to move into his once secret apartment after begging me to let us try any way of reconciliation. He offered to go to couples' therapy, but once he realized I knew about the ultrasound photos, how he was screwing Macy for years, while I went through hell and back to get pregnant with Lola, he knew we'd never piece the shattered glass that had become our marriage. Our marriage was completely destroyed. *The life I loved and knew was completely destroyed.*

We had stayed with Parker for a couple of weeks, and as much as it was just what I needed, I also knew I couldn't use Parker as a crutch to hold me up forever. Lola and I went back to our house, but it didn't seem or feel like a home anymore. Walking in, even the scent seemed different. Parker's house felt like home, because it wasn't filled with memories I wished I could wash away.

Once Lola was settled in for the night, I tied up the garbage and headed outside. That was one thing Eric always took care of—the trash. It was almost appropriate since that was the one adjective I thought of when he crossed my mind. *Fucking trash.* Walking outside, the motion lights went off and I turned to look at them. The security cameras that we'd had for the past two years were still there. Eric swore he checked them when I complained about the window and door being opened or my earrings going missing. We had upped the security alarms and cameras since Brooks broke in, but I realized we never even really checked the recordings. I pulled my phone out and clicked the app for the cameras. Six square screens appeared. I could see our backyard, the sides of the house, the corners, and the front. Then there I was, on the screen. I sighed and slid my phone in my pocket.

"Hello, darling… it's awfully late to be out alone, isn't it?" A voice trailed close to me. I turned swiftly and saw Macy standing in her driveway, leaning against her car. I could feel my fist clench, wishing it would meet with the smug look on her face.

"Macy. Wow, you have some kind of audacity to speak to me. Are you waiting on the side of the street to be picked up as someone else's whore?"

"Now that's not very woman-empowering, is it, Serena? Isn't that your whole vibe? Women empowerment, blah blah blah. Besides, really, your husband is the whore. He basically threw himself at me. Begged for me. Poor guy clearly needed an upgrade." She tossed her head back and laughed.

"Oh, trust me, he isn't just a whore, he's a fucking idiot, too." I scanned her over and back, then turned away. I hated how beautiful she was. She didn't have the look of exhaustion drawn-out on her face. Her body was tight, toned, *perfect.* She invested in herself while I invested in everyone else. That clearly was the wrong gamble. Sure, I made sure I appeared well-groomed, but you could see Macy's beauty was deep because she didn't have to worry about anyone else. I was always pouring from an empty glass while hers was overfull.

"You'll have to thank him for the gorgeous earrings by the way." Her voice was callous.

I turned back toward her and squinted at the pearls she had in her earlobes as her red nails pushed her shiny hair back to show them to me. I swallowed as my teeth grinded together.

"You bitch. Those are mine. Give them to me right now." I walked to her quickly as my steps and voice increased simultaneously.

"They are mine. Get away from me, you lunatic," Macy shouted as I approached her, reaching toward her ears. I didn't know what I was planning to do, but in that moment, I wanted to tear her ears off.

"Macy, my parents gave them to me. Just give them back. You can have my husband, just give the damn earrings back." Pleading with my husband's mistress had to be a new low in my life.

"No thanks, I think I'll keep them both."

I could feel my lip quiver. I had no words. This

wasn't a suburban neighborhood, this was an inferno burning me alive.

"Darling, you really shouldn't be out this late all alone... You just never know what or who you'll find lurking in the shadows." The smile that spread across her bright red lips rivaled the Devil's.

My stomach sank. How could Eric be this cold-hearted? Those earrings were the one important piece of jewelry to me—besides my engagement and wedding ring. I even told him how much I couldn't wait to pass them down to Lola when she graduated from college. He didn't steal from me; he stole from our daughter. He was the lowest form of scum on the Earth.

I ran back inside the house and pulled my phone out.

"Eric?" Hot tears were furiously streaming down my face.

"Serena? Is Lola okay? Are you okay?" He genuinely sounded concerned.

"You stole my earrings and gave them..." I was hyperventilating. "Gave them to that slut, Macy... your fucking mistress!"

"Serena? What are you talking about? I thought you said you lost them. I swear, I didn't... I wouldn't do that, Serena. Can I come over? You don't sound good..." I could hear keys jingling in the background.

I hung up the phone, sinking to the cold, hardwood floor, crying hysterically. *Should I call the police?* And say what? That my husband stole my jewelry and gave it to the woman he was sleeping with? This couldn't be more degrading.

Opening the security camera app on my phone, I scrolled back to the date my earrings went missing, dragging the time stamp to match the hours of night I was asleep. My hands began to shake. I could feel the lines in my forehead deepen as I stared at the screen in front of me. A hooded figure was running through our backyard, and I fast-forwarded the video while my pulse raised and fingers trembled. Zooming in, I paused as the figure's hood slid off.

Brooks Callahan. He was staring over his shoulder at our house and his fist was clenched. He had to have my earrings in his hand. *What in the world?* Why would he steal my earrings and give them to his mom? Most of all, why would Macy wear them and say Eric gave them to her? Was this kid some sociopath, puppy killer out to get me? I shook my head and watched the tape over again, three times.

Suddenly, the doorbell rang. Glancing down at the security camera screens, I saw Eric standing there.

"Serena, oh my god. Are you okay?" Eric stretched his hands out toward me. I instinctively backed away, putting my arms up.

"It was Brooks. *Again.* He stole my earrings. It's on the security footage... and tonight, Macy was wearing them." I was stifling my impeding sobs.

"What? Are you sure?" Eric rubbed his forehead, kicking his shoes off in the foyer.

I handed him my phone and he walked over to the couch to sit and scroll through. I could see his face turn pale as he watched everything I had just replayed.

"Serena... I don't see—"

"I'm calling the police and showing them this."

"Serena, I think you..." Eric looked up at me.

"Don't you dare start with me. He stole my earrings, and I want them back. You can't just steal shit and then say sorry, expecting to be forgiven with no repercussions." My entire body shook with rage.

"Look, let me just talk to Macy. Please. I'll get the earrings back and we can all just move on," Eric pleaded.

"You're despicable. I forgot you'd be defending them. What is he, your stepson now?"

"Serena, please. Macy and I have ended our... we stopped seeing each other. I swear to you. It was a lapse of judgment. You know how much I love you and wish you'd reconsider. You need me. You're not well. It's happening, again. Please, baby." Eric stood and slowly approached me.

"You know, you're absolutely right," I replied.

"Really? Oh, baby, we can start over. You and me." Eric placed his hands in front of me, inviting me closer. I moved as close as I could to his face. I could feel his warm breath on me, which made my skin crawl.

"It was truly a lapse of judgment... on my part. I can't believe I chose to marry you. I can't believe I chose *you*. You killed him. You killed me," I whispered into his ear. I pulled back and looked into the shock of his eyes. He knew exactly what I meant. He knew what I meant and finally admitted that my greatest mistake in this lifetime would always have been choosing him over Parker. My greatest mistake was staying with him after everything. After he stole everything and everyone from me.

"The only thing I will ever consider was good from my decision has been Lola. If it wasn't for her, I don't know how I could live with myself, knowing I wasted so much of my life with someone as disgusting and repulsive as you. Now get the fuck out of my house, and the next time you come on my property, I'll be calling the police," I shouted at him. My brain felt fuzzy and everything began to blur.

"Fuck you, Serena! You're nothing more than a shadow of your insane, self-absorbed mother. It's ridiculous you have yet to accept they are gone and it wasn't my fucking fault."

Moments later, I heard the front door shut and I sunk back onto the cold hardwood floors. I let tears drown me in their comfort as I laid completely flat on the floor, sobbing hysterically. My entire body felt numb. The tears stung my eyes, and the salt from my nose and eyes blurred together, seeping into my mouth. I couldn't believe this was where my life had taken me.

Waking up the next morning, I realized I had fallen asleep on the floor. Even my eyes hurt to open, as the tears dried them together. I sat up and looked around. Sunlight was shining all through the glass windows. I was thankful Lola hadn't woken up yet and saw her mother piled onto the floor like a lunatic. Quickly, I walked upstairs and went to shower. I knew I had less than fifteen minutes before the pitter-pattering and giggles from Lola echoed through the house. She was the light of my life. I had to stay strong, for her. *If it wasn't for her, I'd have drowned long ago... She was my life raft.*

After showering, I threw on a pair of joggers and a hoodie. I had texted Parker and Mindy that I would be late into the office today. We needed time together this morning to settle into our new routine, just Lola and me. Using the spare towel, I quickly dried my hair and turned to the time. It was almost eight. Lola never slept in. I knew she had a tough time adjusting when we were at Parker's. Toddlers were creatures of habit with their routine, and she missed her pink princess room. She must have been sleeping soundly as I tip-toed down the hall to her room and gently pushed the door open. Chills covered my entire body. I felt para-lyzed. The scream that surfaced from my throat was unrecognizable. I don't think I even realized it was coming from my own mouth. I was surely having some outer-body experience.

Lola's bed was *empty*. Her window was opened, and the curtains were blowing carelessly in the dewy morning breeze. Suddenly, it was as if the room spun into white; there were no decorations, just an empty room. Tiny tiles covered the ceiling. I pushed my legs to move, feeling as if they were stuck in mud. My voice echoed as I peered down through the window, shrieking her name over and over again. Someone walking their dog got startled and ran away. My voice was hoarse, and I couldn't let out another sound.

Adrenaline kicked in and I ran as fast as my body would allow. I jumped down the stairs four at a time and raced to where my phone laid. Grabbing it, I called 9-1-1 as I sprinted outside, my hair soaking through the back of my hoodie as the cold air stung my skin.

"9-1-1, what's your emergency?" the operator answered monotonously.

"My... daughter... Lola..." I could barely speak. My hands were trembling intensely as I held the phone against my ear.

"Ma'am, I need you to take a deep breath. What happened to your daughter? Can you tell me your address? Is she home? Ma'am?" The operator churned out questions.

My eyes felt wide as I pried them open, praying I would see her playing in our yard or sitting on the driveway, playing with chalk.

"Lola Hudson. I can't... she... Please help. I can't lose her. *Not again*," I whispered into the phone. My hands couldn't hold it up any longer and I watched my phone fall and crash in front of me.

"Serena?" I looked up, following the voice.

Macy, Brooks, and James were all standing in their driveway, staring at me. I began hysterically screaming and crying. Sirens grew closer and before I knew it, there were three police cars and a fire truck in front of my home. Not long ago our driveway was filled with Lola and her friends tracing each other with chalk. Now my mind flashed to a crime scene, officers tracing the body of my dead daughter. My precious Lola. *My baby.* I couldn't breathe.

"Serena Indigo?" An officer gently tapped my shoulder.

"Ma'am, it is of utmost importance for you to talk to us. Time is of the essence with any abduction," the officer said sternly.

"Abduction?" I looked into his eyes and began sobbing again, using the sleeve of my hoodie to wipe my nose. I wasn't even the slightest bit of embarrassed by the clear, slimy trails that ran across.

"Ma'am, is there somewhere we can sit down?" The officer began to guide me back into my house. I looked around and saw many of my neighbors standing in their driveways, staring at me in shock. The same neighbors, my sweet Lola trick or treated at, were now pitying me with their looks of intrigue and curiosity. My life had officially become a sick specta-cle. My mother was right in this scenario. "When you laugh, the world will come over and laugh *with you.* When you cry, the world will abandon you and laugh *at you.*"

The officer and I went inside, taking our seats at the dining table. It was ironic because we hardly ever used the formal dining room, except for the occasional dinner party or celebration. Yet here I was, sitting with a stranger on the worst day of my life.

"Dr. Indigo, I need you to start speaking. I know this is extremely upsetting, but we have to find your daughter. Time is ticking and she needs to find her way home to you. Safely. *Alive.*" He cupped his hand around mine, shaking it, as if he could shake me into reality. The only thing was, there was no way I could allow this to be my reality.

Looking up at the officer, I read his badge. It was the same officer from the station when we met with the Callahans. My teeth chattered together violently as I allowed my trembling finger to trace the grooves of the wood in the table.

"Officer Lopez, my daughter, Lola Indigo Hudson, is three years old and has golden blonde hair... curls. She has dark blue eyes. She was wearing a white nightgown—" I began to silently cry in my hands. "Oh god, she must be freezing out there."

"Dr. Indigo, please, please. You must continue. Do you have a recent photo of her? We need to send out an alert immediately," Officer Lopez continued.

"Yes of course. I dropped my phone up front," I muttered, rubbing my head.

Officer Lopez held my phone up in a sealed bag. "This it?"

"Yes? Can I please have that back?" Irritated, I reached for it.

"Of course, ma'am." He handed the bag to me. "Let's see a clear picture of Lola."

Tears pricked my eyes as I scrolled through my phone gallery. They were all of her. There were some screenshots of toys or articles I was saving, but every square was filled with her smiling face. My heart sunk. I had been so preoccupied with my career, my marriage falling apart, and the daily chaos of life that I felt as if I barely had spent time with my own child. And now I was being punished. I was a terrible, unfit mother and apparently, a terrible wife.

"Dr. Indigo, a photo please?" Officer Lopez stared at me intently.

"Here." I shook my head and handed him my phone with the newest photo of Lola. It was from yesterday.

"Cute kid. I'll just text it to myself and we will have it blown up, covering every local news channel within the hour." He offered a reassuring smile. I knew that smile all too well. It didn't stem from happiness or optimism, it stemmed from the unknown. It was the same smile I gave to my patients when they sat across my desk and I told them bad news, like a diagnosis of infertility or that their growing fetus no longer had a heartbeat.

"Officer Lopez? We have something to show you." Another officer came inside, carrying an evidence bag but trying to shield it from me. I squinted and saw a glimpse of pink.

"What is that?" I screamed.

"Ma'am, please, I need you to sit down." The officer put his palm out at me as I lunged toward him.

"I'm begging you, show me! I'm her mother! Did you find my baby?" I shrieked.

"It's okay, David. Give it to me." Officer Lopez got in between us and grabbed the bag.

"Dr. Indigo, do you recognize this?" He held up the clear bag. It was Lola's small, blush-pink blanket. She had it since she was born and never slept without it. It was the blanket they wrapped her in and handed her to me at the hospital. The day everything *changed*. The day I changed *forever*. It felt as if my heart was outside of my body, being ripped to shreds. I sunk into the floor as things blurred and suddenly, everything went silent.

CHAPTER THIRTEEN

"*S*eri?" I slowly opened my eyes.

"Lola?" My voice was unrecognizable. I looked around, knowing I was waking up from the worst nightmare of my life. The relief felt incredible.

"Serena? Hey, you're okay…"

Blinking slowly to clear my vision, I saw Parker. His eyes were filled with concern and lined with fear. Realizing, as usual, I was stuck drowning in a nightmare.

"Parker, she's gone…" I didn't want to be alive. I wanted to be washed away and feel free from the burdens of this life. If Lola was gone, I couldn't survive. I wouldn't. I couldn't handle loss.

Not again.

"I know Seri, but they are gonna find her. She's a

strong little girl," he whispered, holding my hand tightly.

A voice cleared and we both followed it.

"Parker, would you give me a moment with my wife? Our daughter is missing, and I think it'd be best we handle this alone. *Together.* I know you don't have a family of your own, so you don't know boundaries." Eric stood fuming in the doorway.

"Well, I'm just so caught up having to take care of yours, I guess I didn't get a chance for my own..." Parker spewed back.

"Fuck off, Parker!" Eric yelled, his face bright red.

"Sully, it's okay. I'll see you in a bit." I nodded to him and gently patted his hand. My body was weak, my mind was weaker. I didn't have it in me to referee the ego-filled fight between the two men in my life.

"I'll be right outside. Call me if you need me. We shut the clinic down today." He stroked the hair off my forehead before planting a kiss on it. Eric cleared his throat again and took a deep breath, exhaling loudly.

He strolled in and sat at the foot of my bed. I could have sworn I wasn't in my room, but instead, laying in a hospital bed. Seeing Lola's baby blanket again triggered something I couldn't handle. I was exhausted from being strong all this time for everyone.

Who would be strong for me?

"We were happy once, weren't we?" I looked at Eric. His green eyes were tinged with red. I knew he was up crying, too. As shitty of a husband as he had been, he adored our daughter. Having children was always the one thing we always agreed on the most.

"We can still be happy, baby. You just have to forgive me. We will find her. We can be a family again. Look what's happening when we aren't together. I wasn't home and now Lola is gone." He looked at the floor.

"You're blaming me? You think you could have prevented her from being taken? What the fuck, Eric?" I couldn't believe him. Instead of comforting me, he was accusing me.

"What were you doing when she was taken, Serena? Screwing Parker?" He pierced through me. I didn't even recognize the man I spent so much of my life with.

"Get the hell out of my room, my house, and my life, you fucking asshole," I shouted.

Eric's fist clenched, and for a moment, my hand instinctually blocked my jaw. He shook his head with a knowing grin.

"You did this, Serena. You were never meant to have a baby, *remember*? You were never meant to be a mother. You had two chances and failed them both." He turned and looked over his shoulder at me.

"Get out! Get out! Get out!" I screamed until my voice grew hoarse, my hands covering my ears.

Officer Lopez came running in. He looked between Eric and me, opening his mouth as if he were going to say something but couldn't, *shouldn't*. Parker came in before he had the chance. He had water and a pill bottle in both hands. I sunk my head into my pillow, turning away.

"Seri, you need to sleep. Take one and let yourself rest. As soon as the officers find anything, I'll wake you up." He held the bottle and two brightly colored pills in front of me. I knew what they were, and I knew I needed them. I could feel Officer Lopez's eyes on me. *Judge all you want. Your daughter hasn't been kidnapped. Your marriage isn't crumbling in front of you. Your life isn't falling to shreds.* I parted my lips, allowing Parker to pour both the pills and water in. I felt numb. My body wasn't working. I closed my eyes, letting the memories of Lola take me away from my reality.

A cold hand brushed my cheek. It felt like ice. I flung my eyes open and felt the cold, autumn breeze blow over my uncovered body. The moonlight was shining through as a guide. I sat up, watching as the curtains shimmered with the wind. Reality sunk in as the medication side effects caused me to have a delayed reaction. I looked around my room, sweat beads budding at my hairline even though I was freezing. *Someone had been here. Someone was watching me sleep. Someone touched me.*

My blanket that I usually had tucked around me was completely thrown off. Taking a deep breath, I let my feet touch the softness of the rug underneath. I felt something sharp and I jerked my foot upward. I could feel something trickle out of my foot.

Turning on the lamp, I saw the blood from my foot drip onto the white shag rug beneath. As if I couldn't breathe already, something caused my heart to race and beat harder. One of my pearl earrings taunted me from the rug. The white of it was covered in my own blood. *How did it end up here?* Letting my hand roam around the area near it, there wasn't a second earring to be found. I held it in my hand, blinking away the numbness as adrenaline raced through my veins and the fogginess of the medication began to subside.

I left a bloody trail on our wooden floors as I ran as fast as I could to Lola's room. Approaching her door, I took a deep breath, begging the universe for one thing. Flinging the door open, I could tell there was something in her bed, tucked away. My heart was beating on the outside of my chest. My palms were sweating. I gripped the single pearl earring so hard that the post dug into my flesh, and I was sure it would reach my vein.

Pulling back the soft comforter, I sighed and sunk into the bed. Tears trickled down my cheeks. Nothing but Lola's favorite bear was there. I had wrapped it with the soft pink baby blanket, as if magically the bear would become my child.

"Mommy?" a small, tired voice trailed behind me.

I didn't want to turn around. I knew if I did, I would see that I had gone mad. I would know that I wasn't sane anymore, that I was in a state of shock. I didn't want to turn around to face the demons that were haunting me. *Always haunting me.*

A small, cold hand touched my shoulder, and that's when I closed my eyes. Taking a deep breath, I turned around, gripping her small bear in hopes it would offer me the same protection and strength it had always offered her.

"Lola?" There she was. My baby girl, my beautiful angel. She was standing in front of me, wearing the same nightgown she had on.

"Baby, my baby! Oh god, thank you! Thank you, God!" I screamed, pulling her into my arms as tears raced from my eyes, burying my tear-streaked face in her hair.

"Baby, are you okay? Lola, honey?"

I got up quickly, turning the lamp on but not letting go of her. I was terrified if I did, she might disappear from my arms. I looked down at her small frame, noticing her nightgown was stained with dirt, her soft curls had fallen flat. She offered a small smile as her eyes filled with exhaustion.

"Mommy, I hungry." She yawned. I had a million questions but knew better than to scare or overwhelm her.

I lifted her into my arms and swiftly looked around, hoping no one was lingering. I could have sworn we were being watched. Pushing aside her curtain, I saw Parker's car parked in my driveway and an unmarked car, with Officer Lopez in it, was on the side.

I walked as fast as I could downstairs with her wrapped in my arms while her small head was resting safely on my shoulder. Parker was on the asleep on the couch—he wanted to stay downstairs to provide me the sense of security. Chap was sprawled out on the rug in front of him, but immediately woke up. His fluffy tail wagged in delight.

"Uncle Parker! Chappie!" Lola shouted, seemingly more alert.

Parker abruptly sat up, staring at us in shock.

"Lola? Serena? Oh my God!" He ran toward us. Pulling away slowly, he stared into my eyes. His were filled with the questions, the same ones I had. I shook my head, looking down at Lola, as my fingers intertwined with her hair.

"I'm going to get the officer. Do you want to come with me?" He glanced around anxiously. He realized the same unnerving thing I did. *Someone had been in the house while we both were asleep.*

"No, I'm going to take Lola to the kitchen. She needs to eat and drink something. Just hurry and come back soon, please."

"I'll be back in a second." Parker ran to the front door, and I could hear him shout to Officer Lopez.

Carrying Lola into the kitchen, I couldn't let her out of my arms. Her weight was resting on my arched elbows. I kept smelling her hair. It didn't smell like the sweet orange-vanilla smell it usually did from her baby shampoo. I had so many questions for her, but at her age, I didn't know what she would manage to tell me. Secretly, I was also terrified to know the answers.

Officer Lopez and another man walked into the kitchen with Parker. Officer Lopez smiled at me, and I took a deep breath, offering a smile back. I didn't want to start crying again and frighten Lola.

"Hello, Miss Lola. You gave us all quite the scare.

Can we all sit down and talk?" Officer Lopez sunk onto a barstool. I looked over at Parker, who nodded at me, as I sat with Lola wrapped tightly in my arms. Parker went to the other side of the island and began prepping a peanut butter and jelly sandwich for Lola, while also quickly pouring a glass of milk.

"Should we call Dr. Hudson?" Officer Lopez looked at me while opening his laptop.

I closed my eyes and felt my hand run through Lola's soft hair.

"I hope she'll be a fool, that's the best thing a girl can be in this world... a beautiful little fool." He boasted all those years ago.

I had been sitting in the quad during my freshman year of college at UNC. I was reading The Great Gatsby, sipping a steaming hot coffee. The skies were a bright Carolina blue, the sun was shining in between the green of the trees that covered the area. I could still smell the scent of earthly freshness. The bustle of college students all around and the excitement of a new chapter in life circulated around creating an exhilarating momentum.

There he stood, staring at me, clutching the straps of his new backpack. We had already been acquainted living down the hall from one another in our dorms. I closed my book and observed him. It never made sense why he chose to recite that quote out of all the ones from The Great Gatsby, but it finally sunk in.

He had always wanted me to be a trusting and naive fool, and that I was.

"Dr. Indigo? Should we call your husband?" the second officer prompted.

"Seri, I think maybe you should just let him know Lola is home," Parker added softly.

"Yea, um… you guys can call him. After Lola eats, I think we need to take her to the H-O-S-P-I-T-A-L." I spelled out the word, not wanting to scare Lola. She was silently devouring the sandwich and milk in front of her.

"Yes, we will do that. They'll want to do a few tests on her, and we can do some questioning while we wait for results and whatnot," Officer Lopez replied, not able to make eye contact with me.

A pit in my stomach twisted as I knew exactly what kind of tests he was talking about. The second officer was already on the phone talking to Eric.

"Dr. Indigo, your husband is delighted your daughter is home and safe. He'd like you to know he's working in the ER right now and will wait for you both there. His colleague is on standby to check Lola," he said while pacing, his eyes shifting between Lola and me.

"Great. Okay, honey, we are going to go visit Daddy at work, and these nice people are going to ask you some questions."

Lola looked up at me, and I could tell she just wanted to sleep. The car ride to the hospital was only ten minutes, so she'd at least get a small power nap.

Once reaching the hospital, Eric raced toward me, grabbing Lola out of my arms. She was deep asleep, and he kissed her entire head, fighting back tears which made my eyes sting again. I rubbed her back gently as he carried her through the doors of the emergency room and into the bright light. Parker took my hand, and I took a long breath before looking up at him. I resented Eric for not even taking a second glance at me. I was the mother of his child—the child that was taken from us. He had no compassion or sympathy for me. *Ever.*

"I'm so scared, Parker," I muttered.

"I know, Seri. It's going to be okay. She's alive and with us." He squeezed my hand.

Dr. Vivian Rigsby, Eric's colleague we had known for years, was standing by the hospital bed that Lola was fast asleep in.

"Serena, it's good to see you, unfortunately on these terms, but nonetheless, it's good to see you." She offered a reassuring smile.

"You too, Vivian." I twitched my mouth slightly, unable to force a smile.

I sat in the chair next to Lola, holding her silky hand. She was still a baby to me. In her short three years of life, she'd already gone to hell and back, and I didn't know where I had gone wrong in parenting.

Dr. Rigsby began running tests and was softly talking to Eric. I was in a haze and wanted to be in ignorant bliss. Right now, I didn't want to be a doctor, I wanted to just be a mom.

"Are you seeing him?" Eric's angry voice drew me out of my thoughts.

"Oh Eric, I don't owe you a damn explanation and to be honest, do you think this is an appropriate setting? Have some shame. Our daughter is in a hospital bed," I fired back in a hushed whisper, looking to see if Parker had coming back with our coffee.

Officer Lopez quickly cleared his throat, waking Lola up. She opened her eyes slowly and looked at me.

"Baby, Officer Lopez wants to ask you about…" I began.

"Hey Lola, you can call me Gabriel," Officer Lopez stated and sat in the chair next to me. "So, Miss Lola, you were off on quite an outing. Can you tell me who took you from your house?"

Lola glanced between me and Eric.

"Baby, just answer Gabriel here. He's a good guy and is going to help us," Eric cooed at her and I nodded in agreement.

"He did." Lola's eyes widened as her small finger pointed at the glass window. We all turned and looked. There were so many people, mostly nurses, doctors, and patients. The other officer's hand went to his gun as he looked at Officer Lopez.

"Who? Do you still see him?" Officer Lopez quickly asked.

"No, he was looking at us and ran as soon as Mommy turned her head," Lola stammered.

"Okay, lock down the hospital. No one goes in or out. Now!" Officer Lopez shouted at the second officer. "What does he look like, Lola?"

She began to cry. "He told me if I said anything, then bad things would happen to my mommy."

"Oh, honey, nothing will happen to me. Please just tell us who you were with. Did they hurt you?" I began to tear up, unable to compose myself.

"No, he was nice. He said he had to take me so Mommy would remember about me going away a long time ago... He did it to help Mommy remember..."

Eric looked at me confused. "What is she talking about, Serena?"

"I have no idea…" I stared at Lola, as if I could figure out everything that happened by studying her small face. "Baby, do we know this man?" I nudged her hand some more.

"Yes," she answered.

"Okay, who is he? What is his name?" I nudged her again as she closed her eyes.

"The man next door with the brown notebook." She yawned before drifting back to beautiful dreams of bliss.

Eric looked at me. "Fuck! James Callahan? What the hell does he have against you?" He raised his eyebrows as Officer Lopez stood and moved to make a call.

"I don't know! Probably getting revenge for the fact that my husband was off fucking his wife!"

Officer Lopez covered the speaker of his phone, rotating to look at us. Eric's face turned red before he stormed out the room.

"James Callahan? Didn't his son break in recently?" Officer Lopez questioned.

"Yes. No one took me seriously. The earrings his wife had on were stolen from me! I found one on my rug just before Lola magically appeared."

"Damn it. James Callahan is one of the city's best attorneys. This is a nightmare. He has the judges and courts in the palm of his hand. We have to tread very carefully." Officer Lopez rubbed his head.

"I mean, he has a motive. My husband, the idiot, was screwing his wife for the past few years." I shook my head.

"Doesn't matter, we can't arrest him until we have evidence. I have officers checking Lola's dress and blanket for anything that can help us," he replied.

Dr. Rigsby returned and smiled at me. "Her results were perfect. She's a healthy, perfect little girl. Slightly dehydrated, but some Pedialyte will be good enough."

"Thanks, Vivian." I sighed with relief. I then turned to Officer Lopez and said sternly, "I want you to arrest him."

"Dr. Indigo, we are going to scan everything and anything for his DNA and prints. I'm going to head over now to question him. I advise you to stay away from the Callahans and maybe go stay elsewhere. Officers will be scanning your house inside and out."

"Okay. Can we go now?" I glanced at Vivian.

"Yep. She's all set. Eric's checking her out right now. Call us if you need anything. I'm so sorry again, Serena. I can't imagine what you guys are going through." Dr. Rigsby turned away, softly shutting the door behind her.

"You guys get somewhere safe and text me the

address. I'll have an officer stay outside to watch. I gotta go question Callahan."

"Thanks, Officer Lopez." I stood, meeting his face.

"Call me Gabriel. Don't worry, Dr. Indigo, we will solve this. We always do." He turned and left the room.

The dark sky outside grew lighter as we pulled into my parents' house. Parker offered to have us stay with him, but I didn't need to burden him any longer. I stared at the house I grew up in. It was enormous. It had been in the Indigo family for generations. I was in a beautiful bubble of happiness when I lived here, or at least, I thought that was what happiness was. Then again, looking at my life now, living with my parents was a walk in the park compared to this.

When I moved out from my parents' house to go to college, my dad handed me that small rectangular box. He took me into his office and sat me down. The memory would always be engrained in my mind. I remember looking at him as he pushed a wrapped gift toward me...

My fingers traced the smooth ivory paper.

"Open this when you get to school. I'm proud of you, baby girl."

I unpacked my belongings in the tiny dorm room,

reaching for the wrapped box. My roommate had gone off to grab a bite to eat with her parents.

Staring down at my desk, I slowly unwrapped it, pulling out a wooden rectangular box. It was engraved with *Be the hunter or the prey*. I tugged at the small note that had my dad's monogram embossed onto it.

"Grandpa gave me this when I was your age. Stay safe, my girl. Love, Dad."

I could feel my forehead crease as I hesitantly opened the wooden box. On deep indigo-colored velvet laid a shiny knife with a wooden handle that looked worn. I ran my finger over the smoothness of the cold metal that connected to the callous, yet beautiful wooden handle.

My grandfather was a paranoid man, a multi-millionaire who had made plenty of enemies along with his wealth. This was no surprise he'd start a family tradition with a dagger. I heard my door creak open, so I quickly shut the wooden box and hid it behind the random school supplies in my drawer. One day, I'd have to give this to my own child but until then, I'd just keep it hidden away so no one thought I was a psychopath. I turned toward the door as my roommate came in and I smiled at her.

· · ·

Walking inside, the housekeeper quickly grabbed my bags as my mom came running. She clutched Lola, wrapping her tightly, while grasping my waist with her free arm.

"Serena? The officers wouldn't let us come inside your house when we found out what was going on. Why didn't you call us? We saw our granddaughter's photo plastered on the news." My dad's voice rose behind my mother.

"Dad, it was a whirlwind. I called Mom, but then I just…" I rubbed my face.

"Oh, Ian, let her rest. Our girls are fine and here now; that is all that matters." My mom carried Lola upstairs while I followed my dad into his study.

"I already have my private investigator working on this." He sat in the oversized leather chair while I collapsed into the sofa against the wall.

"Lola says it was our neighbor, James Callahan."

"James Callahan? That's just great. The man is untouchable in this city." My father pounded his fist against his desk.

"That's what the officer said, too. Dad, I'm scared. Things have been really… off." I looked at him.

"Well, when we're you going to tell me about that cheating, good for nothing husband of yours?"

"Dad… can we not do this right now? I'm

exhausted and I have to get back to the office tomorrow. Mom and you have to stay with Lola. An officer is going to be parked outside 24/7, too," I stated with sheer exhaustion.

"Of course, baby. We won't let her out of our sight. Besides, this house is secured from bottom to top. I want you both to stay here as long as possible."

"Dad… am I alright? I just feel like I'm watching myself… but I am not going through all of this. I know that sounds insane."

"Baby girl, Indigos are not weak. We aren't the prey. If you feel that way, then you need to get in control and be the hunter. We don't let anyone or anything bring us down. You will be okay, because you have to be okay, Serena. There isn't another choice." He looked at me sternly.

"I'm really just tired. I think I need to just head to bed. 'Night dad."

"Love you, baby girl."

The next morning, I sat up in my bed, replaying the words my dad said. I knew I had to pull my life together. *I was weak. I was the prey.* Eric Hudson had hunted me and ripped me to shreds. My heart was aching at the mere realization that I had let myself and my life get this out of control. Opening the small nightstand drawer, I let my fingers glide through old photographs, high school and college memorabilia, and finally, a small lighter.

Picking it up, I flicked it open as the flame grew. Shaking my head, I knew I shouldn't. I needed to be better than this, yet I couldn't. I wasn't strong enough. Pulling down the shoulder of my nightgown, I lifted my arm up and stared at the scars that were embedded there. Letting the flame graze the damaged skin, I wished so badly it'd burn the layer off for a fresh start in more than just my physical body.

My head tossed back as the heat peeled my flesh. The floorboards creaked near my door, and I quickly jolted upright, hiding the lighter under my blankets. My mother waltzed in and my pulse increased as I could easily smell the now simmered flame.

My mom walked toward me, wearing a beautiful pale pink skirt with a cream blouse tucked in. Her dark hair was pinned up, while pearls donned her neck and ears. She looked at my sleeve that was pushed off my shoulder and back at my face, waiting for me to say something, *anything.*

"Hey, Mom…" I could hear my voice quiver. She paused, her nostrils flared, and I knew she had smelled the smoke. Not just the smoke, but the burn that came from her own daughter's flesh. Clearing her throat, she fidgeted with the pearls around her neck.

"Serena, I brought you this for your first day back at the office. I'm hoping it helps to draw you out of this…" She grew closer with a dress and golden tube in her hand.

"You know what they say… A woman without her face on, is a woman without her armor." My mom handed me the shiny tube.

"Yea, Mama, I think this lipstick will just solve all of my problems. Thank you so much!" I said sarcastically as she eyed me, the forced smile melted off her face.

I spent the next few days sliding into the office through the back doors since news reporters were lurking out front. I saw my patients who had all asked me details of what was going on. I delivered babies, performed surgeries, and tried my best to do everything I could to find normalcy. Lola was with my parents and was never out of their sight, while an officer was staked out in front with the house. Lola begged to go back to preschool, but the police suggested it was too risky until we figured out more.

A knock on my door lifted me out of my ever-racing mind and thoughts.

"Come in?"

"Dr. Indigo, I don't mean to disturb you…" Officer Gabriel Lopez said.

"You're not, please sit down," I replied, pointing to the chair across from my desk.

Officer Lopez stared at me. "He has a clear-cut alibi."

"What? How?" I gasped. "I mean, there is no way Lola would make this up. It has to be him."

"He was at home and his security cameras show that. There was no trace of DNA on any of Lola's items or in your house. Dr. Indigo, I have to ask, how well do you know Dr. Sully?"

"Parker? You've got to be kidding me. He was at my house the entire night and has…" I sat back and stared at Gabriel's face.

"Look, Dr. indigo. All I'm saying is the only DNA we found is yours, Eric's, and Parker's. It's time we look at those in the house, rather than out." He tapped his finger on my desk.

"There's just no…"

"That's what everyone says. There's always a way. Well, you let me know if anything strange happens and I'll keep digging."

I began thinking about everything. The woman outside of Parker's window waving at me… It couldn't be him, obviously. The person was clearly a woman. He loved me and Lola as his own… This was crazy. My daughter had been abducted. *Kidnapped.* Someone was doing this to mess with me, mess with my head. Parker was with me the whole time. Why would a three-year-old lie and say her neighbor did this. I rubbed my head, feeling a wave of dizziness wash over me. This was all becoming too much to handle. First, Eric's affair, then my child being ripped away from me with no answers. I was treading a very, very weak rope and didn't know how much more I could handle.

Weeks passed and nothing unusual had happened. I was feeling a sense of relief. Lola was back in school, but my dad had hired a private bodyguard to accompany her and stand outside the school. In another world, I would have considered it insane but the fact was we still had zero idea who took her, which meant whoever did was still lurking.

I got to my parents' house, it was completely silent since they weren't home, minus the light footsteps of the housekeepers. My parents had taken Lola to the zoo in a nearby city and were staying in a hotel overnight. I walked around the living room, letting my fingers trace the large gold frames that adorned the walls. Most of them were filled with photos of me. I was posing in all of them, with a giant smile on my face, holding award after award. I shuddered, realizing it felt like a shrine. Walking to the kitchen, I pulled out a wineglass and reached down to my parents' wine refrigerator, which was always well-stocked thanks to my mother's "secret" alcoholism.

Pulling the bottle out, I let the liquid slosh into the glass, watching as the deep red filled it. Sticking my finger in my mouth, I began slowly tracing the rim of the glass. The light music that emitted from the gesture helped cut through the unnerving stillness that radiated around me. As much as silence was nice, it also meant I could hear myself...thinking. I spun my phone around, lifting my drink up, pressing the cold rim to my lips, and allowed the sweet yet bitter liquid race down my throat. My phone began to vibrate aggressively against the marble counters. Lifting it up, I stared down at "Private Caller." I squinted at the screen as if I would be able to somehow decipher who the caller was.

"Nope..." I said out loud and flipped my phone over. I stood with my glass in one hand and decided to find a new show to watch. I couldn't remember the last time I actually committed to a tv series. That was what normal people did after work... *I could be normal.* I shook my head and walked to my parent's in-home movie theater. Maybe if I had grown up in a small house with a white picket fence instead of the over-the-top gated mansion with lion statues lining the porch, I wouldn't have become this perfectionist whose life was in shambles? How could anyone keep up with this? I looked around me and froze. I could hear the sound of my phone vibrating again against the hard counters, again. My damn phone wouldn't even let me be normal and watch a show.

I turned back and lifted it to my ear. "Hello?"

I could hear light breathing that sent chills up my spine.

"Okay, asshole, stop calling me." I shifted the phone to end the call.

"Hello, darling... Now that's not very polite, is it?"

Macy fucking Callahan.

"Macy, what the hell do you want?"

"Well, Serena... I hate that you and I are on such... rigid terms."

"Rigid? Macy, we aren't on any terms because I could give a shit less about you. Please don't ever contact me again. Especially since I'm pretty certain your husband is a goddamn kidnapper." As much as I wanted to slam my phone away, I couldn't help but wonder what she wanted from me. Macy Callahan was a drug, and I think I was getting high off her, or worse, maybe I was addicted to her.

"Don't be silly, Serena. You know very well that James would never take away something that can't be taken. You know, I think the two of us have so much more in common than you realize… I think you and I could actually be friends," she said confidently, as if she was certain.

"Macy, you and I are absolutely nothing alike." I paused, trying to absorb what she meant by taking away something that couldn't be taken.

How on earth did she think we could be friends? We had nothing in common. She was a stunning woman with no worries or fears and seemed to be loved by everyone around her, even though she was the most imperfect and horrible person I knew.

"Drinks at Queen's Rocks in thirty? Come on, darling, this is your chance to call me a bitch to my face."

"Well, I won't pass up that opportunity." I hung up the phone and couldn't believe I had agreed to meet up with my husband's mistress. Maybe James hadn't taken Lola. The police said he had an alibi. There was video footage of him at home with his family. *But then, who took her?* Maybe seeing Macy would give me the answers I needed, since clearly, the police had no leads.

I went upstairs to my childhood bedroom and sat at the white vanity. Opening my makeup bag, I flinched.

"Prim. Pluck. Pucker up, my perfect buttercup." I

looked into the mirror and began painting my face. The makeup couldn't cover the lack of sleep, the stress, and aging. It irritated me knowing I'd be sitting with Macy, and when everyone saw us, they'd think she was the more beautiful one of the two. Shaking my head, I let my face plant into my hands, feeling tears surface. I straightened myself up and grinned back at the otherwise defeated woman I didn't recognize in the reflection. Pulling on a sheer yet beautiful white dress, I quickly turned back to my vanity and put on the single pearl earring, leaving the other earlobe bare. I brushed my long, dark hair neatly and let it flow over my shoulders.

Queen's Rocks was located in a not-so-desirable area of Charlotte—an area I never frequented. I guess living behind a gate was something I was overly accustomed to.

I could hear her as soon as I walked into the crowded bar. Her voice and shrill laugh radiated through the cheap beer and sweat-scented air. I cringed as the red beneath my designer heels stuck to the sticky floors. The once pale blue walls were chipped away and covered with random historical Charlotte images.

"Darling! I'm so glad you came! Boys, scoot on over. My friend has arrived." Macy laughed as the doting men all turned toward me and lifted their drinks to move away. This is who Eric left me for? Rolling my eyes, I grabbed a small cocktail napkin and wiped the metal stool before sliding on it. Half my ass hung off because I didn't want to fully sit on it, especially after seeing the gross drunks who moved off it.

I turned and saw Macy staring at me with a small smirk. Her perfectly arched eyebrows were lifted as she observed me. She studied me as if I were a paining in an art gallery. She wore a tight gold dress and sparkly heels. Her plump lips were painted in the cherry-red she'd always adorned them in.

"Dave, this fine young woman would like a glass of your best wine."

"Oh no, I'll have water, and maybe…" I looked at the small glass of whiskey sitting in front of Macy.

"Red wine?" Jake, the young bartender, smiled kindly at me with a knowing glimmer in his eyes.

"No actually, I'd like tequila."

"Very well then." Macy lifted her glass up as Jake slid me mine.

"Cheers to you, Serena Indigo for being so… kind."

I tilted my head as I looked at Macy. Lifting my glass up without toasting hers, I threw the strong, disgusting alcohol down my throat and slammed the glass against the table. Wiping the corners of my mouth, I let the stool swirl toward her.

"Kind?" I questioned.

"I mean, you gave me your husband..."

"You are a despicable woman." I began to stand when her long red nails gripped my wrist. I looked down at her hand and met her eyes.

"Serena, have you ever thought that you aren't all mighty and perfect as you think you are?" she said in a hushed tone.

"Well, we all can't be perfect, little homewrecking trash like you, now can we?" I jolted my wrist out from her grip, and turning back around, I looked at her as she slowly tucked her hair behind her ear. There in one ear, was the other missing pearl earring. I could hear her shrill laugh trail behind me as I ran out. Reaching my car, I collapsed into the seat and pressed my head against the steering wheel and allowed myself to cry. Rolling the window down, I inhaled the cool air, the scent of rain hovering around me.

I drove home, and as I pulled through the gates, I looked at the house that had created the person I had become. Wiping the lingering mascara that streaked my cheeks, I thought how Macy Callahan was a small-town girl, who married her way into money. I wasn't going to let some low-class slut bring me down. I was better than her. I would always be better than her. Walking inside, I felt suffocated, so I did what Indigos did best. I swept all my problems under a lavish rug and acted like nothing was wrong.

Curling up on the sundeck that overlooked the pool, the cool breeze was rippling into the water. I pulled open a book that had been left out by my father and began to read. The birds chirping in the trees soothed me. I needed time away from all the chaos and noise of my life.

Landon Hills, my attorney, had proceeded with my divorce paperwork, which allowed me to feel a sense of clarity. Parker was swamped with work, and I was, too. It was easier to avoid him. I missed him, but ever since Officer Lopez brought the idea of him or Eric somehow being involved, I wanted to be alone. The only person I could trust was *myself.* Which wasn't saying much, considering I was a complete wreck.

I dozed off on the soft lounger, wishing I had changed out of the sheer, short dress into something more comfortable. Opening my eyes, I saw the shadows of the trees reflecting into the pool. It had grown colder; the impending chill of November was right around the corner. Wrapping myself in the cozy blanket, leaves rustled in the distance. Suddenly, the motion lights set off, making me jump. The pulsating in my neck grew harder and faster. It had to be a stray animal. My parents' home was basically a gated castle. No one could get in or out without purpose. I looked down, seeing the book folded neatly beside me, and realized my phone was inside.

Taking a deep breath, I turned around and looked through the glass. A small cat raced past the pool, laughing at my paranoia. I was so on edge that something as normal and simple like rustling leaves and nature were now setting me off. My dad's book was still sitting outside, and I remembered the weather predicted a storm. Opening the door, I turned to grab it. I couldn't help but smile at how much joy he found in reading. Maybe that's what I needed, too—find joy in something besides being a mom, doctor, and wife.

I clutched it against my chest. The lights inside of the pool were on, and the water looked so welcoming. It was heated in the fall and I would have loved to go for a swim, but there was no way in hell I would be that dumb to go alone when I was already scared of the sound of a stray cat. Shaking my head, I turned the knob, placing my hand on my rumbling stomach. Delivery Thai food sounded like the perfect end to this night. Just as I was about to step inside, a strong grasp pulled my hair so aggressively, the sound of ripping echoed around me. My mind went blank as my body met the cold concrete below me.

As if my brain wasn't aligned with my body, I couldn't open my mouth. Pain was growing from the back of my head to my legs, I was being dragged down the hard pavement. Darkness kept going in and out of my vision. I couldn't tell if it were the night sky or if I was getting lost in my own body. Sounds of deep breathing that weren't my own towered over me. I tried with every ounce of strength to speak, yet my mouth wouldn't open. Parting my lips slightly with thick saliva coating them, they felt like a sticky marshmallow spreading between fingers, unable to clear through for words.

Blinking harder, I saw a figure dragging me with both hands, while my delicate dress ripped against the concrete as the bare flesh on my back scraped against the unkind, cold surface below my frozen body. Peeling my eyes open, it was all a blur. *Red lips? No...*

"Please... wait..." I called out, my voice hoarse. What seemed to be an agonizing eternity later, I felt my body hit the warm water. Before I knew it, I was sinking, drowning in the vivid blue around me. I reached up and opened my eyes, chlorine blurring them. Dizziness overtook me, but I saw red reflect in the water around me by the light of the pool. I could see an outline standing outside of the pool watching me descend. My hand stretched toward the reflection that stared at me, pleading without words to save me, to help me.

Instead, all I could see was a smile, a red smile curving as I sunk deeper and deeper into the unknown. My body felt weightless, as if I were a mere feather from a bird, plucked off and floating in the sky. *Then everything went dark.*

CHAPTER FOURTEEN

The sound of beeping and the familiar humming of my mom intertwined together. I opened my eyes and saw white ceiling tiles. Forty-four tiles. I was in and out, counting them slowly. The muscles of my body colliding and twisting in pain. My body felt as if a truck had rammed into it.

"Serena?" My mom's voice lifted, echoing in the stark, white room.

I croaked back, my throat sore. "Mama?" My southern drawl more apparent, I didn't have the strength to fight it.

"Oh, my goodness. She's awake! Nurse! Doctor?" my mom shouted out the door.

The loudness of her voice twanged with her deep southern accent rang in my ears. A doctor I didn't recognize came inside and checked the machines I was connected to.

"Dr. Indigo, how are we feeling?"

"Like complete shit." I closed my eyes again. Everything fucking hurt.

After the doctor poked and prodded at me, I saw Eric standing next to my bed. He looked concerned. My mom wasn't in the room anymore. Things were fuzzy, blurry, and so out of place, I didn't even want to attempt to piece this together. Until suddenly, I realized something.

Lola.

"Eric? Where's Lola!?" I tried to sit up but had no strength.

Eric reached out and pushed me back down slowly. "Serena, we aren't doing this right now. Their housekeeper found you floating in the pool. Serena... the pool was filled with blood and the back of your head was cracked open. What the hell happened? Who did this?" Eric's eyes were filled with terror.

"Who do you think?" I fired back at him.

"James and Macy Callahan are out to kill me. No one can prove it, but just think, Eric... His wife's affair humiliated him and now he is out for blood, *my* blood." I began crying, gasping for air as my chest tightened with pain.

"Serena. James and Macy were out of town. They have receipts and everything." Eric looked at me.

"They are questioning Parker…" he added quietly.

"Oh, you're loving this, aren't you? Just admit it, Parker being pegged as the fucking villain must make you elated. How about you tell me where you were last night, Eric? How about the last thing I saw were bright red lips?"

"I was working. Damn it, Serena, you know I'd never hurt you. I've always had a feeling about Parker. He was always too good to be true, and you never saw it… You let that psychopath into our lives and home. As for red lips, that must have been the blood you saw around you, the pool was covered…" Eric sighed, pushing his fingers through his hair.

"Get out, Eric. The only person I regret letting into my life is you." I closed my eyes again as tears glued them shut.

Officer Lopez showed up to question me. We were running around in a circle, there were no answers and everyone had an alibi. Part of me was convinced I had lost my mind, and this had all been in my head, but the stitches in the back of my head said otherwise. Someone had attacked me, and I was the victim.

"Dr. Indigo, how much did you have to drink last

night?" Officer Lopez sat on the stool next to my hospital bed.

"Seriously? You think I drank, then threw myself against the concrete floor, and fell into a pool?" I angrily questioned him.

"Serena, the camera's picked nothing and no one up. We have to go through all the options."

"I had maybe one or two drinks..."

"Right. You went to Queens Rocks just before this happened." He scanned the small notepad in his hand.

"Actually yes, and I'd like you to go and question Macy Callahan because she was the last person with me. She could have easily followed me home through the gate." I sat up and thought of how I felt long nails gripping my scalp just before everything went black.

"Oh my god, it really was her. It had to be her. She's a sociopath," I panted as anxiety filled me. Gripping my chest, I felt like I couldn't breathe. This bitch stole my husband, shattered my life, and was now trying to *kill me.*

"Right. We will look into it. You take care, Dr. Indigo." Officer Lopez lifted an eyebrow and watched me in a way that made my skin crawl.

"What?" I hissed at him. My lips were cracking from the dry hospital air, and my throat couldn't feel any more uncomfortable.

Lola eventually told a child psychiatrist that she saw a man had taken her to a large room and let her stay there when she went missing. She was scared and he had blindfolded her until they got to the room. It was apparently some kind of empty space, cold and dark. He left her there alone and finally brought her back home. She said he had tape over her mouth as they stood and watched me sleep before he took her into her room. He wore a mask over his face and didn't say a word. She assumed it was James Callahan because she couldn't tell who else the man looked like. We were all confused and had no idea where to piece things together. Nothing made any sense. She said he took her to help me remember... *But remember what?*

Parker came to visit me at my parents' house as I laid in bed. I looked like an absolute disaster, yet I didn't care anymore since it matched the theme of my life. *An absolute fucking disaster.* He brought a bouquet of flowers, along with my favorite chocolate mousse cake.

"Hey, Seri, I've missed you." He leaned down, planting a warm kiss on my forehead.

"I've missed you, too. Sorry, if someone wasn't trying to constantly kill me, I'd be at work more." I offered a small smile.

"Serena, I'm really worried about you. Why didn't you come to me?" He sat down next to me.

"You know they questioned me like crazy. They searched my house, our office, questioned our staff. You know I'd never hurt you right?" He stared into my eyes. Sadness lingered across his face. Letting his fingers graze my cheek, my face fell into his palm.

"Parker, I never in a million years would accuse you. They are just covering their grounds. I'm so sorry to have dragged you into this mess." I sighed, reaching my hand out for his. His head met mine as the tips of our noses touched. Turning my face toward him more, there was no space left, and our lips grazed each other's. I could taste lingering coffee. He was kissing me back as if he were starving for me. Being wanted, being desired by someone this much was a godly, holy sensation that pierced my soul. I turned toward him and pulled him closer, his hand trailed up my chemise and brushed against my naked breast. The heat between our bodies rose. I wanted him badly... but really, I needed him. I needed to feel—I needed to feel anything but pain. He pulled away quickly, breathing heavily. His eyes filled with lust and desire quickly faded into restraint and concern.

"Seri, we can't. You literally have stitches in your scalp. You're not in a good place. You have to rest." His lips turned into a devious smile that made my heart race. With Parker, I always felt like I was twenty-four again.

"Parker Sully, you're such a tease." I smiled back at him and let my aching head sink into the pillow. After watching a movie together in bed, he went home while I was snuggled between Lola and Chap. Chap's tail was wagging happily as I rubbed his soft head. Guilt panged me as I looked between the two of them. My littlest loves, both neglected by lack of attention because... *life.*

My mom came in for Lola to take her out for ice cream, which was a cue for me to get rest. The security staff that my parents spared no expense on were all through the house, with my personal guard being, Brett. He stood outside of my door, which allowed me to actually sleep at night.

I stood and instantly felt lightheaded, but knew I needed to move my body. Looking out the window, I stared at the drained pool from above.

Officer Lopez said the whole thing was tinged with my blood and a trail from the patio led the house-keeper to my floating body, I was still in the beautiful dress that I wore to Queens Rock. The eeriest part were the flowers that surrounded and intertwined with the blood. They were small, pink roses that had barely even budded. Security cameras had been tampered with, so there were no leads on the perpetrator. In order to sleep, I was taking sedatives because every time I closed my eyes, I felt like I was drowning, reaching up in desperation to be saved. *Saved by her.*

"Brett, let's take Chap on a walk," I called out. Brett was a massive man wearing a shirt probably two sizes too small that made his muscles bulge out obnoxiously.

"You sure that's a good idea, Ms. Serena?" He raised his eyebrow at me.

I wrapped myself in a thick cardigan and waved to Chap. "Yea, I have to get out of the house. It'll be really good for me." I smiled at him.

Moments later, we were strolling down the sidewalk. I had Chap on his leash as he was pranced excitedly in front of me. Brett was walking close, and I knew the outline on his waist was that of a gun. I felt safe. *I was safe.* The air smelled fresh and welcoming, and the coldness of it did wonders for my lungs.

From a distance, I could see a boy jogging toward us. I gripped Chap's leash harder as he began to tug, trying to run toward him.

Brett moved in front of me and stopped. The boy kept running toward us when I quickly realized it was Brooks Callahan.

"Dr. Indigo?" he called out, stopping a good distance from us. My hand felt slippery against the plastic handle of the leash.

"Ma'am, I want you to stand right behind me. What do you want, kid?" Brett called out aggressively.

"I don't mean any trouble, sir. I just need to talk to Dr. Indigo. Please," Brooks pleaded.

I stepped outside of Brett's large, protective frame and peered at Brooks. He was just a kid with fear painted across his face. I took a deep breath and nodded.

"It's okay. Just stand next to me though," I whispered.

"What do you want, Brooks? What are you doing here? How did you even know where I was?" I spoke to him, keeping my distance. I couldn't help but look at how blue his eyes were—a deep shade so similar to my Lola's... *and my own.*

"It's my mom and dad. You have to be careful, Dr. Indigo. They hate you. They want to hurt you. They *will* hurt you." Brooks' voice shook as he spoke.

Stunned, I stared at him. "Why? Why do they want to hurt me? Brooks, I need to call the police. You have to tell them," I cried out. This was my only option now to prove that I wasn't crazy.

"No! You can't! They'll make me go away... Just

watch out." He turned around and sprinted in the opposite direction. What was happening? Why did they want to kill me? If they had something against Eric, then why not go after him? *Why me?*

I told the police about my encounter with Brooks. Again, without him confirming anything, they had nothing to go on. He denied ever seeing me, and I refused to involve Brett. If Brooks was telling the truth, I didn't want James Callahan hurting his son over me or anyone else for that matter. He was just a kid.

Time had come and gone. We all learned to find a new normal. I finally felt that things were cooling off, and that maybe everything was going to be okay. I had learned that I needed to simply move on. Life was going forward, and I had to, as well. There was nothing I could do about James or Macy Callahan, either. No one could. He was untouchable without hard evidence. He basically owned the North Carolina judicial system.

I hadn't been back to my house because the movers packed and emptied it for us. The 'for sale' sign in the house was now marked with giant SOLD letters. It was the end of an era—an era which provided me pain but also pockets of joy, and much of what I once was proud of.

CHAPTER FIFTEEN

I was sitting next to Landon Hills, my divorce attorney. The nail polish on my thumbnail was almost completely peeled off, and I could feel the rapid pulsing in the sides of my forehead. Eric was sunken in the chair across from me with his attorney. It was finally happening... our divorce was becoming official. As much as I resented the man I was staring at, I mourned the man who put the ring on my finger all those years ago. I mourned the man who held my hand as I brought our daughter into the world.

However, I reminded myself, this was no longer the same man. Humans were more than capable of wearing various masks, yet we are who we are. You can't change anyone, especially when they don't see the faults embedded inside of them. This man was a lying coward who single-handedly changed the course of my life. *Our lives.* We agreed on seventy-thirty custody. Lola needed to be safe with me at my parents' house. Eric worked irregular hours and neither of us felt safe leaving her with any kind of babysitter. He was living at the apartment he once used with Macy. I was living with my parents and didn't have any desire to leave until I felt safe again. *If I ever would feel safe again.*

"Serena…" I froze in the middle of the parking lot. Inhaling the fresh air around me, I looked over my shoulder.

"What now, Eric?" I sighed with zero interest in starting a fight. I was over it all. I was over our marriage. Most of all, I was over Eric Hudson.

"Let's go to dinner, one last goodbye?" He shrugged, running his hand through his hair. I couldn't help but tilt my head and study him. I guess divorce made him more appealing, because in that moment, he didn't seem like the man who shredded our marriage, he just seemed like the college boy I had been in love with all those years ago. As much as I knew I should just go home and let this parking lot be the last of us, part of me needed more. *Closure.* Closure is such an ironic thing. Without it, you're in limbo, but with it, you feel as if your fate is sealed, often wishing the result could be different or altered, but it can't. You have to accept what you've been given. *An end to the beginning.*

"Okay." I tucked my keys into my purse and nodded in the direction of his car.

He smiled excitedly, as if he'd won me over for a first date. I rolled my eyes as he laughed and climbed into his car.

"So… what now, Seri?" He smirked as he glanced over at me.

"Don't call me that… Watch the road, not me."

Why had I agreed to this?

"Why? Only King Parker Sully can call you that?" He shook his head with irritation.

"What are we even doing, Eric? Just turn around." I pressed my head against the glass window.

The darkened sky was starless. I watched as restaurants passed by, knowing he wouldn't turn back. Once he wanted something, he always got it. We pulled in the parking lot of The Jewel. It was Charlotte's most expensive restaurant. I looked down at my outfit. Thankfully, I wore the new designer dress I'd bought. Dressing up for your divorce seemed ironic. Purchasing a designer dress seemed slightly irrational, but necessary. I took so much time to paint my face with makeup, crafting my hair perfectly, and climbing into this expensive dress, it was almost like a strange ode to my wedding day. Dressing up that day was to excite and show Eric everything he had to look forward to. Today, I dressed up to show him everything he'd be missing out on.

Heartbreak and anxiety dancing the tango inside me as I realized something riveting. *It was okay.* It was okay to mourn the loss of your marriage. Just because I felt relief, didn't mean I wasn't scared, too. *Labels.* Labels are branded on all of us every day of our lives. Daughter, wife, mother, doctor, woman, and now I had a new one…divorcee. That is a label no one wants, and one that you swear you won't have when you stare into the eyes of the one who you think with certainty, with clarity, will be by your side through it all. Your crutch. Your rock. Instead, they become your weakness, your fear, your demise.

"Dr. and Mrs. Hudson?" The thin hostess wearing a plunging, tight-fitted dress smiled as she glanced at Eric. Her cheeks turned pink. I looked over at him and could see the delight he felt from her attention.

"That's us, the happy couple…" Eric laughed and pulled me tightly toward him.

We followed her to our table, and I watched as my husband's—ex-husband—eyes trickle down to the peach-shaped ass of the twenty-something-year-old waitress. *Yep, my demise.*

"How did they have a reservation for Dr. and Mrs. Hudson? I mean, you are a sociopath and a misogynist." I looked down at the menu in front of me.

"Serena, contrary to what you think, I know you better than anyone. I knew you'd never say no to me. You never have been able to, and you never will."

"I divorced you. Pretty sure that means I can say no and much more to you." I pretended to be engrossed into the menu. My finger sliding across various selections.

"But seriously, what are you going to do now? Don't you think you'll be lonely without me?" he asked as the waiter brought over a bottle of wine and began pouring. I watched as the deep red streamed into my glass.

"Serena?"

Lifting the glass up, I placed it to my lips while staring at Eric, taking a sip of the bittersweet wine. *Bittersweet.* That's what this dinner was supposed to be —the bittersweet end to the beginning.

"I have Lola. I'll never be alone." I peered at his distorted face from over the glass.

He sighed loudly and placed his elbows on the

table, running both hands through his hair as he looked down. He looked tired. *Defeated.*

"This again? Serena. Whatever… not my problem anymore," he huffed under his breath and glanced over the menu once again.

"Not your problem? What the hell is that supposed to mean?" I placed the now empty wineglass back on the table in hopes our waiter would be back and leave the bottle this time. I could feel Eric's eyes piercing into me.

"Exactly what I said. You're not my problem anymore. I don't have to worry about you. I don't have to spend my life living in the fucking past." He shrugged with a smirk on his face. He had a way of making me feel inept with just his body language.

"There he is. There's the jackass I married." I rolled my eyes and shook my head. Pulling my phone out of my purse, I searched for a driver, but just as I was looking at the screen, I glanced up and saw Macy Callahan. She was smiling at me, donning a bright red dress that hugged her impeccable body. Waving ever so slightly with her fingers, I could feel my mouth part in shock and anger.

"Wow, really? You invited her here? What is this, Eric? Some sick game?" I hissed at him, grabbing my purse.

"What are you talking about, Serena?" His eyebrows creased as he looked over his shoulders. Turning back toward me, he opened his hands in utter confusion. I looked through the sea of faces, but she was gone. They were two merciless assholes.

"Goodbye, Eric Hudson. Please stay the hell away from me and my child." I took a deep breath, as if I were inhaling the man I was once addicted to and released it, hoping the air exhaling from my lungs would forever rid me of him.

"Try not to pick up fast-food on the way home, that dress is bursting at the seams," he added with a snicker. Pausing in my tracks, I could feel eyes on me as I stared off, counting my breaths. Nope. Wasn't working.

I turned, walked up to him, and allowed my clenched fist to meet his jaw, the cracking sound echoed, bringing me joy.

There. Much better. Be the bigger person, my ass.

"What the hell, Serena!" His hand jolted to his reddened face. I couldn't help but smile at the way his face looked in disbelief. He had caught me off guard so many times and enjoyed savoring in my pain. Everything was about to change. I wasn't going to let him have all the fun anymore. Things for him were about to fall, crash, and burn. *He would pay.*

CHAPTER SIXTEEN

I stared at my phone, holding the screen to my chest, it had been hours of searching everything I possibly could about the Callahans. The internet didn't provide enough. It was time to take matters into my own hands and find the answers the police were clearly incapable of finding. I needed answers, and I needed to do whatever it would take to protect myself, protect my family, and most of all, protect my Lola.

I climbed out of bed and looked at myself in the mirror. I began covering my face with makeup, lining my lips with the creamy tube, and smacking them together. *Pucker the fuck up, buttercup.* I pulled a black hoodie over my head and pulled my leggings on. Tying my dark, loose waves into a tight ponytail, I pulled a pair of sunglasses over my eyes. I gripped the banister tightly and tiptoed down the stairs.

"Serena?" My heart was thumping rapidly against my chest.

"Hey, Dad…" I turned and smiled at him, pushing my sunglasses to the top of my head.

"Where you off to this early?" He was drying his hair with a towel after coming in from his daily morning swim. My parents had the pool cleaned endless times after the accident before refilling it.

"Oh, I'm just going to run out and grab a few things from storage. I'll be back soon…" I felt my nails gripping deeper into the banister.

"Okay, honey… I could have sent someone to do that for you." He walked away and instantly, I released the breath that I had been holding. Suddenly, I felt sixteen again.

My hands shook so hard that I dropped my keys to the concrete before I even reached my car. I reached down and clutched them in my palm. Looking into the cool steel, I caught a glimpse of bright red lips. My breathing ceased as I looked again, peering behind me, but no one was there. I had to find answers. Now. I couldn't afford to lose my mind and be the pawn in a vile game that was being played with me. I had a lucrative career and a daughter to thrive for. I didn't have time for this nonsense.

Pulling up to my old street, I punched in the code and drove through the high gates that once made me feel safe. Yet here I was, trying to find the demons behind them.

I parked at the end of the street, tugged the strings of my hoodie once again, slid long leather gloves over my hands, and walked over to the Callahans' house. It was early, but Macy was probably off with Eric since he had asked me to watch Lola while he was jetting off on yet another vacation. I wasn't a fool; I knew they were definitely still together. James would be at work by now, and I knew for a fact that Brooks had school.

I looked around and climbed over the fence that traced their backyard. My leggings caught on a loose piece of wood, ripping through the material and cut my skin. Frayed wood poking out. I watched the blood trickle down and soak into the fibers. The pain from the wound radiated through me as I clenched my mouth shut. Pushing myself hard, I pivoted over the fence, flinging onto the grass coated in wet dew below me.

My feet pulled me quickly to the back patio. Bending over, I pulled the doormat up and looked under it. *Empty.* I looked around and saw the giant flower planter sitting by the door, and moving it over, I saw a gold key looking straight back at me. The Callahans had a teenager who probably forgot his house key more than once. I also knew with certainty that Brooks was the last to leave the house, meaning he most definitely didn't set the alarm. It was the perfect chance to sneak in. Turning the key, I held my breath, praying I'd be right. *Silence.* Carefully, I opened the door and could feel Macy Callahan's scent invade my nasal passages. Her perfume was intertwined in their air. Waiting for a moment, I felt my hands shake against the door.

For once, things weren't going against me. Sliding inside, I looked around. The Callahan house was a stark contrast to ours. They had all black and white décor, it was minimalistic, and the only thing that stood out was the bright red painting above the fireplace. I shuddered. I couldn't imagine how Brooks lived here. It wasn't a home, it looked like the Devil's lair. *It was.*

I grazed my hand against the smooth leather couch and trekked toward the unambiguous white stairs. The soles of my shoes treading and tapping against each stark white step. I carefully opened a closed door, which revealed Carolina Panthers memorabilia and an unmade navy-blue bed. There were sports jerseys and sweatpants strewn across the carpet. I shut the door and made my way to another door, which was definitely James and Macy's bedroom. Just like the rest of the house, it was bare.

The walls were painted black, the gold lamps mounted above the nightstands were both left on, while the bright white bedding stood out. At the end of the bed there was a lacy robe. I picked it up and let the silk touch my face. Inhaling it, I pulled my hoodie off and slid into the sweet-smelling, sexy robe. I sat on the plush little stool that was perched in front of the vanity as I peered down at the endless rows of lipstick... all the same shade of vivid red. Reaching in and rolling the tube up revealed the clearly well-used lipstick.

Just before pursing my lips, I wiped the pink off and carefully lined them in the bright cherry shade. Smacking them together, I smiled. The lipstick that had been used to lay kisses all over my husband, the lipstick that was used on the mouth of the woman who whispered sweet nothings in the ear of my child's father. The lipstick that belonged to the woman who ruined us. *Ruined me.*

"Hello, darling..." I tossed my head back and laughed. *Dumb bitch.*

Placing everything back as it was, I got up and shut

the door to their bedroom. Picking up my pace, arriving at the end of the hallway, I opened the last door. Finally. The deep brown mahogany desk and bookshelves that lined the walls were a complete contrast to the rest of the house. There were degrees neatly lined behind the oversized desk. The scent of whiskey and expensive cigars seemed to collide with the cold air.

I knew I needed to hurry. The longer I took, the more likely stay-at-home-moms pushing strollers and older couples walking dogs would be outside. Pulling open the drawer, I looked down, carefully rustling through papers. Nothing out of the ordinary. I didn't even know what I was looking for. I sat in the leather chair, gripped the handles, and spun around as I stared at the diplomas. James Callahan was obviously intelligent, he had multiple degrees proudly hanging on his wall. There was a small box sitting under a stack of legal textbooks. Reaching down, I pulled it out and scooted the chair closer. *There you are.* The worn cognac leather notebook I had always seen James carry with him. Leaning back into the chair, I opened the notebook and found light cursive writing, I squinted at the curly lettering and began to read.

James Callahan

I woke up and turned over, staring at the most radiant woman I had laid eyes on. Naomi Callahan, my high school sweetheart and wife. I watched as her chest rose and fell with soft breaths. Her eyelids were tinged with red, the small purple veins protruding. Reaching over, I gently kissed her cheek even though she turned away. Her nightstand was covered in pill bottles. It was the only way she was able to sleep after what we had just endured. I pulled the covers off and tiptoed down the hall to the kitchen. The counters were decorated in floral arrangements and small plush toys. Food trays were covered with aluminum foil. Turning my head to the living room, I saw a small toy train strewed across the rug. Colorful blocks sat lonely in the corner and a sippy cup rested on the end table.

Closing my eyes, I inhaled the air around me. It was dark and filled with lingering cries. I immediately went to make coffee in hopes the heat of the liquid would invigorate the coldness that encased my heart. Naomi appeared donning her pink robe—the one she hadn't change from since the funeral. It had a small stain on it that I recognized immediately. Grape juice. *His favorite.* She locked eyes with me. Her long hair was stringy and unwashed, and the dark circles under her eyes aged her well beyond her years. The small home we bought as soon as we found out she was pregnant with our first child was now a constant reminder of heartache. She turned and looked outside. The pool was drained completely and covered. She shuddered and walked toward me, and I placed two coffee mugs on the counter and pushed away the flowers.

I opened my arms, welcoming her into them, yet she walked past me. I was nothing more than the grim reaper. She still blamed me for what had happened. The doctor told her it was no one's fault, that things like this happen. She didn't care. I was the one who was supposed to be watching him. I blamed myself, too.

A quick shower later, I kissed Naomi's cheek while she cringed in disgust. She was sitting in the chair staring at the vacant pool. Her beautiful eyes that were usually filled with love and happiness were now filled with anger and resentment. Her delicate hands gripped the hot coffee mug and I could see her palms were red. I knew she wanted to feel pain. She said she wanted to feel something. That's what she said when I found her laying on our bathroom floor the morning after the funeral with the razor blade trailing blood across her thigh. She couldn't feel anything, she was completely blank. After Mason died, she swore she'd never be able to feel again.

I drove to my office, a small law firm that I had just leased in hopes to start my own practice. I had worked for a big-time law firm in town for a while and wanted my own. I would build it into something huge and pass it down to my son; I dreamt of this countless times. The small sign "Callahan and Son Law Firm" taunted me. I knew it was ridiculous to add "son" to the name, but Mason was my pride. He was the light to the darkness. Naomi and I tried for years to get pregnant. We married after high school, and it took an eternity to have Mason.

We were celebrating his third birthday. A pool party during the hot Charlotte summertime was the obvious choice. We had all our friends over, and Naomi went inside to get the cake. Kids flooded the pool with laughter as water splashed out. Country music was lingering in the air and the scent of burning coal from the grill mingled in the sweet summer breeze. I saw Mason playing in the small sandbox near the pool but didn't think twice, needing to flip the burgers quickly on the grill since Naomi would be back in a minute. There were so many adults sitting nearby, surely everyone had their eyes on all the kids.

I stood at the grill, inhaling the smoky aroma. My

best friend, Chris, slapped me on the shoulder and handed me an ice-cold beer. I got carried away in our own conversation, and then life took a turn. I heard the shriek that would forever haunt my dreams and days for the rest of my life.

I turned toward her and saw the cake she was carrying smashed onto the ground. The horror painted on her face as she sprinted to the pool. I dropped the spatula and trailed my eyes after her. My response was delayed. I was still processing the ringing in my ears from the screaming that continued from my wife's mouth. Suddenly there was so much noise—running, screaming, hysterical shouting.

"James!" Naomi screamed, and finally my feet were able to move. I sprinted toward her as I saw my wife pulling the limp body of my beautiful son out the cold pool water. His golden blonde hair was matted to his small head and his eyes were shut. I yelled at Chris to call an ambulance. The terror and panic I felt surging through my veins in that moment was one I didn't think my heart would ever be able to survive.

What felt like eternity but was only hours proved to be the cruelest time of our life. The doctors did everything they could, but he was gone before he got to the hospital. I knew it as I clung onto his usually warm pink hand that was now cold and pale. Naomi's tears soaked through my linen shirt as my eyes burned.

We went from planning a birthday party to a funeral in the matter of two days. Life played a cruel, hideous game with us.

Naomi and I became strangers in our own marriage. The day the moving truck came, I was thankful we were both going together since I was certain for the past months on end, I'd wake up one morning and not see her beside me. She was heavily medicated and no longer the vivacious woman I had fallen in love with. I didn't think she was capable of smiling ever again. Work consumed me and I welcomed it. Going home felt like going to prison. I missed Mason every day of my life, but I also wanted to live. Naomi didn't want a life without him, so each day, we died together.

Months later, she finally let me touch her again. Therapy was beginning to help, and I could finally see the light at the end of the tunnel. We left the house that haunted us behind and moved to the other side of town. We bought a townhome and eventually, wanted to custom build a property on our own land. We weren't just surviving anymore, we were thriving. My law firm was taking off and money started to trickle in faster than we ever thought. We began going out together again. I'd catch her smiling or softly laughing at the television. We joined a support group for parents who lost their children. Life was beginning to go upward. I no longer felt as if we were rowing a boat against a current, we were cruising along together.

I was sitting at the small dining table reading the Charlotte newspaper while sipping a hot cup of coffee. It had been a year since we lost Mason. I peered over the paper every day, envisioning him sitting across from me, spooning large bits of cereal into his mouth. Milk dribbling down his chin and laughter erupting every time I reached to wipe it away. I closed my eyes, the sunlight danced across the room as its warmth seeped into my body.

I heard Naomi's footsteps run down the stairs. Turning toward her, I saw her face lit up with excitement. My eyebrows creased and I felt my lips curve into a curious smile. She looked light and happy. Her hair was brushed neatly into a low ponytail while her sundress hugged her perfectly. One hand was tucked behind her back and the other reached toward my eyes. She covered them gently. Her body was so close to me I could smell the soft scent of jasmine from her favorite perfume. It was the first time in a year I smelled it on her.

Pulling the hidden arm from behind her back, she

waved a small white stick at me, not saying a word. I could see tears building in her eyes as I quickly dropped my newspaper. Reaching for it, I turned it over and saw the two dark pink lines… lines I had seen once before. My eyes shot up and connected with hers. Resentment and fear were no longer embedded in the deep blue; instead, excitement and hope had taken its residence.

I threw my arms around her, pulling her small frame into my chest, kissing her soft face all over. I remember her hands grazing the stubble on my cheeks. I remember tears streaming from her eyes that weren't ones of grief, but ones of gratitude and hope. The universe wanted us to be happy, finally.

I admired Naomi as her belly grew rounder by the day. We painted a room in our small townhouse bright yellow. I spent hours building a crib, changing table, and all the things Naomi excitedly had waiting on me. Sitting in the rocking chair, she'd happily watch me build each item. I'd look up and see her eyes lovingly on her belly, rubbing it gently while singing to our baby. Our miracle. This baby had given her the hope and strength she needed. This baby put the beat back in her heart and oxygen back in her lungs. *This baby saved her. Saved us.*

We took one last beach trip as just the two of us

before we became a family of three, *again.* It felt bitter-sweet whenever someone congratulated us on adding our first child.

Driving home from the beach, I remember looking over at Naomi. She was staring at me. She told me she didn't blame me for what happened to Mason, and she was ready for us to start fresh and be a family again. I remember gripping her hand, raising it to my lips, and kissing it.

One month later, it was two a.m. and the light of our bedroom woke me abruptly. Naomi was standing up, looking at the carpet beneath her feet. It was time. Her water had broken. I leapt out of bed and grabbed our bags. Holding hands, we both walked into the bright yellow nursery. I leaned over, kissing the top of her head and we prayed. We were going to be home in two days carrying our baby into the room, beginning the rest of our lives. Our second chance.

The contractions were intense, and Naomi was groaning in pain. I sped through to the hospital. There was a nurse waiting for us with a wheelchair, and I helped her into it, grabbing the bags quickly. Naomi held my hand tightly and squeezed it with each rippling contraction. Once in the room, the doctor came in; she was one we both liked from the practice. *Dr. Nix.* She came in and checked Naomi, reassuring her, soothing her. Naomi wanted to have an unmedicated, natural birth. I knew deep down inside after she hadn't felt anything for so long, she was on a high of feeling any emotion she could, whether pain or happiness. I fed her ice chips and we laughed excitedly. Finally, Dr. Nix came back and checked the screen. The baby's heart rate was dropping. Her face was expressionless, and she looked at us with no concern. Surely if she was worried, she'd tell us. It was time for Naomi to push. The room filled with nurses, techs, medical students, and a resident physician.

We had a whole team surrounding us to bring our baby into the world, and I felt confident. Moments later, Naomi screamed as she pushed, breathing through the pain. Her teeth were clenched, and her hair was matted to her sweat-drenched forehead. I remember there was so much noise suddenly. There were people running. I remember Dr. Nix's face filled with concern while a dark-haired young woman wearing scrubs stood by her holding our baby in her hands. I remember them whispering to each other and looking at Naomi. Naomi's head flung back onto the pillow as she sobbed hysterically.

I was holding my wife's hand so hard, I swore I could hear cracking, as my gaze drifted between the small bundle still connected to my wife. There was so much noise. Until there wasn't. The younger, dark-haired doctor handed the wrapped bundle over to my wife. She was trembling and softly crying. I was terrified her tears would drown our baby. Amongst all the noise, one sound I didn't hear was the baby crying.

I looked over at the bundle and saw Naomi's head planted on the pillow with her hands gripping the soft pink blanket. There was a small head tipping out with a tiny pink hat. *A girl.* We had a baby girl. Georgia May Callahan. That was the name we picked if we had a daughter. She was here. Our sweet Georgia, named after Naomi's mother. May was the birth month of Mason. We wanted her big brother to live on through her. Oh, the irony. The sweet irony.

A cold hand gripped my shoulder, and I met the face of Dr. Nix. She offered her deepest condolences. She moved her hands and spoke about the cord being wrapped around the baby's neck. There wasn't anything she could have done. The second, younger resident physician stood in the shadows of Dr. Nix, and looked at me and offered a small nod. Her hands were behind her back as if she were guilty of a crime. Weren't they all? They had all failed my daughter. They had all failed my wife. They had all stolen our second chance at life.

Another child's day of birth marked the planning

of another funeral. This had to be some kind of punishing joke from the universe. We gathered around the tiniest casket I had ever seen. The light wood was gently engraved with a cross and a small pink teddy bear was perched on top. Naomi was draped in her mother's arms wearing the same black dress she buried our first child in. The preacher spoke of redemption and sacrifice. We were being rivaled to God. Apparently, our children were equivalent to Jesus. Fucking bullshit. People trickled in and out, the look in their eyes filled with fear as they held their own young children. It was as if they were scared that losing your child was contagious.

Weeks had gone by, and the door of the nursery stayed closed. I went back to work while Naomi stayed in bed. The food drop-offs and flower arrangements became less and less. We rarely heard from our closest friends. After all, most of them had children of their own, so they didn't know how or who to be around us. We were cursed, a blanket of death wrapped around us. Once the dust settled from the loss of Georgia, life went on for everyone else.

Not for us though. I became engrossed into malpractice lawsuits against the doctors and hospital with no luck. I knew if the doctors had been competent, they could have saved her. They could have saved us. But instead, they watched her die and would now watch us collapse into ashes.

I drove home after a long day of work. The fast-food bag was crumbled next to me. Naomi survived off plain toast and an occasional bottle of water. I picked up food for us every day, stacking it high inside the fridge in case the day came where she wanted to eat. We had gone through this once before with Mason and survived. I knew eventually, we'd survive this, too. I had already began looking into land to build our dream house on. I wanted to surprise Naomi, hoping it would be a welcome distraction. It would be just her and I. We'd have to be enough for one another.

Unlocking the door to our home, I walked into darkness. The sun had already set thanks to the winter months proving to be a fitting backdrop to our current state, gloomy and dark. I tossed my keys into the glass bowl that sat perched on the foyer console table and loosened my tie. Calling out for Naomi, there wasn't a reply. She usually stayed in bed or stayed planted on the sofa, curled up under a blanket staring off into what seemed to be a place she was drowning in. I tried every single day to pull her out but couldn't. She wouldn't let me. Time would heal her just as it did with Mason's loss. *Time.* That was all we needed.

I walked upstairs and saw a stream of light trickling from the nursery. Holding my breath, I paced toward it. We hadn't opened it since Georgia's death. I called out to Naomi again and gently pushed the door open. She was sunk into the rocking chair with her eyes closed, her arms draped on both sides of the chair. The light from the lamppost just outside the nursery window outlined her. She looked so peaceful. I flipped the small light on and looked back at my wife. Chills raced along my spine as my eyes widened and glued to the deep red that painted both sides of the rocking chair and seeped into the soft beige carpet below. Wanting to scream but couldn't, my brain and body weren't aligned as I dropped in front of her exposed legs. She was wearing the pink robe that I hadn't seen in so long. The grape juice stain was still embedded in it, with the addition of deep red plaguing the ends of the sleeves. I grabbed her cold, lifeless face in my hands and gasped for air through my sobs.

The ambulance came later. It took me eternity to find the ability to walk away from her and make the call. Call for what? Help? Help with what? Removing my dead wife from our home?

Another funeral to plan. This time no one came,

just Naomi's family. Three funerals in one home this close together was a record. When most people celebrated holidays and birthdays, we were the family who constantly celebrated death. I left the gravesite after seeing the fresh dirt piled neatly over my wife's casket. She was planted in the middle of our children. I saw the look in Naomi's mothers' eyes. She stared at me as if to ask, why weren't I in the ground with my family, too? What kind of man was I to be roaming the earth, breathing the air around me, when my wife and children were sunken into the insect-ridden ground. *What she didn't know was I didn't need to be dead to go to hell, I was already living in it.*

I drowned myself in bottles of liquor, I slept with women I didn't care to know the names of. It was a vicious cycle. I obsessed over those involved in the death of Georgia. If they hadn't failed her, my wife would still be here. My daughter still would be here. The doctor had four children, and a house near the hospital with a fucking white picket fence. I drove by her house often. She and her husband would be sitting outside on their porch as their children laughed and played with a red ball. I followed her to the hospital, I watched her shop for groceries. I dreamt of my hands wrapped around her throat.

One day, I had left my office late. I decided to see

what Dr. Magnolia Nix was up to. I flipped through a newspaper as I watched her walk to her car from work. She was wearing a long white coat over her scrubs. I had watched her leave at all hours of the day and night. She parked her car on the opposite side of a wide street. Their driveway was narrow and displayed her husband's truck. I pulled over and watched her outline climb out of her car as the lamppost high-lighted her body. She bent back into her car, reaching in for her bag.

I turned my car back on, the headlights blasting and watched as she closed her door. She had just turned to walk toward her home when I saw Naomi standing beside her. I blinked harder. I saw my wife's pale, lifeless body standing in the middle of the road with blood draining from her wrists onto the road. My foot collided with the pedal and the tires screeched. I saw the doctor's eyes widen in shock as the front of my car beat into her body. My tires drove over and what sounded like crunching rang into my ears. I looked back into the rearview mirror and could see a pile laying on the darkened road, and then I caught the look in my eyes. They were filled with deep satisfaction.

One down. One to go. There was one more qualified doctor in the room that day. Her long black hair and deep blue eyes burned into my memory. I would find her. Sure, she was only a resident physician, but she was qualified and hadn't she also sworn in her oath to "do no harm?"

Thankfully, I had taken an oath of my own.

Do harm.

CHAPTER SEVENTEEN

*T*here I was, sitting in my car trembling. There was no way James was talking about me. What was happening? I didn't know what to believe anymore. Who would I tell? No one would believe me without evidence. I couldn't just flaunt around that I had broken into my neighbor's house. My head was spinning, and I couldn't take it anymore. Why did this story sound so familiar, as if I had lived it on a personal level? *Why did it sound so damn familiar?*

I sped back to my parents' house and raced up the stairs. Opening the wooden box, I closed my eyes and pushed my shirt up while tugging at my pants. Sitting down, I dug the metal into my hip, cutting along a healed wound. The blood dribbled out rapidly and I sunk backward, lying flat on the floor. Cutting myself had covered me in a way that brought me to a safe haven no matter where I was. Cutting myself proved that maybe, just maybe, I could feel something, even if it was pain. Counting my breaths, I prayed that if there was a God, he would save me from whatever madness was spiraling in my life, and most of all, save my Lola.

"Serena..." I opened my eyes, which were sticky and dry. Rubbing my head, I turned and looked at Parker.

"Serena, what the hell happened? There's blood... Seri... there's blood everywhere!" His voice was laced with panic and urgency. I tried to sit up, but my body felt weak. Pulling me up into his chest, I sunk inward and exhaled.

"Seri, talk to me please. What is this?" He lifted the knife that was covered in blood, *my blood.*

I felt lightheaded and didn't know how to explain to Parker that the perfect, unflawed woman he thought he knew was nothing more than a façade of a damaged, scarred human being.

"Parker, I need water..." My voice sounded raspy and hoarse.

"Stay here, don't move." He jolted up, and I could hear his footsteps race down the stairs.

Moments later, he appeared with a bottle of water, his forehead creased and his dark eyebrows lowered as he studied me carefully. I was laying on the carpet, turning my head slowly, eyeing the stained carpet. Parker held a washcloth on my wound.

"My mom is going to be pissed that I wrecked her new carpet... She spent a fortune on it." I laughed softly. Parker lifted my head into his lap, I watched as he unscrewed the lid off and dribbled water into my parted lips.

"Seri, talk to me please." He pushed the loose waves from my face and leaned down. I could feel the warmth of his breath, letting my eyes close because I couldn't face him. I was a coward.

"It was just once, Parker. I was overwhelmed. I didn't mean to..." Humiliation seeped into the opened, exposed wounds.

"Serena, please let me just help you."

"Oh, Parker, don't you see? You can't save me. After all, you can't piece together a broken mirror and expect to see the same reflection." I turned away from him and everything blurred.

Days had come and gone. I didn't even know where, it felt like pockets of time were blank holes. I was drowning myself in work and Lola. I didn't know what to do about James Callahan, but I didn't think there was anything I could do, besides hope I'd have time to figure something out. I also never saw Eric. I blamed him for the demise of my life and for destroying everything I had worked so hard for, but now I hated him even more. He had essentially fueled a fire inside a monster who was already after me. I wondered how you go years of your life sleeping next to someone, sharing your most intimate and vulnerable moments with them, investing years of your life you'll never get back with that person to suddenly have them out of it forever?

It was heart-wrenching. I dropped Lola off to his apartment that he shared with Macy and would just wait long enough to see the apartment door crack open before reversing out of the place that had destroyed us. I had recently rented a cozy house near my office, which was perfect for Lola and me. I didn't want to commit to buying anything just yet. I wasn't sure Charlotte was still home for us. Maybe the best thing I could do was escape this hell, leave everything and everyone, besides Lola.

I couldn't just leave, though. I had a private practice here, and most of all, Parker. I couldn't let him go.

Pulling a loose button down over a pair of denim shorts with my large straw hat on, I threw on my gardening gloves. I sat in the lush green grass, the smell of pollen and dew brushed my nose as I began to carefully dig the softened dirt.

"Serena, those are simply beautiful!" My new

neighbor, Bianca came over. I titled my head up at her as she admired the four new flowerpots waiting to be planted.

"Hey, Bianca! Thank you. I thought the color was just stunning... It's almost a purply blue... *indigo*." I smiled at her.

"Oh, that's so perfect, Serena Indigo!" She laughed.

"I think my Lola will love them." I dug ferociously and reached to place one of the flowers into the cold ground and looked back at her.

"Oh... okay. Well then, see you around." Bianca clutched the brown grocery bag closer to her chest and offered a small wave.

"Bye now." I rubbed the sweat off my forehead with my elbow and continued to plant the flowers into the earth.

I spent hours fixing my yard, finally taking a break to sit on my front patio and drink a tall glass of sweet tea.

Being in my new home felt rejuvenating. I was finally at the place in my life where I knew I could have everything I deserved, everything I had earned. I wasn't going to let Eric or Macy or anyone else haunt me any longer. There were even moments I was able to let go of everything I had read in James Callahan's notebook. There was no way I was connected to his life. Maybe Eric was right, maybe I was too paranoid for my own good.

The next morning, I pulled on my surgical scrubs and headed to the hospital. I got through a C-section and was finishing up some notes when my eyes caught his.

"Eric? Oh my god, is Lola okay?" I quickly walked toward him.

"Yea, yea sorry, I didn't mean to scare you. Sorry, I was just here for work and thought I'd see if you had a minute to talk."

"Um... okay. Sure." I looked up at the clock plastered on the wall. I had just enough time to grab some food in the cafeteria before heading over to the office to see my scheduled patients.

Eric and I sat at one of the hospital cafeteria tables with sandwiches between us. Looking at him, his soft green eyes and blonde hair looked just as they did when we were in college and medical school. I remember laughing with him over our meals, holding hands and gazing into one another's eyes, as if there was no one else in the world besides us. Suddenly the hate that had grown in my heart melted away.

"What happened to us, Eric? Weren't we happy once?"

"Serena, you left me."

"You cheated on me! You had an entire secret life..." I waved my hands around in shock. He couldn't be serious.

"You neglected us; you weren't the same woman I'd fallen in love with. You know you changed... after everything." He shrugged.

"You're such an asshole." I began to stand, vowing I'd never let tears fall for him again.

"Serena, wait. I wanted to tell you before you found out from someone else." Eric tore off a piece of bread and placed it in his mouth. I watched as he chewed slowly, while I sunk back into the hard chair, peeling the polish away off my thumbnail.

"Macy and I are getting married," he exhaled, leaning back into the small cafeteria chair while studying my face.

I blinked as the air around me feel overpowering. My eyes felt moist, but I wouldn't give him that satisfaction. I stood abruptly, turning away from him.

"Serena... she reminds me so much of you. She reminds me so much of you before... *everything changed.*"

I turned back to face him and looked at the man I trusted with everything; the man I'd been with since I was eighteen years old.

"Fuck you, Eric Hudson. I never want to see you again."

I raced to my car, opened it, fell into the driver seat, and cried. The pain I felt inside was as if daggers were embedded in my soul. Sobs were choking me, but I had to let it all out.

He didn't deserve a happily ever after. *He wrecked me. He wrecked us.*

CHAPTER EIGHTEEN

"*H*ey gorgeous!" he called out from the foyer.

Walking toward the front door, Parker had a bouquet of flowers and a bottle of wine.

"Hey, Sully…" I leaned in and kissed him slowly. I could feel a smile emerge beneath our intertwined lips. He placed the wine and flowers on the small foyer table, wrapping his hands around my waist, and swiftly pulling me closer.

I began to walk backward from him toward my bedroom. His eyebrow lifted as he followed me. I pulled my shirt off as Parker watched me. I didn't have anything to hide anymore. The scars embedded under my arms, the ones that dug into my hips…he'd seen them all. Most of all, he made me know even without words, that he didn't just see my scars...*he saw me.*

He came closer, placing his hands on both sides of my face, kissing me the way you'd hope to be kissed in a lifetime. Tilting my head to the side, he caressed the crevice of my neck and squatted lower while pulling my pants down with him. I watched him as my chest heaved and chills formed across my skin. He used his finger to trace the small stretch marks that were embedded in my hips, looking back up at me and I saw sympathy in his eyes. He kissed the marks carefully as I ran my hand through his soft brown hair. He knew about my self-inflicted pain and wounds.

He knew everything about me.

The vibration of my phone against the wood of my nightstand woke me from my dreams. I looked over and saw Parker sleeping soundly. My reality was better than my dreams now; finally, the nightmares had ceased. I turned and lifted my phone up.

I hate how we left things, Serena. Can we meet and just find a way to be civil? I know I hurt you, but I love her. You changed so much. I needed someone to lean on.

I cringed at the word 'love' in regards to another woman. He was my husband, the father of my child. He didn't see how he poured salt into my open wounds. He still blamed me as the reason he was forced to cheat on me. He didn't care about the fact that I had stretched myself so thin between being a wife, mother, daughter, and doctor. Of course, I had changed... *I had to.* I had to evolve to balance life. What did he expect, a wife in lingerie every night? I resented him for the way he saw things. He cheated on me. He had a separate life. He gave up on us without even giving us a chance to fix things. The double standard was repulsive.

Maybe he was right though. Maybe for the sake of Lola, I had to find a way to tolerate Eric. I looked over at Parker again. Perhaps this was what our lives were meant to be. I was finally with the man I was supposed to be with, and I was happier than ever.

Come over this evening. I'll make a blueberry pie if you bring the wine.

My favorite. I'll swing by around five. Thanks, Serena.

I saw the three dots indicating he was still typing, but they quickly faded. I clicked my phone off, clutching it against my chest.

"Vengeance is best served with a slice of blueberry pie." My mother's voice rang in my head.

Busying myself in the kitchen and prepping everything for the pie, I felt good, finally good. Indigo blueberry pie from scratch—my grandmother's famous recipe—was the first thing I had ever made for Eric, and he loved it. The color of bright blueberries tinged my hands as I looked outside my window. My flowers were blooming and it made me smile. The purple and blue hues of my new plants stood out against the green grass.

Parker headed out after we spent the day together. Although he didn't think seeing Eric was a good idea, he also knew I needed to find some closure with him. I couldn't stand how every night when I closed my eyes, I saw him wrapped around Macy. *His perfect woman.* I couldn't stand how my mind raced with his indirect jabs of how I failed us. He was always a narcissist and took advantage of me in so many ways.

The way I still stepped on the glass scale and pinched my loose skin from pregnancies… *pregnancy.* I could hear his cruel comments about my weight and everything in between. I needed to heal once and for all. That meant letting go of Eric *forever.* I knew I tended to obsess over things until I took care of them, and this was the only way. The only way to free Serena Indigo.

The doorbell rang, and I quickly glanced in the mirror, brushing my dress carefully, trying to smooth out the creases. My long hair cascaded over my shoulders, and my lips were painted in a deep shade of pink.

My dress flowed over my thin figure, and I brushed my earlobes... nothing. I couldn't believe Macy still had one of my earrings. Eric swore over and over that she didn't. He even said he looked through her things, but I didn't believe him.

I'd never believe him.

"Hey, come on in." I smiled, opening the door. He was wearing a green Oxford button-down that brought out his eyes, his blonde hair was cut shorter and brushed neatly.

"Wow, you look great. Nice place, Serena." Eric lifted the wine bottle in the air and took a deep breath in. "Blueberry pie... God, I forgot how much I love it."

He took a deep breath in, smelling the comforting scent, and walked past me into the kitchen. I watched him sit on the island stool and cut into the pie that was neatly on the counter next to some cut flowers from my garden.

"How are you, Eric?" I stood on the opposite side of the island.

"I'm doing good. How are you?" he asked with formality that made the pit in my stomach rise.

"I'm fine."

He was shoveling huge bites of pie into his mouth. "God, this is good. Macy doesn't cook. She doesn't even know how to turn the stove on." He laughed.

"So, when are you getting married?" I rubbed my hand against the cold countertop, feeling a few straggling crumbs while avoiding eye contact with him.

He placed his fork down. "We already did."

"What? When? You just said..." I could feel my heart race as I stared at him.

"Yea, well, I didn't want to upset you, but we already got married. Lola was our flower girl. She looked so cute." He smiled with no care.

"What the hell, Eric? Did you not care to even ask me if my daughter could be a part of all this?" I shouted, knowing my tears weren't far behind.

"Macy's pregnant." He leaned back in his chair and shrugged with a mouthful of pie.

I couldn't breathe. He had no care for my feelings. He didn't care that he destroyed my life and was creating an entire new one with his mistress and our child. He was crafting the life we were supposed to have together with someone else. Someone who was clearly perfect, unlike me.

I walked around the island, moving closer to Eric. The lines between his eyes grew deep as he looked at me curiously. He planted his hands around my waist, pulling me in between his legs.

"You look good, Serena... really good." His eyes trailed hungrily over my body as he tugged me down into his lap. I leaned in closer, wiping the blueberry filling that lingered next to his lips with my thumb, and shoved it into his mouth. His tongue circled my finger as he smiled. His cold hand trailed up my dress as I kept my eyes on his.

I grabbed his hand, clutching it tightly. My nails dug into his flesh, and I felt nothing but rage.

"Get the fuck out of my house and life, Eric," I whispered close to his face through my clenched teeth while my lips forced a small smile.

"You were never a good fuck anyway... And look how easily Macy got pregnant... Guess I did marry damaged goods." He laughed and pushed me off his lap.

I clenched my fist as my body trembled with hate. The front door slammed behind him. Tears poured from my eyes as I gripped the kitchen island, shaking my head. I grabbed the pie and threw it into the trash, tightly tying the bag and went outside. Dumping the bag into the empty bin, I slammed it closed.

"Hey there, neighbor!" I turned and saw a woman standing there with a smile on her face.

"I'm sorry, do I know you?" I was breathing hard as I stared at her.

The woman laughed loudly. "You're funny!"

My body felt cold, yet I was sweating, I ran back

inside and shut the door behind me, locking it. I sunk down against the floor, wrapping my arms around my chest. Rocking back and forth, I counted my breaths, not knowing what number I had started at and which I had left off from.

"Seri?" My head was pounding as I opened my eyes. I looked up and saw Parker crouched beside me. I was sprawled out on the kitchen floor with an empty wine bottle beside me. I rubbed my head and slowly sat up. My eyes felt sticky with dried tears and makeup crusting along my lashes. My mouth felt like sandpaper as I looked down filled with shame at the straggling wine bottle that taunted me.

"Baby... are you okay?" Parker sat beside me and pulled me between his legs, rubbing my shoulders.

"Yea, I think I may have had a little too much to drink. Eric being the culprit of my one-night alcoholism." I laughed lightly and pressed my head against his chest and inhaled the scent of sandalwood, feeling safe.

"Serena, I have to tell you something. Can we go to the sofa?" He sounded the way he spoke to patients, I felt my heart sink. I was terrified that it wouldn't be able to handle any more.

"Sully, you're scaring me." I squinted at him as he helped me off the floor, guiding me into the living room. Parker held my hands tightly and looked at me carefully. I could see his chest rise and fall with shallow breaths.

"Eric died in the middle of the night. He had a massive heart attack."

"What? No... No... How?" I could feel my hands tremble against his. He pulled me closer, hugging me tightly, as if I'd disappear if he let go.

Emotions raced through my mind, but they didn't mix with how I felt. I didn't feel anything. What was wrong with me? The man I loved for almost twenty years and the father of my child was dead, but I couldn't even cry. Running my fingers over my eyes, there was nothing there. I took a deep breath and closed my eyes, picturing Eric's laughing face just hours ago in my kitchen. We had ended the night off so badly, and I felt somewhat guilty. Eric was dead.

"The funeral will be in two days; his parents are planning it." Parker didn't release his hold on me.

"You'd think his wife would have planned it..." I scoffed bitterly.

Parker loosened his grip around me and looked down. "Wife?"

"Yea, apparently he got married again. He told me last night." I said under a hushed voice. I was scared Parker would notice my lack of emotion.

"Oh my god… Lola," I said blankly, dreading the fact that I'd have to crush my daughter's life once again.

"I'm sure she'll be there for him, baby… along with…" Parker kissed the top of my head and hugged me.

"I don't want her there. It's too much. She needs to stay away from this mess," I whispered back.

Parker studied my face, creasing his forehead, deep in his own thoughts. He pulled me closer. "Okay, Seri…"

The next two days blurred together. I had my parents keep Lola at their house. I didn't want her to see her dead father laying lifeless in a wooden box. My ex-in-laws planned an open-casket funeral. It was so gruesome. Why did anyone have open-casket funerals? I barely wanted to see Eric when he was living, and now I had to see him dead. I stared at the black sheath dress that laid on my bed. I wore the dress to a fancy dinner one night on our honeymoon. I once wore it to celebrate the start of something, and now I was wearing it to celebrate the true end of the same something. It sounded horrible, I knew. But deep down inside, I felt free. I didn't have to ever see his face. The one that ridiculed me and made me feel irrelevant. The face that tormented my imperfections.

I didn't have to share Lola with the man that deceived me. *Deceived us.* Part of me wanted to believe karma had its hand in his death. He left me for a woman who probably tried to kill me. He always made me feel less than and worthless. I spent so much of my life trying to please him, but it never was enough. Now he wasn't enough. He was dead. In the end, in the game of life, I had finally won against Eric Hudson.

Parker held my hand as we cut through the wet grass. My nude heels dug into the wet earth.

"We probably shouldn't have cut through the grass. What if my heels stab through someone?" I widened my eyes at Parker.

"Damn, that's dark, Seri." Parker looked at me. He was wearing a sleek black suit and a white dress shirt with a silk tie. He looked like he was going to a wedding, not his girlfriend's ex-husband's funeral. I stared up at him as we walked. Maybe he was celebrating not having to ever hear about Eric again. They never liked one another from the beginning, and Parker always felt as if he lost out on being with me because of Eric.

We met with the group of people who were seated in neat rows. A large portrait in a bronze frame surrounded by flowers displayed Eric. It was a photo of him from our wedding. I was stunned his parents chose that picture of him. Looking over at the front row, I saw them seated. His mother was dabbing her eyes as his father stared off emptily. They were despicable human beings. His mom was a certified narcissist who went out of her way to make me feel unwelcome. His dad was a secret drunk who invested in friends and gambling instead of his own son. Eric had to work his ass off to get through school. He had so much debt from his student loans, even though his parents were extremely wealthy and could have easily taken the burden off their son.

They showered themselves in an oversized house, luxury cars, lavish vacations, and designer clothes, but made Eric drive a beat-up car, work at a crappy convenient store, and take out every ounce of loans he could in order to put himself through college and medical school. No wonder their son turned out the way he had. He had bad blood. Part of me felt sad, maybe he never had a chance to be truly good when he came from that. He once had a sweet side, but what he did and chose to do to me was despicable.

Parker guided me to a seat in the back and I looked through the sea of black dresses and suits, noticing Macy wasn't there. *How strange.* "Where's his wife?" I whispered as quietly as I could as the preacher spoke.

Parker looked at me in awe. "I really didn't even know he was in a serious relationship."

Parker must have been blocking out everything I ever told him about Eric. He was clueless. I didn't blame him though, I wouldn't want to hear the woman I loved complain about her ex as much as I had. Sliding my sunglasses over my eyes, I sunk back into the chair. His parents stood, walked over to the podium, and began to talk. I rolled my eyes as I heard them speak about the son they barely knew and hardly understood.

"Serena, would you please come up and say a few words? We know Eric would've wanted that—" His dad's voice boasted from the front. I looked over at Parker and his eyes widened back at me.

"Oh, fuck me," I huffed under my breath and stood. What the hell were they thinking?

I looked through the sympathetic faces of the attendants. So many of his coworkers, our friends from medical school and college days, family members, and then random people his parents must have known.

"Um, hi. I... well, I wasn't prepared to speak today so I apologize in advance." I smiled nervously as I clasped my hands together on the podium and began peeling away at the polish on my thumbnail. I quickly wiped the smile off my face, replacing it with a somber façade. *Funeral, my ex-husband's funeral. Right.*

"Eric and I met when we were only eighteen. As many of you know, we didn't have the best ending to our relationship, but we shared a lot of history. The best being our daughter, Lola…" I stopped and looked into the crowd. Suddenly, I felt as if I were missing something, *someone* from my speech. Eric's mom was dramatically wiping her eyes while other guests had their hands on their chest as if their hearts were physically breaking for me.

"I loved Eric, I really did. We had a turbulent marriage to say the least, but he tried. He tried to be good and to most, he was. Just like everyone else, we had good times and bad times. I think perhaps we both expected much more than either could give the other. I will miss you, Eric." I walked to his portrait, kissed my hand, and planted it against his smiling face. I turned and walked away, leaving Eric Hudson behind me *forever.*

I sat down beside Parker, who reached for my hand, stroking it gently.

Another voice echoed from the podium, and I looked up. It was a strikingly beautiful woman who had to be in her early twenties. Her eyes were red and swollen. Her stomach was round while her hand protectively guided across it.

"Thank you, Mr. and Mrs. Hudson, for allowing me to speak. My name is Tessa, and I was… Well, I was seeing Eric for some time. He was so excited about…" Her eyes looked directly at me and averted quickly from my stunned expression as she looked down to her stomach.

What the fuck is happening? Tessa. He really was seeing a woman named Tessa, too? Macy must have found out about Tessa and couldn't face coming here looking as stupid as she had once made me feel. *Oh Eric, what have you done?* I was thankful in that moment he wasn't my problem anymore. He'd never be my problem, again.

"Eric and I worked together, and he had been nothing but incredible to me. He was the most loyal, loving, and supportive man I had ever met. I loved him so much." Tessa began sobbing hysterically.

"Did she just say loyal and Eric in the same sentence?" I giggled into Parker's ear. His eyes widened at me and he shook his head, though I could tell he was suppressing his own smile.

We stood up to leave when the funeral was finally over. A delicate, cold hand tapped my shoulder, and I quickly turned to meet the devastated face of the young woman who had spent the good portion of the funeral weeping into a tissue.

"Serena, I'm so sorry about everything. I'm so sorry. I miss him so much. Like, he was genuinely the kindest man I had ever met. I didn't know he was married, I swear... I would love to get together, and maybe we can share memories of him together. I truly loved him. He was the love of my life." She began crying into her hands.

I pulled my sunglasses on top of my head. "Oh, honey, you are apologizing to the wrong wife now, though. You should say sorry to his new wife Macy." I laughed lightly and began to turn away.

"Macy?" she questioned through her sobs.

"Oh, you really are what Eric loves. He sure did have a type. *A beautiful, little fool.*" I smiled sympathetically and walked away as Parker clutched my hand.

arker Sully

I parked my car and looked up at the building in front of me; it was tinted with a yellow hue that showed its age. I looked down, staring at the Starbucks latte. Grabbing it in my hand, I walked inside.

"Dr. Sully!" a warm voice greeted me.

"Hey, Carla! How is she?" I looked at the older nurse who was rapidly typing on an old computer.

"She's better today. You know you can't take her that." Carla eyed the latte cup as if it were a weapon. Glancing down at it, I supposed in this environment, it very well could have been.

"Carla, just this once? Please? It's her favorite." I offered my most charming smile at her.

"Fine. You're just a handsome devil and know it. But don't you dare give it to her with the lid…" she warned me with a lifted eyebrow.

"You are the best, Carla." I winked at her and traveled through the daunting hallway. The air around me reeked of burnt, cheap coffee and cleaning supplies. It felt so sterile and suffocating.

The security guard eyed me and badged me in. He led the way quietly down a second hall. "Thanks, Brett. Good to see you." I paused, taking a deep breath, bracing myself for what was behind the door. Every week she changed. Some were good days, some were bad. Some visits I saw the Serena Indigo I knew, though other times I feared she'd been consumed by someone I had never met before. I didn't know how a woman as strong as she was had shattered into a thousand sharp pieces.

"Hey, beautiful." I smiled at her, gently brushing her hand. She was looking outside the tiny window that had been fogged with splotches.

She looked at me. "Sully." The bags under her eyes were deep and her once shiny hair hung over her shoulders in a tangled, dark mess. The stark white scrubs she wore hung over her tiny frame. It pained me to see them replace the green surgical ones we usually wore together.

"How's Lola?" She dug at the already raw and ragged skin around her thumb.

I moved closer. "Seri… please."

"How is she? No one will tell me anything!" she shouted at me.

"Serena, you know what we talked about… what your doctor has been reminding you? Please, Seri, please just try. Try for us. Try for me." I crouched to the floor and held her hands, fighting back my own tears.

"Tell me… Just tell me again because I can't remember," she said blinking hard, the whites of her eyes tinged with red and a wildness that terrified me.

"Seri… Lola died during delivery when you were in residency remember? The cord was wrapped around her neck. There was nothing they could do, sweetheart. You have to try to remember." She felt lifeless, cold, and I truly didn't recognize the woman in front of me.

She nodded slowly as she looked at me, though it was as if she were looking through me. And although she and I were together in the small white room, it felt as if I were alone.

"Look what I snuck you?" I smiled, lifting the latte

that had become lukewarm. I slowly peeled the lid off before handing it over to her.

"You think I'm going to kill myself with a plastic coffee lid? For God's sake, I am a fucking doctor." She reached for the drink and I couldn't help but smile. *There was the Serena Indigo I knew, the one I was in love with. The one I had loved for as long as I could remember.*

Eric had left her for a nurse he worked with, Tessa. She was only twenty-two, and he had gotten her pregnant. He didn't even tell Serena. He came home one day when she was at work, packed his things, and left to move into the apartment he had kept for his multiple affairs. He texted Serena telling her that he wanted a divorce—it was cold and calculating. After everything they had been through, everything Serena went through with Lola and their son, he didn't care that he was breaking an already destroyed woman. Eric created a life with another woman that was meant to be the one they were supposed to live together, and rubbed every aspect in her face, finding joy in her demise.

After Serena lost her daughter—her miracle baby they had after the devastating death of their first-born son, Mason—she threw herself into work. The cruel irony. She spent her days and nights delivering baby after baby, completing the families of others. She was the first to hold countless new lives, seeing them open their eyes for the first time, hearing their cries. Every life she helped bring into the world took a piece of her.

Serena was in college when she had Mason. Eric was supposed to be watching him while she went to get his birthday cake, but he got preoccupied during the party and minutes later, their life had changed. Mason had drowned during his birthday party. Serena never, ever mentioned him. She had repressed every ounce of his memory. Her parents and Eric allowed him be forgotten, assuming it'd help her heal, but instead, it set her up for self-destruction.

She consumed herself with school, except finally she cracked and attempted suicide. Eric found her with her wrists slit in the nursery before medical school. Medicating herself, and a hospital stay later, her parents pushed her to stop dwelling. They lied to everyone, saying she was studying abroad when really, she was institutionalized. Serena was not permitted to be anything less. *Anything less than perfect.*

One breezy fall day, we were eating outside at a local restaurant when Serena's face turned pale, the life drained from her face. I followed the beautiful eyes I'd fallen in love with all those years ago. There he was. Eric lifting a giggling toddler his arms as a woman looked on proudly. The little girl's curls bounced with the wind. The sunlight caught the shine of a wedding ring on both their fingers, and I prayed they wouldn't see us.

Eric turned and caught Serena's gaze, though he looked away quickly. I felt immense relief as I reached and held her hand that had grown cold, trembling against mine.

"Serena? Parker? What a surprise." Eric's voice boasted beside us. I looked over and leaned into my chair, gripping Serena's hand tightly. It was shaking as if an earthquake had washed over her body.

Eric was balancing the child on his hip. "Serena, don't you want to meet my daughter?" he asked in a way that spiked with cruelty. The child was from Tessa's previous relationship and apparently, Eric had legally adopted her. He often paraded his new family near Serena.

Serena didn't move she stared at him and paced her eyes between the toddler and Eric.

"This is Julia. Isn't she perfect? Tessa really made my dreams come true. She's actually pregnant, too! Can you believe it? Two kids." Eric grinned.

"Eric, please. I think you need to leave," I pleaded with him.

Eric looked at our clasped hands and smiled coyly before he shook his head and let out a soft chuckle.

I turned back to Serena and met her eyes. She looked as if she died. The blood drained from her face completely, leaving her skin, pale. At that moment, I knew I couldn't save her. I remember trailing my finger to her pulse on her wrist, feeling the faint beat.

Eric died two months later... He had a heart attack in his sleep.

One night, Serena was at my doorstep, I remember bringing her inside and tucking her into the guest bed as if she were a bird with a broken wing. She woke up screaming hysterically. I found her in the hallway, wrapped in a faded pink baby blanket. She looked ridiculous as an adult woman with a tiny blanket around her as if it would shield her from her pain.

I lifted her into my arms. She looked at me... and *smiled*. It sent chills up my spine as she spoke softly with glazed eyes. "Honey, will you check on Lola? I think it's time for her bottle."

The next morning, I packed her bags and drove her to Great Falls Psychiatric Hospital. I arrived at the door with her body weight completely crashed into mine.

"You're gonna be okay, Seri. I'm going to help you.

I love you." I kissed the top of her soft hair and inhaled the gentle scent of coconut.

Tears stung my eyes as the nurse came up with a wheelchair and Serena looked at me. She looked at me, similarly to what a dog at a kill shelter looks like before he's put down. *Knowing there was no way out.* She sunk into the wheelchair as they pushed her away, her face once again painted with betrayal and anguish.

I went to Serena's rental house to pick up some things as her release approached. The bright purple and blue flowers she had planted were beginning to wilt, so I quickly grabbed the hose to water them. She loved them so much, and I didn't want her to think I didn't care enough to tend to them.

"Hey, Parker, haven't seen you 'round here in a while." I turned my head and saw Serena's neighbor.

"Hi, Bianca, how are you? I'm just watering Serena's flowers before I grab her clothes." I smiled and turned back to the pitiful plants.

"I hope she's doing better. I heard she gone to the looney bin. She always seemed kinda off..." The way she chuckled made my fist clench.

"She'll be okay," I said, my tone coated with clear annoyance as I could feel her eyes lingering on me.

"You guys be careful around those..."

I turned back and peered at Bianca. She had her body pressed against the small white picket fence that divided the two houses.

"What do you mean?" I asked.

"Those are called Monkshood. Super lethal to humans. Surprised she planted them, bein' a doctor and all." She stared at the flowers that I was apparently trying to drown with water. I quickly moved the hose off them and looked back. The water puddling in the grass beside me.

"Yea, we will be. Thanks, Bianca. Take care."

Turning the hose off and heading inside, it felt stuffy and sticky. The smell reminded me of visiting an old childhood home, after it had been left unlived in for ages. A familiar scent fading into the stench of abandonment. Sinking into the barstool, I pulled my phone out and Googled 'Monkshood flowers.' Images that matched the flowers outside were plastered across my screen. Leaning forward on the counter, I scanned the words over and over as my heart began to race and my palms moistened. The slickness of my fingers made it harder to slide through the article that streaked across my screen. Wiping my hands against my pants, I paced through the words feeling my heart beat even quicker than the rate my eyes could process each small, black word.

"Monkshood, when ingested, can cause fatal cardiac complications," I read out loud. It sounded familiar from medical school, but it was obviously not something one absorbs into their long-term memory.

I dropped my phone on the kitchen island, letting my hands brush through my hair. Staring down at the screen, I whispered, "What have you done, Seri?"

The night Eric came over, Serena had a blueberry pie waiting for him. It was her go-to dessert—an Indigo family tradition. I remember smelling the tangy aroma linger through her house and asked for a slice, but she had aggressively swatted my hand away when I went to cut a piece. She made me promise I wouldn't eat it, saying something along the lines that she didn't want a mess until she needed to serve it. I didn't even think twice. Serena had always been a perfectionist.

I quivered. There was no way the woman I knew— the woman I loved—was capable of murder.

Or was she?

So many memories crashed in my mind, piecing together slowly. I leaned against the counter, letting my forehead touch the cold, kitchen island. I think I always knew there was a darkness inside of her, I just didn't know she'd lose control over it. Through the years, I would see her wander off and get lost in an unknown world, but she always found her way back.

I didn't care what she'd have done, I was in love with her. I would always be in love with her, and I would love her until my last breath. I didn't care if there was a monster inside her... to me she'd always be perfect. Together we'd find a way to control the monster she had unleashed to protect herself. Amongst the broken glass, I'd always find a way to help piece her together to whoever she needed to be. If you push and tear down the perfect woman enough, of course she'll be nothing more than imperfect. Yet, amongst the cracks of imperfection, she'll find something greater...

Vengeance.

CHAPTER TWENTY

"Get off me! Do you know who I am? I'm a damn doctor! Get these restraints off me!" I screamed at the large security guard named Brett. He, along with three nurses, had me pinned down with what resembled zip ties along my ankles and wrists.

"Serena... Dr. Indigo?" a soft voice called out. I opened my eyes slowly—they were blurry and sticky, yet I could feel my eyes widen in sheer fear. I couldn't breathe. Suffocating on the waves of emotion and panic that rode through me violently. Flashes of a cognac brown leather notebook and a hand gripping it seeped into my vision.

"No... no keep that man away from me! He and his

wife... they'll kill me! Help me!" I yelled, the words echoing in the stark white room.

"Serena... please, *just breathe,*" he said. The calmness of his voice made my heart race more. I was trembling as tears blurred my eyes, and I blinked repeatedly as if the simple motion of my eyelids could waft away what—or rather who—was staring back at me. I saw the hospital badge on his white coat.

Dr. James Callahan, MD, Psychiatry.

Closing my eyes, I felt a sharp, cold needle puncture my skin. *Please God don't let me wake up.*

I inhaled the sweet smell of spring with the blooming cherry blossom shadowed over me. The pink silhouette wrapped me in its protection. *Protection from what?* I suppose it was ironic, really. I needed protection from no one other than myself. The worn bench felt hard under me, I had lost so much weight that my bones met the wood with ease. The sunlight danced through the gaps of the tree and warmed my skin that felt permanently cold.

"Good afternoon, Serena."

I turned my face upward and looked at him, squinting as the sun found its home on my face. A deep breath of air escaping my lungs, I leaned back into the bench and loosened the grip around the wood. "Good afternoon, Dr. Cal—" I cleared my throat and looked back at him.

"Serena, you're more than welcome to call me James, you know that," he replied with a reassuring smile. The wrinkles around his eyes and mouth deepened. He was an attractive man for his age. I looked down and saw a beautiful dog. His tail was rapidly wagging while his pink tongue hung out of his mouth. Little droplets of saliva trickled down onto the floor. A Goldendoodle... the dog we had always thought we'd get one day for our children. Anxiety pooled into me as I began peeling at the bare thumbnail.

"Serena, you remember our friend Chap? He has taken to you, and I thought you'd like to have him join us."

"Mmm-hm." I let my hand graze his soft fur, pushing away the thoughts that rampaged through my mind.

Dr. James Callahan was North Carolina's top psychiatrist. A month after arriving at Great Falls Psychiatric Hospital, I sunk into a leather chair across from him. They had me in therapy and heavily medicated. I was finally lucid, not lost. He smiled kindly and didn't say anything for a few minutes, just watched me. Finally, a few moments passed, and he looked at the giant folder in front of him. He squinted as he slowly turned the wooden name plate that was carved in gold wording. *Dr. James Callahan, MD*.

I remember the blood in my body feeling as if it were funneling out. I remember thinking I was in an alternate universe. I remember really realizing I was officially no longer perfect. I was the most flawed and damaged person. I knew I didn't have to be terrified of my husband, my mother, my neighbors, or breaking the façade of perfection.... I needed to be absolutely terrified of myself.

Serena Indigo, a monster who wore pearl earrings and a white coat.

According to Dr. Callahan, I had met him the day I arrived, yet within a week, I had suffered an enormous psychotic break where I crafted some sort of unrealistic reality where my neighbor, James Callahan, was to blame for a surplus of events. My mind had plotted a life story about Dr. Callahan that didn't even exist. People that didn't exist. Events and people were meticulously crafted in my head to protect myself from being a victim. I shuddered at the thought. *A victim.* I hated that word. I used him and others to help me remember my own story, my own losses. I projected my own life onto a stranger in hope I could recollect it, but not claim it. They found a small note-book with an entire journal entry that I had crafted from his perspective. Yet, it wasn't his story. It was mine. Disguised and repressed.

Apparently, Dr. Callahan came to one of the many conclusions that years of Eric's gaslighting, emotional abuse, and PTSD from two particular life traumas caused me to craft these protective stories—which I found to be ridiculous. This wasn't some horror movie; I wasn't a crazy person. I was a tired, over-worked physician, mother, and wife who just needed a fucking minute to breathe without the world throwing its weight on my damn shoulders.

"James, are you married?" I looked at him. My brain felt fogged as usual with the plethora of anti-psychotics I was being numbed with. I felt twanged with embarrassment now that I had begun to emerge from the mentally insane woman Parker had brought here to a more coherent woman. Embarrassed that I, Dr. Serena Indigo, one of the best damn OB-GYNs in the Southeast, was being treated like a toddler. Not just a toddler, I was that damaged piece of fruit in the supermarket that you lift up and almost put into your cart, yet you pause. *Why?* Because although its shiny, red, and beautiful, you realize there's a bruise hiding away on the other side that will eventually rot and consume the beautiful apple. You won't give it a chance or a second thought, you just dispose of the imperfect fruit.

"Serena, why don't we keep the focus on you." Dr. Callahan peered at me while tapping his shiny pen against his notebook.

I nodded. It had been months. Every Tuesday and Thursday like clockwork, I met with Dr. James Callahan as he drilled away at the iceberg we were hoping to pull out, knowing it had been submerged for too long.

He used too many metaphors and blinked too often. Besides that, he was—he is—a pretty good man to have to spend the afternoon with dwelling on why the perfect woman turned into a shit show. Some days, before my medications would take effect, I'd catch a glimpse of him in the hallway and shudder in fear, thinking he'd come kill me or destroy me.

"To answer your question, I have been married. Twice, actually." He offered a gentle smile.

"Are you still married?" I studied his face as his forehead wrinkled.

"Yes, I am."

"Is your wife's name Naomi or Ma—"

"Serena… you know we've discussed what you wrote in your journal… the story about me. The one about my kids, my wife, and everything. You know none of that is true. You wrote that when you were first re-admitted here… We talked about it being an interesting coping mechanism for you, remember?"

"I know… I just… Do you have…" I sighed and paused. He knew I was trying to move past the embarrassing—no, humiliating—revelation he'd just made and had made multiple times already.

"Children? Yes, I do. Four, actually. All grown up, probably close to your age."

I swallowed the sticky spit that was lingering in my dry mouth. "You're a blessed man. So many of my patients and their partners would have gone through hell and back for just one child." I traced the wooden bench markings carefully.

"Serena, are you talking about your patients or you?"

"I did go through hell and back for my Lola," I fired at him.

"I know you did. I…" Dr. Callahan furrowed his eyebrows. "How about we talk about Mason?" he asked with a hushed whisper, slowing his words and examining my reaction as if he were terrified the name alone would wreck me. He had tried multiple times to bring Mason up, but I was healing, I was doing better... Bringing Mason up would unleash something, someone I was terrified of.

"No. I cannot... I will not—" I stifled the impeding sobs that were brewing inside of me. I couldn't even say his name. So, I redirected to the child I never got to know because with Lola, I could narrate the story. Mason, well... I knew him. I loved him for a couple of short, yet perfect years before...

"You know after I had Lola, I remember my recovery was brutal. I had a second-degree tear and bled for longer than usual. I was laying in our bed, with no blanket over me. I was abnormally hot because of the hormones...wearing a damn adult diaper and some shorts..."

"I admire all women for what they go through during the entire journey of pregnancy and delivery. It's something a man simply wouldn't be able to ever handle," Dr. Callahan said with a kind nod.

"Do you know what my husband said to me when I was freshly post-partum?"

"No, but I'm sure you'll share?"

"He said... Oh wow, look at all that cellulite on your thighs and hips." I cringed as I told Dr. Callahan what Eric spewed at me all those years ago. I still felt my face flush and grow red with embarrassment—the exact same sentiment I felt when Eric said those cruel words to me. That night I went to our bathroom and dug the dagger into the grooves of the cellulite markings that hid on my hips. The blood dripped down my legs onto our white bathroom floors. My tears blurred with the blood as the pain distorted with the hate I felt inside.

"When… After I had Mason, we were in college… we were so young. In the hospital, I asked him to grab me a snack in the middle of the night… I wasn't supposed to stand hours after having a baby… He told me I didn't need to eat anything, and to shut the hell up so he could sleep…" Thinking back to him, even in college, I couldn't believe I had stayed with him. I was such a helpless fool.

"Serena… Eric was a narcissist. He found pleasure in hurting you. He found pleasure in scheming ways to make you feel less than. Those are not faults in yourself, rather faults in a broken and tormented man. You lost two children, yet he didn't choose to nourish and support you during your weakest times. Instead, he hurt you further. He enjoyed gaslighting you, ripping you to shreds." Dr. Callahan closed his eyes and nodded again as if he were proud of the declaration he had shared with me.

"I know. That's why he's in the dirt now." I smiled back at him and winked. Dr. Callahan tilted his head again, studying my face. His lips parted ever so slightly as he closed them quickly. He was incredible at keeping his face stoic and emotionless.

"Is there anything you'd care to discuss, Serena? Perhaps the way Eric suddenly died?" He leaned in closer to me, as if he knew even the trees and birds had ears.

I smiled again and placed my hand over his. "I don't like digging things up that were always meant to be buried. Some things are best left locked away... including myself, I suppose." I laughed and waved my hands toward the large hospital behind us.

After nibbling through details of repressed memories one by one, I was back in my small, isolated room. I laid in the bed and peered at the ceiling. Forty-four. That's how many hideous tiles crafted the ceiling above me. I remember dreaming of all the times I'd manage to push through them all and crawl down, finding some form of escape out of this hell. *Great Falls Psychiatric Hospital.* I couldn't help but laugh. I worked my entire life to serve and save people, yet no one saved me.

There was a knock at the door. I turned my head to the locked door. It wasn't locked from the inside, it was locked from the outside. Another bit of my life's irony. I spent so much time worried about locking the inside of our house to protect myself—even living behind gates—yet here I was, being locked in from the outside because apparently, the only demon I had to fear was the one inside the four walls of this room. *Me.* My mother was on to something all those years ago when she told me I was indeed the only person I needed to be scared of.

"Hello, Dr. Indigo! How are you feeling? I have your medicine and then it's lights-out time." A man wearing a stiff beige uniform came in. He almost looked like a zookeeper. Well, I guessed that he often felt like one. Hearing the nightly screams of patients and the bone-chilling laughter rising around me made me feel as if I were a caged animal displayed in some exhibit. I studied his face carefully and looked at his name embroidered on his shirt. Carlos Garcia. Pushing in a small trolley cart, he had the room door opened. Apparently, he was scared of me, too.

I sighed, opening my moist palm. He placed four colorful pills in it. They stuck to my skin, and with my free hand, I took the small Dixie cup of water. Tossing the pills into my mouth, I chased it with the warm water. Parting my lips, I moved my tongue side to side, then up and down as Carlos inspected it.

"Carlos? Do you ever get scared working here?" I asked him, watching his expression change from the generic smile to one of intrigue.

"I did many tours in the army, so nothing I see or do here will ever be worse than what haunts me in my sleep, Dr. Indigo."

"How can you function so well with that kind of past?" I propped myself against the flat pillow that was probably once white but was now a shade of yellow that reminded me of hospital sheets stained with urine from my days in medicine.

"Well, I probably shouldn't be talking to you, Dr. Indigo... but you know what I think? I think we all have ghosts that haunt us, you just have to be willing to choose to let them haunt you while you are awake or haunt you while you are asleep." He shrugged before he turned back to his cart.

"What if they haunt you in both places? Then what?" I called out.

"Well then, I suppose that decides if you're the person locked in this room or outside it... Sweet dreams, Dr. Indigo." He looked at me over his shoulder and paused. I hoped he'd say something more. Something like, "Hey, remember that time I was your private investigator when you were a big-time doctor?" But I knew my mind had failed me, yet again.

I closed my eyes and prayed to the God I didn't believe in that the ghosts wouldn't come—in my dreams or reality. No matter how hard I tried, unlike Carlos, I wasn't strong enough to keep them away.

CHAPTER TWENTY-ONE

*A*nother day, another morning came. Weeks went on and most days felt as if I were reliving the same day over and over again. I woke up and looked through the smudge-stained window of the stark room I was in. I had tried countless times to wipe the glass, yet just like me, the markings were embedded so deeply they'd never be able to come out.

"Good morning, Serena. How are you feeling this morning?" Brooklyn, a younger nurse came in with a clipboard and a small Dixie cup balanced on top, holding colorful pills that were apparently going to magically suck the insanity out of me. Her ponytail swung with her movements.

"Fine." I grabbed the cup, tossing them back down my throat and chasing it with lukewarm water she handed me in a second cup. Even the coffee here tasted like the water. I missed my expensive, freshly ground coffee we'd pick up weekly from the small boutique café around the corner from my office.

"Please show me your mouth and under your tongue," the nurse asked while staring at my lips.

I sighed and opened my mouth, making the over-dramatic sounds that a child does at the pediatrician office. I fought back all the thoughts of Lola at the doctors. The Lola in my mind wasn't mine. Apparently, the image that followed me was all crafted by that of Eric's stepchild. There was no Lola. My Lola died, and that was the day I died, too. Mason... my son, my baby boy... After he died, I was able to repress him, bury him away—not only in the ground but in my mind, too. Lola, my only shred of hope. How can you heal from burying two children? I didn't know why these people were so set on bringing me back to life.

I was already gone.

I closed my eyes, knowing the darkness was the only place I felt safe. I thought back to when I was younger. Tall, skinny, beautiful, and intelligent. I was homecoming queen in high school, valedictorian, came from money, but also had worked hard to become a doctor. How did someone so perfect crash and burn? Dr. Magnolia Nix and Eric were the two people in the world I blamed for everything. I had the world in my hands and they ripped it from me, making sure I would never live a life I deserved. *A life I earned.*

I opened my eyes and stared at the small amount of light that came through the window from the moon. A tear escaped, trailing down the hollows of my cheekbones. I thought about Parker. Parker Sully. If only I had married him, had children with him… Why didn't I leave Eric when I knew all those years ago that Parker was the one? The medication fogged my brain and I fell into sleep, hoping I wouldn't wake up and have to face this life… this pathetic, miserable life in the morning.

"Dr. Indigo, you asked for the photo frames from your office desk to be brought here. I had someone grab them for you." Dr. Callahan leaned into a bag and pulled out the two gold frames I looked at every day for years at work. His eyebrow raised as he glanced down at them before handing them to me. I flipped the frames into my lap and stared down into them. Numbness coursed through my weak body. One picture was the same photo of Eric and me on our honeymoon, the other had a photo of a little girl, but not my little girl. It was the image that comes with the frame when you buy it—the one I had always seen Lola laughing and smiling in. It was nothing more than a generic child model. It even had the picture frame barcode printed in the corner.

I looked at Dr. Callahan. "Was there not another photo in this?"

"No, Serena. Your receptionist, Mindy, even admitted how she always thought it was odd you had a frame with some random model on your desk and would often be smiling down at it. Remember we talked about the concept of you crafting what you wanted versus what you have? Reality versus dreams. Expectations and desires blurring together." Dr. Callahan spoke softly as he patiently reminded me that I had truly lost my mind.

"Dr. Callahan, how long have I been here?" I rubbed my eyes and face.

"You've been in and out of here twice for a few years. You went home and relapsed just around the time Eric died. Do you remember?"

"Lola…" I stared at the frame and closed my eyes. "Dr. Callahan, do you know what Lola means?" I whispered.

"No, but I'm sure you'll share that with me…"

"*Sorrows.* I always thought it was odd how we chose that name. It is fitting, isn't it? After losing Lola, my life has been nothing but sorrow. Well, actually, interestingly enough, Eric chose her name." I lightly chuckled. "The creator of sorrows named his child with me just that."

"Do you want to talk about Mason? We've done pretty well talking about him in recent sessions."

"Mason. Oh, Mason. My beautiful son. He was the perfect baby. I was so young and naïve when we had him. I was only a college student. We were hosting his birthday party, a day to celebrate his life. Can you imagine? He drowned because of my asshole ex-husband. His own father let him die. I let him die. He wasn't watching him, James. All he had to do was watch him." Tears streamed from my eyes. I knew I couldn't handle talking about him. It was too much. The pain would always be too much.

"Serena, according to your mom and Parker, you did pretty well after his death. You continued with medical school and your career. Do you feel that was a cover to repress your memories of Mason?"

"After Mason, I just pushed forward to everyone, but secretly, I had died with him. You don't understand. Being an Indigo, there is no room for failure, there is no room for giving up. When I got pregnant with Lola… it was my rebirth. How cruel, right? I just don't think happiness is in the cards for me, Dr. Callahan." I looked away as tears raced down my face. The salt of my tears met with the tangy snot from my nose, seeping over my lips. I was a mess. My life was a mess.

"Well, perhaps you can begin a path to change that? We've done so well with therapy, and even found the right medication balance."

"Do you know what it was like to confirm pregnancies to excited moms? Deliver new lives into my hands after holding my dead daughter in those same palms? Pulling babies out from their mothers' bodies, after seeing my own son's body go limp in my arms, from pulling him out of the water? Do you know what it feels like to see the same woman for nine months as she smiles and chats about her dreams and happiness? All while your children never had a chance? Then your bastard husband cheats on you with the neighborhood supermodel and also someone from work? I don't know. If I'm a mess, Eric was sheer chaos. The fucking infertile OB-GYN who gave birth to a baby with a cord around its neck after losing her first born? Such irony, don't you think, James?" I looked at his curious face. I knew I sounded frenzied, my words pouring out of me the way my wine did every night.

"Well, they say psychiatrists become psychiatrists because we are so utterly wrecked that we need to figure ourselves out. As you know, well... what inspired your journal entries about my first wife was because you overheard a nurse gossiping. My wife Naomi really did take her life." Dr. Callahan stared up into the sky.

I didn't know what to say. I felt as if I were sitting with a friend and we were competing who was more fucked-up, but I would always win that competition. More so, it was embarrassing to me that I crafted an entire life story and wrote it about my psychiatrist all because I overheard nurses gossiping. I glanced at the cognac leather notebook that sat protected under his hand.

"What do you write in there, Dr. Callahan?" I wish he'd magically hand over his prized worn notebook for me to read and confirm there weren't the stories of my nightmares.

"Just notes about my patients… I find it to be a lot less distracting than typing ferociously on a laptop. The sound of the keys seems to be disturbing and almost… terrifying to many of my patients." He smiled sympathetically while clutching it tightly in his hands as if he knew what I was thinking.

"So, Serena, since today is our last session, I thought we could wrap a few things up. Maybe talk about Eric?" Dr. Callahan rubbed his chin.

"Why?" I looked down at the pink flesh

surrounding my thumbnail. I couldn't remember the last time a beautiful, feminine color sat on the otherwise sad looking nail. Manicures and polish to peel off were a memory of the past.

"Well, I think discussing Eric Hudson, your ex-husband, is something you really always avoided so I just want to make sure we've done our due diligence as much as possible." Dr. Callahan tapped his pen on the leather notebook.

I looked up at him slowly. "He's dead."

"I'm aware of that. How does that make you feel? I mean, you saw him the night he died…" he said it in a way that wasn't a statement, but rather an open-ended question.

"He came over and he looked completely healthy. I still think Macy did it." I titled my head and looked at the small mole lingering on Dr. Callahan's neck. "You should get that looked at." I pointed to the spot.

"Oh, this old thing? Just a birthmark," he replied, running his hand over it.

"That's what they all say and then poof, one day you're dead." I chuckled lightly.

"I'll have it looked at I suppose. So, you think Macy killed him?"

"I dunno. Just seems odd, right? A perfectly healthy, fit emergency room doctor dropping dead in his thirties. That bitch probably wanted his money without the strings."

"Serena, it seems Macy moved away or *vanished.* You know he was with a woman named Tessa, right? It seems you may have been infatuated with Macy because in your eyes, you considered this woman to be your idea of *perfect.*" Dr. Callahan squinted at me as if he were studying an unidentified species out in the wild.

"Dr. Callahan, look, my husband—my ex-husband —was a lying, cheating asshole. He had probably slept with a dozen women during the course of our relationship. Honestly, I don't want to dig him out of the grave now. He was dead to me the moment he abandoned us. As for Macy, Parker knows all about her. He's met her. She was far from perfect, but I'm sure she's skipped town and found a new man to leech onto with those bright red lips and devil claws." I leaned back into the worn wooden bench and looked up at the bright blue sky.

"You said, Eric abandoned *us?*" Dr. Callahan questioned.

"Lola and I, of course." I squinted at the sunlight.

"Serena, please look at me." He sounded vanquished.

I turned back to him and looked at his face. He

stayed quiet for a moment, raising his eyebrows at me, as if I were a puzzle he just couldn't piece back together. My whole life I always felt like something was missing—a piece of the puzzle *missing.* The frustration one feels when they have this beautiful, perfect image put together after all the hard work and patience, but then they get to the last bit and see one small corner piece is nowhere to be found. That frustration evolves into so much more than agitation, it evolves into fury. Having a child, even just one child was the last piece of my perfect puzzle. Apparently, that piece was ripped away from me and crushed to shreds, it was the piece that was dropped and vacuumed away with no second thought.

"Serena, would you please talk with me." Dr. Callahan gently patted my hand.

"You've got my attention, doc." I offered a tired grin—the side effects of the arsenal of medications I was on were wreaking havoc on me. I couldn't wait to leave this place and never be forced to take them again. I'd be just fine, therapy helped and I could get back in control. *I was in control.*

He took a deep breath as if he were praying the days, weeks, and years he'd sat on this same bench with me mattered. "Serena, I want you to tell me where Lola and Mason are."

"Lola. My perfect, beautiful Lola. She's dead, she didn't get a chance. She died during childbirth. Mason. My sunshine. James, you'd have loved him... He lit up my world. After he... Well, my world was dark and cold," I repeated the statement to him. It was the one I practiced in my head over and over to remind myself that if I didn't say what they wanted to hear, I'd definitely never leave this place.

"Yes. This life you crafted as a mother no longer exists. You're still a mother, just not the way you wanted to be. You exist, you can fight to exist in a more fulfilling way." Dr. Callahan glanced at his watch.

"The doctor, Dr. Nix, who delivered my baby. She ruined my life, James. It was a simple delivery. She had seconds to get the umbilical cord off her neck. She failed me. She failed my Lola. I had to work under her for the rest of residency. She didn't even show sympathy. I was just another patient, another number. Parker, you know Parker? He was the resident on-call, he begged her to let him help. She didn't budge. She was an egotistical bitch. Parker would have saved Lola. He would have." I looked down at my palms, watching my tears pool into them.

"Serena, the sooner you accept everything, the sooner you'll be able to be free of the pain that has consumed you. You're a bird in a cage. The cage being

Eric, his baby, his new life, his infidelity, Dr. Nix, Macy, Mason, and Lola. You've got to eventually let yourself fly. Don't you want to fly? Don't you want to be free of the gilded cage?" He tapped his pen against the cognac leather journal again.

"Wounded birds can't fly..." I said under a hushed breath.

"You're right, wounded birds can't fly, but you were meant to soar."

I sighed and looked at Dr. Callahan.

"There is just one more thing I always wondered... We searched through and through for a boy named Brooks to no avail... Serena, the house next door has been vacant for a while due to the previous owners going through a foreclosure."

"Mason Brooks Hudson." I closed my eyes allowing a single tear escape. "I think in my mind I always dreamt of how Mason would have been the most protective son, getting himself into trouble but always looking out for me. Eric only hurt me. I think he's haunted me for failing him. I think inside, somewhere in my soul, I always knew if Mason were still here, he'd have loved me so much, protected me, but I'm not deserving of that and look... God knew. I couldn't protect him. I couldn't save him. I couldn't save Lola." I placed my hands over my face, hiding behind them as a shield as I cried. The sound of my sobs cutting through the grooves of my fingers.

"Serena, the fact that you've accepted Brooks being a figment of your imagination and repressed emotions is a victory of its own." Dr. Callahan tapped my shoulder reassuringly.

"Do you think I can be... normal? I mean, what if I get out of here and spiral again..." My heart pounded as my mind raced with doubt. I no longer doubted everyone else, *I doubted myself.* I was terrified of myself. There was a time my body had betrayed me when we tried to get pregnant, and now my mind was betraying me when it was time to heal.

"Normal? I'm not sure anyone is normal. Do I think you can lead a happy, healthy, and fulfilled life? Absolutely. Look how far you've already come. Unleashing repressed memories was our hardest step, but we did it. You did it. Finding a way to compartmentalize reality versus dreams was our second step, and you did that, too. Serena, you are loved by many. You have so much to look forward to."

"I'm not sure anyone loves me... I'm a train wreck."

"Oh, I think you're quite mistaken..." Dr. Callahan glanced behind me.

I followed his eyes and met Parker. He was wearing

a navy suit and held a bouquet of peonies. Roses still haunted me.

"Seri..." Parker smiled.

I stared at him. He was the reason I was breathing and alive today. He saved me. He visited me every week, even the days I stared at the wall, too sedated to move my lips. Even the days I cried in his arms over a toddler daughter I didn't have or screaming for Mason when I remembered him. He was the only reason I still had a pulse.

It was somewhat embarrassing at first. I'd look at my reflection, a woman who was completely disheveled. My hair looked like stringy, dark yarn; my face was sunken in, and I didn't have a plethora of beauty products to make myself look presentable. I could see it on the nurses faces, they were stunned. A man like him visiting a woman like me. At one point in time, we'd have made a power couple—the couple everyone would be envious of. Instead, I chose to marry a complete monster and destroyed my life.

I cried night after night when everything was silent. It's sad, isn't it? You get one chance at life. *One.* Someone comes along and fucks it up, or you finally have your dream children... and no one can save them. Everything in my life that was wrong was because of two incompetent people—Dr. Magnolia Nix and Eric

Hudson. Well, actually, I had to add Macy to that list. She was Eric's gateway drug to affairs. I mean, if he'd have never met that bitch, we'd probably still be married and happy. Maybe we could have had another baby? Maybe we could have started over? Together. Then again, he deserved to die. Mason drowned because of him. My mind was still nothing more than a hamster wheel churning. I had just learned to put a disguise on as I always did in front of Dr. Callahan.

I had so many questions that haunted my sleep. No one would let me have my phone or a computer, so I never had the chance to look up and find Macy. If she wasn't James Callahan's wife, then who was she? Where did she meet my husband? My dead, ex-husband? Parker refused to speak about her because he said Dr. Callahan advised him to not speak about anything that was a "trigger."

"Seri, are you ready to go home?" Parker looked at me with enthusiasm and hope.

I turned back to Dr. Callahan. "I'm really scared…" I skimmed around the courtyard. Patients wearing the stark white scrubs with darkness in their eyes scattered throughout. I looked down at my soft pink dress and traced my fingers along the hemline. Parker had dropped it off the week before, knowing I'd be eager to finally be free from the scrubs that made me feel weak—unlike the green surgical scrubs that had always made me strong when I delivered babies or operated on women.

"Say goodbye to this cage, Dr. Indigo, it's time for you to soar." Dr. Callahan stood and reached his hand out. I took it, pulled myself up, then I turned back to Parker who had grown closer.

"Let's go home, Seri." He smiled as we walked hand in hand. For the first time in a long time, I didn't feel cold. I felt warm and free. Finally, free. I didn't have to be perfect anymore. Everyone now knew I was the most imperfect woman they knew. The standards were no longer hit and sailing like a boat on the water. The standards were low, sunken into the dark ocean like an anchor. A woman who was in and out of a psych ward... who could be more flawed? A woman who lost not just one child, but two. I was damaged goods.

I paused and peered over my shoulder. I had fallen so many damn times, it was my time to soar. My second, or maybe third chance at simply living my reality versus drowning in dreams that would never happen. *It was my time to be free.*

"Serena, we will always be here for you. Keep up with your scheduled therapies and Parker has my personal number if you ever need me. I'm hoping you don't need it, though." Dr. Callahan smiled as the wrinkles near his eyes deepened.

"Thanks doc... I'll be in good hands." I turned to Parker, grasping his arm tightly. He leaned in, kissing the top of my head.

We had just one stop to make before the fresh start, the new chapter of my life. *Our lives.* Pulling into the parking lot, my chest tightened. The sound of Parker's tires against the unfinished gravel shook me. I held onto the small, pink flowers that looked as if they had yet to bloom still. Parker looked over at me, nodding in a way that helped push me out of the safety of his car.

I told him I didn't want him to come with me because ultimately, I needed to do this one final thing before I could truly set myself free.

Looking down, I stared at the two gravestones that were side by side. "Hi, my sweet little loves." Tears were unstoppable as they unleashed their fury down my face.

Mason Brooks Hudson.

Lola Indigo Hudson.

There could be no greater pain than burying your own children. It wasn't supposed to be this way. Sinking down in between them. I pulled out a poem that was crumpled under the flowers.

A love like no other.
A pain deep in your mother.
Time was all I wished for.
Time for us.
Time for more.
Instead, everything stripped me to my core.
I'll love you forever.
Protect each other, too.
All I could do is get retribution for you.
My two loves, my whole life, you'll both always be.
You are the only perfect part of me.

Mere words I had scribbled in a breakthrough session at Great Falls. They meant so much to me because I finally saw the sliver of peace knowing Mason and Lola were together. Gently laying the small pink rosebuds down, I kissed my palm twice and laid it on both.

"I'm so sorry, Mason and Lola. I'm so sorry. Mommy loves y—" I choked on my sobs.

The soft, small pink roses were just like my babies. They didn't get to bloom fully, yet they were perfection. I stood, closed my eyes, and said one last goodbye before getting back into the car with Parker.

We drove home. *To our home.*

CHAPTER TWENTY-TWO

Sitting in the rocking chair on the wraparound porch, we sipped glasses of cold, sweet tea. Glancing up at the pink sky that was tinged with the orange of a perfect sun set, I inhaled the freshness of the evening summer air. I looked down at the sparkling diamond ring and band that encircled my finger and turned to the creaking chair next to me. Parker was drinking his tea, smiling at me as he felt my eyes trailing him.

I grinned over at him. "How about a treat to go with that tea?"

"Sure, babe."

I walked inside to the kitchen and stared at the blueberry pie I baked early in the morning for Parker. He loved it so much when we were younger, and I couldn't remember the last time I had made it. I slowly cut a slice and slid it onto the shiny white-and-blue plate. Lifting my finger to my face, I saw the sticky blueberry filling linger on it. Opening my mouth, I paused.

"No…" I whispered to myself, wiping it away on the hand towel. I had eaten a few bites of ice cream, I didn't need any more dessert. I carried the plate over to Parker and handed it to him.

"Some dessert for my amazing husband who is simply as sweet as pie…" I laughed, imitating my mother's southern drawl.

Parker paused, looking at the pie and back at me.

"Everything okay?" My laughter halted as he slowly reached for the plate. His hand was slightly shaking.

His eyebrow arched as he looked back at me. "You didn't want a slice, Serena?"

"Oh, Sully, you know you don't have to do that… You don't have to overcompensate and make sure I'm eating everything just because Eric was the opposite. I'm fine. I'm full from dinner and had some ice cream earlier. Eat it… I made it just for you." I smiled, sitting in the chair next to him.

His cheeks seemed to flush as he unhurriedly cut a tiny piece, holding it to his face before placing it in his mouth. His eyes were intently on mine as he chewed it slowly.

"Well damn, Sully, I know I don't cook much, but if there's one thing this girl can make it's a tasty Indigo blueberry pie. I'll have you know that there was once a time you'd eat an entire one when we were younger..."

"It's delicious, babe, thank you," he said under his breath while reaching for his sweet tea. Maybe it had been too long since I had made it. I reached over and took a bite of Parker's.

"Oh... now that's incredible. I'm taking major offense to the fact that you haven't swallowed it whole." I smiled at him, wiping the corners of my mouth.

His face lit up and he looked far more relaxed as he took another bite. He was too compassionate, probably feeling guilty to eat my favorite dessert when I wasn't.

"So, you don't miss gardening out here, do you?"

"Parker Sully, on what planet do you think I'd be good at gardening?" I laughed at him. *What was his deal today?*

"Well, I just mean... You know that rental house you had? You loved planting those bluish-purply... indigo-colored flowers. Remember?" Parker asked quietly.

"Oh… um. I think I was probably just tending to whatever the landlord had already planted. Wow, you have some memory. I don't think I even know how to garden." I smiled back at him.

"Really? That's… Yea. Okay." He placed the half-eaten pie on the table between us and slowly rocked again. I looked at the shiny silver band that looked comfortable on his ring finger as he began flipping through the new book he was reading. Leaning back into my rocking chair, I curled my legs up and laid back to soak up the therapy in front of me. The fierce, crashing waves were drowning out my thoughts.

Parker and I sold our private practice and moved to Charleston, South Carolina. We bought a gorgeous home on Sullivan's Island where the sand was our backyard and the endless ocean waves were the view from basically every room. Parker signed on as an obstetrician and gynecologist at the local hospital. I had spent a good amount of my twenties and thirties delivering beautiful, healthy babies into the eager arms of new mothers, and I honestly didn't know if I'd ever be ready to go back to my job. Part of me feared relapsing into the dark hole it took eternity to dig myself out of. Truthfully, I knew no one would hire me, though. I was officially a liability.

Mason was our surprise baby. We had just gotten

married, and he was our honeymoon souvenir. My parents helped us financially so I could still pursue my education and only take a little bit of a gap between school. He was the most incredible little boy.

On some days when everything was still except the sound of the waves, I could still hear his laughter in the air, in my nightmares I could hear his screams for... *me*. After he passed, I allowed myself to be consumed by my education and work. My parents hated self-pity and made that clear along with Eric after the usual "mourning period." Forgetting about Mason and burying him away in the dirt and from my mind was the only way I could live. Photos of him were packed away, his belongings donated, every bit of him was erased from our lives.

Year after year, treatment after treatment, I finally got pregnant again. The infertile OB-GYN was quite the paradox. We had been diagnosed with secondary infertility, even though I knew it was God punishing me for our sins. I remember going to the hospital carrying my bag that enclosed a small pink bow and soft, matching fuzzy blanket. Our world was supposed to be complete, be changed for the better. The final piece to our beautiful puzzle was about to be here. A second chance to happiness.

We had checked the car seat what felt like a thousand times to ensure our baby would be taken home safely. Getting into the hospital, I was ready. Everyone made sure Eric and I were taken care of. Everything would be perfect this time. Dr. Nix was the physician that was on-call. I was counting my lucky stars since she was the best and had been my attending physician on many rotations already. Parker was the resident that was working, too. *It was all perfect.* Orchestrated to perfection.

I remember the look of horror on Parker's face when I had finally pushed Lola out and there wasn't the long-awaited cry. He moved quickly to Dr. Nix. Dr. Nix's face was filled with distress as her hands were moving and working so hurriedly, I felt every-thing blur as Eric gripped my arm tightly and was shouting out to Parker for answers. Dr. Nix had made Parker move. I watched her shove him out of the way, while my head felt light, feeling as if curtains were closing in on me.

"Serena, I'm so sorry. She didn't make it..."

I never realized the shrill scream that echoed through the room that scorched my ears came from my own mouth. The hot tears that I swore I'd drown in, burned my cheeks and eyes. The stuffy, cold hospital air suffocated my lungs. I went back to work two weeks later and continued to deliver hundreds of babies into the arms of their eager mothers. Turns out maternity leave and recovery only applies to mothers with children who live. No one brings you food, flowers, or joy. They run from you, ignore you. They don't want to be around a cursed family. Each cry haunted my dreams. Eric having multiple affairs, then leaving me for his mistress and new family was the final strike. Macy Callahan being the epitome of the perfect woman and replacing me seared through my soul. *I couldn't face my reality. The only place I was safe was my dreams.*

We had a small funeral for Lola similar to Mason's. Dr. Callahan made me recall it. I thought it would kill me when I told him the details, the ones that haunted me. I told him how every single person brought roses in shades of red. Wasn't that odd? Roses seemed romantic. There was nothing romantic or sweet about my baby girl dying and never having her chance to live. I never knew a casket could be built so small. I thought Mason's was small, yet I suppose one crafted for a newborn proved me wrong. This chapter of our marriage and family was supposed to be a celebration of life, and instead, I was mourning her loss. Another loss.

I remember my mom crying in a handkerchief, wearing a two-piece black designer suit and a small hat... and pearls lining her neck. I remember everyone trickling in, dropping off red roses one by one on the fresh mound of dirt that covered the life that could have been. The life that should have been.

I thought it was so strange that people were plucking out red roses from a large arrangement and participating in some strange farewell ceremony the preacher had instructed. My Lola would have probably loved something bright and beautiful, just like the life she was promised from me. Instead, I let someone take her away from me. No matter how many times I'd gone through the scenario, gone through therapy sessions with Dr. Callahan or sobbed into Parker's shoulder, I'd never be able to overcome this. It was buried inside of me, inflicted into my soul the same way the scars under my arms, thighs, and hips were.

I was wearing a wrinkly black dress and black heels, both of which I threw in the trash after—the same tradition I did after my son's funeral. Eric didn't hold me. He didn't show compassion; he looked at me as if I was a failure—the same way my mother looked at me through her tears. Who loses two children? Parker held me as I sat beside the fresh dirt and cried at how small the patch was. I pushed away all the red roses and replaced them with dainty pink ones.

Everyone left, as I laid there, my cheek pressed

against the cold earth. I prayed I would magically hear her heart beating through the ground. At one point I did, and began digging rapidly in hysterics. Looking down, my thumbnail was covered in the rust color. It had stained my nail polish on that one finger.

I began crying uncontrollably, ferociously peeling the polish that combined with dirt off my thumbnail. Parker came running and lifted me up. He had been waiting in his car, watching me mourn and sleep next to her grave, letting me have a night alone with her. I envisioned the countless hours and sleepless nights holding her warm body in my arms as I nursed her, comforted her, burped her. Instead, we were worlds apart. I remember looking over at Mason's grave next to hers, not even realizing it was that of my son. I became the epitome of living in oblivion and protecting myself. If I didn't protect myself, who would? Look what happened when I relied on people to protect my babies?

The first time I had been admitted to Great Falls, a piece of my recovery was supposed to be going back to her gravesite, but I couldn't do it. I was terrified that I'd hear her heart beat or a giggle that never was. I was scared my angel would turn into the ghost that had stalked me. No one pushed me to remember Mason. They all assumed unearthing Lola and letting her go was the first step. I couldn't believe it. How could a mother bury her child, not only in the ground but so far out of her own heart and mind that I didn't even remember him. Eric hid every last photo of him, as did my parents. They didn't know that hiding him from our lives would only make me find him somewhere else, in someone else. *I realized my perfect life was all simply a perfect lie.*

"Seri, you up for a walk tonight?" Parker gently nudged my hand. I turned to face him. He was wearing a white linen button-down and khaki pants that were rolled at the bottom. He belonged here. I just hope I did, too.

"Yea definitely, let me just go and grab my cardigan." I smiled, gently squeezing his hand.

I walked into our bedroom, sliding on the oversized cream cardigan. I caught a glimpse of myself in the mirror. Quickly sitting down at my vanity and added mascara to my lashes while swiping on some lipstick. My long hair had done well with the sea breeze as the dark waves tumbled over my shoulders. Pumping some lotion into my hands, I rubbed them carefully. I studied the rings that sat on my left-hand ring finger. A simple diamond band and a large emerald-cut diamond nestled together, reminding me how lucky I was to get a second chance at an otherwise destroyed life. I no longer used an army of products to mask who I was. I was learning to accept myself and how freeing that truly could be.

I got up, meeting Parker out on the porch. He smiled at me and wrapped his arm around my shoulder as we trekked to the ocean that was steps away. The sound of the rolling waves provided solace to the debilitating anxiety and fears that otherwise consumed me. The way the ocean met the sky reminded me how small I was and how endless the world was around me.

"What do you think you'll do tomorrow, beautiful?" Parker looked ahead as we strolled hand in hand. I looked down at my feet as the sand sunk every time my foot landed into it. The first day we got here, I was terrified if I pressed hard enough into the sand, the world may swallow me whole.

"I don't know, maybe go to that new yoga studio and catch up on some reading?" I looked up at him with a reassuring grin. His forehead creased, but he didn't look at me. I knew he worried about me every single day. I hated that I dragged the most perfect man into a complete mess of a life.

"That sounds nice..."

"Parker... what ever happened to Dr. Nix?" I looked over at him as the sea breeze picked up and blew my hair. A piece stuck onto my lipstick and I gently pulled it off, letting my hand intertwine back with his right after.

"Serena, you know I don't like talking about things from our past. It's just… it's not good for you, baby. Please, after this, we have to let the past stay just there…in the past. Dr. Nix she died right before you… you went to Great Falls Hospital."

My free hand flung to my mouth in shock. "Oh, my goodness. How'd she die?"

"Seri, she was found in her home. Wrists slit. It really shook the community. She had an abnormal amount of sleeping pills in her system, too. Her husband said they'd gone out to dinner, came home and had pie for dessert, then he had to go back into work while Magnolia Nix headed off to bed. They ruled it a suicide, but…"

Parker looked down at me, holding his breath before releasing it slowly. I knew he was terrified that anything would trigger me into a state of psychosis. I had never felt more alive or better. I hoped he'd see that and trust me sooner than later. Dr. Callahan told me how I had been admitted to Great Falls twice and stayed there for long stretches, so I knew my track record didn't match with what I promised him. I felt like I was finally living for the first time since losing my children. I was healing. I wasn't going to spiral out of control again. There was no way in hell I would go back to a psychiatric facility a third time, I'd rather be dead. The sun had set, and Parker yawned.

"She was an awful woman. I mean, you remember..." I began, anxiously peeling away at the blush pink polish.

"Serena, don't go down this road again. Please, baby, we need to move forward. Remember what Dr. Callahan said? You have to live in the present and live for the future, not recreate the past. Please, sweetheart." Turning toward me, he pulled me closer, planting his chin on top of my head.

"God, you must think I'm so broken. I can't believe you married me, Sully. I'm starting to think you just may be the crazy one." I gave him a small smile, nudging my shoulder into his side.

"No, actually that isn't true at all. Whenever I see a strong person, I pause and wonder what kind of rigid ocean and untamed waves they must have sailed through in order to be that strong. You, my sweet Seri, are stronger than anyone I know, and that's one of the many reasons I love you."

"See, when you say that kind of stuff it makes me sad because I feel like I really just wasted away so many years of my life without you." I could feel tears sting my eyes. I nestled my face into his comforting chest.

"We have forever to go, my love. Anyway, baby, I gotta get some shut-eye before heading in tonight. I'm on-call so we should head back home. You need to get some rest, too." He gently lifted my face toward his. Reaching down, he kissed my forehead and lips softly.

"Yea, I'm getting tired…" Even though I knew the only way I would sleep was drowning myself in the pills that decorated my nightstand. Without them, I'd wake up covered in sweat, screaming, calling out for Mason and Lola, or waking in fear that Macy was hovering near me. The worst part now about Macy was that I had nothing to connect myself with her. She disappeared. I didn't know her real last name since she was clearly not my shrink's wife. Going on a hunt for a stunning blonde who donned red lips didn't yield much of a search result. I supposed she found out about Tessa and couldn't face the embarrassment. I didn't blame her.

We went inside and changed our clothes. I watched as Parker pulled off his shirt and climbed into a pair of pajama pants. He really was the perfect man. All along I chased perfection, and the one person who truly encompassed it was standing right beside me all along.

"You checkin' me out, Miss Indigo?"

"In your dreams, Sully." I giggled, tossing a pillow at him.

Parker got into bed, I followed and planted myself right next to him.

"I love you so much, Serena Sully." He kissed me as I turned my face to him.

I changed my last name for him, deciding it would perhaps change me as well. I knew that was far from reality. I prayed every night that I would be able to become the woman I was, or maybe a woman I had never been? It felt as if every corner I turned, I was terrified of which version of myself I would find. Depressed Serena? Anxious Serena? Sad Serena? Happy Serena? Normal Serena? *Perfect Serena?*

I waited for him to fall asleep, as I always did, before leaving our bed. I walked down the hall to the unused guestroom. My parents hardly visited us, partially because they simply did not know how to interact with their own daughter—the broken, imperfect embarrassment to the Indigo name. My father was crushed that I'd wrecked any chance of a career I'd built so well, and not even lipstick and pretty dresses could make me perfect and beautiful to my mother. The wood beneath my feet creaked, and I could still smell the scent of the salty ocean air linger in our home even with the windows closed. It was therapeutic. All I needed was right here, right in this house with me.

I unlocked the door, closing it behind me. Standing on my tiptoes, I pulled out the small box out from the closet. Collapsing onto the floor with it in my lap, I pulled out the aged, tiny faded pink blanket that wrapped a delicate doll. Rocking her in my arms, kissing her head, I sang sweet lullabies to her. *To my Lola.* I spritzed baby powder, scented hair spray onto the small golden ringlets and inhaled her every night. Laying her on the bed, I took out the newborn-sized diaper and hummed while changing my daughter. Re-wrapping her in the old, pink blanket, I lifted her in the air and admired my *perfect baby girl.* It was the same blanket that she was wrapped in when she was handed over to me for the very first time.

I had finally, in some sense, allowed Mason to cross over into the heavens. I had accepted his loss. My beautiful boy. I freed myself from the pain and burdens of his death knowing Eric was gone, too. He was paying for his sins. He wasn't watching him and let him drown. Lola, my second chance of everything, of perfection, didn't even get that once small window of time with me. I didn't have the chance to protect her, but now I would. *This time no one would take her from me.*

I sat in the chair in the corner of the room and held her tightly in my arms. Slowly gliding while humming her favorite song. We had gotten a late start to bedtime tonight.

"Sorry, baby girl, I went for a stroll by the beach tonight. I'll take you tomorrow in the morning like we always do," I whispered into her ear.

Pulling my phone out, I Googled Dr. Nix. I couldn't stop peering over at the closed door, terrified that Parker would open it. Every night I did this, I felt as if I was a member of a circus. The one on the tight rope, treading carefully, holding my breath because if I fell, I'd be nothing more than a… *disappointment.*

News articles instantly loaded onto my screen and I clicked the first one. *Dr. Magnolia Nix found dead in her home. Community is stunned.* I let my finger trace over the photo of her. My chest tightened. Closing my eyes, I could see her standing there in front of me all those years ago, holding my Lola in her arms. *Lifeless.* Finishing residency under her was hell. She was the damn grim reaper in disguise. Wearing paisley-printed colorful dresses and a condescending smile, she was the epitome of grief. I shuddered at the mere thought of her.

I clicked another article which stated that the police were mystified that there was no knife found consistent with the wounds. A small description was left in hopes that if anyone knew anything, they'd be able to phone it in.

Suddenly, my breathing quickened to the pace of my already wild heartbeat. My palms grew moist as I watched my phone shake in front of me.

They never found the knife?

I stood, although my legs felt like putty, I used every ounce of strength I could muster. I carefully placed my Lola back into her box, hiding her away in the closet. Guilt panged me when I did this every night. Quickly kissing her once more, I left the room and looked around, making sure Parker was asleep. A thief in my own home, except the only person I was robbing was my husband and his trust. My trembling hands quietly opened the French doors to our study. My palms were so slick with sweat, and the metal knobs barely turned until I added force.

I walked over to the small wooden box displayed next to the black and white photo from our wedding day. Lifting my shaking hands up to it, I cracked it open, my fingers traced the indigo velvet. The old, small dagger stared back at me. Reaching for it, the jagged wooden handle felt rough against my palm. It had been so long since I had let this blade touch my own flesh, it needed to be content on someone else's.

Be the hunter or the prey.

I felt my eyes widen as chills raced against my arms. Flipping over the cool steel, I held it in front of my face. I saw my reflection in the shiny silver, deep red was stained across my face... Jumping back, I blinked hastily and dropped the knife. The gasp that filled the dark study echoed from my throat. I couldn't hear the racing thoughts over the pounding of my heart. *Whose blood was that?* I swallowed the lingering saliva from my mouth, hoping it would coat the extreme dryness of my throat. A natural response with anxiety. I began to inhale and count my breaths, and crouching down, I lifted the dagger back up. Panic coursed through me.

Leaving the study, I opened the front door. A sporadic summer storm had been brewing, unleashing its wrath through the high wind and pounding rain. I walked into it, praying it would wash the sin, the pain, and the confusion away. Seeing the drains on the street flooding with the fresh rain, and hoping everything bad would be extracted down, yet maybe it couldn't. Maybe there was too much sorrow that it simply had to pool out somewhere, it had to overflow and take residence in a different outlet.

The pellets pounded against my body. My hair clung to my face and scalp as my clothes gripped my skin uncomfortably. I looked at the darkened sky and let out a scream. The thunder collided with the shrieking that rose from my lungs, muting it from the world.

Falling to the ground, I sobbed uncontrollably. I was nothing more than a wounded bird who'd never be able to fly, let alone soar. I'd be in this cage forever. Choking on my own tears and hysterics, I peeled myself off the muddy, wet ground and begrudgingly walked back inside to our bedroom. Water trailed behind me as the wind howled through the front door I had left open. I had no one and nothing to fear outside of our home. *What or who was to fear lived right here.* In this home. *Our home.*

Parker was sleeping soundly as the curtains swayed with the sea breeze outside and water puddled onto the floor through the cracked window. I walked up to him and looked down at the dagger that was cutting into my palm. Blood dripped onto the white rug that peeked out from our bed. The place where our feet were welcoming with warmth every morning was now streaked with my blood. With my free hand, I grazed his soft skin, tilting my head to the side. I couldn't help but study his breathing. He moved slightly, turning away. I allowed my lips to kiss the side of his neck, inhaling his comforting scent.

Opening my closet door, I pulled out the old pink robe and wrapped it around me. Looking down, my finger traced the old grape juice stain. The sleeves were rolled up, but underneath were the tinges of my own blood from years before.

Walking to the bathroom, I placed the dagger on the counter and began brushing my hair, tugging through the many tangles. I turned the faucet on, the dribbling water echoed against the sink. I splashed the cool water onto my face and gently patted away the droplets with the plush hand towel. Looking up, I stared at the reflection in the mirror. *Prim. Pluck. Pucker up, buttercup.* I tweezed a stray hair and grabbed a tube of lipstick.

Letting darkness cover my eyes, by mere habit, I carefully applied the creamy texture to my lips. Thunder roared through the tumultuous stormy skies as I jolted my eyes opened. My eyes wandered to the bathroom window as lightning flashed and I glimpsed back to my reflection. Dropping the cloth in the sink, I immediately turned around and peered behind me. There was no one there. The glimpse I saw…

No. This couldn't be.

"Serena, *just breathe.*" An unknown voice surfaced in my ear, a cool breath grazing the crevice of my neck. I began furiously peeling away the polish that coated my thumbnail, frozen in the moment.

Lightning followed the roaring thunder providing light in the otherwise dark bathroom. Leaning toward the mirror, I allowed my hands to trace my face while the blood from my cut palm painted my cheek. My fingers grasped my ear lobes, both of the pearl studs were securely in them. *How...?* I hadn't seen the second pearl earring in what seemed to be an eternity. Macy had one. She stole it. She taunted me while wearing it, she told me she'd keep them along with my husband. I nodded as my thoughts blurred together, reassuring me with the truth. My chest was heaving with the racing thoughts that swirled in my mind, just like the storm took over the clear sky and calm ocean outside. I was drowning *on myself.*

"Seri?" Parker's tired voice trailed behind me. I saw his reflection in the mirror. His eyes widened. Turning around, I looked over my shoulder at him, curving my bright red lips into a smile…

"Hello, darling…"

ABOUT THE AUTHOR

*Monica Arya is a Charlotte, North Carolina native
currently residing in South Carolina with
her husband, two beautiful children, and goldendoodle.
Besides writing and her family, she is passionate about the
beach, spicy food, chocolate, and spontaneous dance parties.
She is a multi-genre author in both romance and thriller.
Girl in the Reflection is her debut psychological thriller and
second novel.*

Monica enjoys connecting with readers, you can learn
more about her and upcoming releases:
Website: www.monicaarya.com
Instagram: @monicaaryaauthor
Facebook: Monica Arya Author

Please consider leaving a review on Amazon, and Goodreads.

ACKNOWLEDGMENTS

To my family, the beat to my heart and all of the stars in sky. I love you so much.

To my parents. You both have shaped me into the strong woman I am today. You believed in me, when I didn't believe in myself. You've sacrificed so much for me and I'm forever grateful for everything you do and have done for me. The support you've given me is the greatest gift you could have blessed me with. I love you both.

Writing and telling stories allows me to find a new level of joy so finally, ***thank you to my readers*** for reading a story, I absolutely loved telling. Life is better with love and thrill.

Printed in Great Britain
by Amazon